John Baird lives in Notti
A former Physical Educatio
look after his wife who suff
information on John Bai
www.johnb

C000173099

CHASING SHADOWS

JOHN BAIRD

First published in 2009
by Discovered Authors, ISBN 978-1-905108-80-0

This paperback edition published by CallioCrest
an imprint of CallioPress

37 Great Russell Street, London WC1B 3PP, United Kingdom
555 Fifth Avenue N.E. Suite 343, Saint Petersburg, Florida 33701, USA
www.calliopress.com

ISBN 978-0-85778-059-1

Cover Design by Ravikiran Pawar

A CIP catalogue record for this book is available from
the British Library.

Available from CallioPress Online, all major online retailers
and available to order through your local bookshop.
Visit www.calliopress.com to buy our books
or email sales@calliopress.com

Printed and bound in Great Britain

For my wife, Mel, supplier of all the love and laughs a man could need.

ACKNOWLEDGEMENTS

Writing is a solitary pursuit. In the case of Chasing Shadows it took years of two finger tapping before I had knocked out enough rewrites to claim a finished manuscript. It is at this point that a novel, especially one fortunate enough to be published, needs the help of others. To that end I thank the following:

The fabulous author, Helen Hollick, for her invaluable counsel and championing of my book. Without whom.....you know the rest.

My wonderful editor, Jo Field, whose commitment is matched only by her talent; I suspect she may even be able to disprove the saying that you can't polish a turd.

Michaela, Kate, Ravi, and the team at my publishers, Discovered Authors. Your faith is much appreciated.

Julie Malone, for her hard work on behalf of the best writers group around. Visit us at www.newwritersuk.co.uk

Finally, to my lovely wife and the most incredibly supportive parents I could ask for.

CHAPTER ONE

Blood engorged my throat, clogging my airways. But dying was exactly what I needed. The lack of oxygen ignited involuntary reflexes. Suddenly I came to, gasping for air.

Nothing.

Panic rising.

I coughed up my insides; desperately sucked oxygen into my burning lungs.

Where the hell am I?

Wiping swollen eyes, I searched for familiarity; recognised the oak tree spinning in the moonlight. Clambering to my feet, I stumbled to the path. My thumping head weighed me down. My legs buckled.

I never made it.

* * *

My eyes opened to a brilliant light in which floated a beautiful angel. Gazing up at her, thoughts of my own mortality evaded me. All I ever wanted was there in the form of this heavenly creature. As the light faded her face illuminated and I was immersed in love.

My senses returned and unwelcome feelings gate-crashed my body. Love was displaced by suffering and confusion. This wasn't heaven, it was the Northampton General Hospital. Opposite me an elderly man lay on his side; naked but for a pyjama top and head bandage.

Elaine, I mouthed to my beautiful angel. A searing pain confronted me as she slid open a green curtain and disappeared behind it.

Attempting to sit up I felt my brain bang against the inside of my skull. Steadying myself, I managed to pull my arms free of the bed sheets and fished for injuries. I located bandaging to my face as Elaine returned, a tiny nurse in tow.

Her hands shaking with emotion, Elaine pulled her blonde hair away from a wet cheek. 'Ed. It's me. You okay baby?'

She looked pale, her blue eyes swimming with tears.

'I'd like a glass of water,' I uttered hoarsely. It felt like a hot water bottle was lodged in my throat.

At full stretch, the nurse reached over with a plastic cup, guiding a straw to my grateful lips. I swallowed painfully. 'What happened?'

Puzzlement registered on Elaine's face. 'We thought you would know.'

'I'll go and fetch the Doctor,' said the pocket-sized nurse before giant doors swallowed her up.

Shuffling up close, Elaine cupped my face. 'I have been so worried about you. They told me you were found unconscious in the park. Beaten up.'

'I don't remember.'

Then a picture developed in my mind, with feelings of panic. Having entered the park I had become unable to breathe, as if a hand gripped my face. Soon I recalled the oak tree and regaining consciousness.

'What is it, Ed?' Elaine broke my memory. 'You all right?'

I smiled reassuringly. 'How do I look?'

She nodded across at the recuperating geriatric. 'Much like him, only worse.'

'Thanks. Bet he gets sympathy, where are my red grapes?'

Elaine whispered in my ear, 'They're haemorrhoids.' She kissed my cheek. 'Speaking of which, your best mate's here. I told him I'd fetch him when you woke up.'

'Go get him,' I replied, eager to find out what Sam knew. Sergeant Sam Chapman had been with me before I entered the park. That much I remembered.

In my thirty-seven years I had never been in a proper fight, let alone been beaten up.

My one and only punch was thrown at school; my six-year-old knuckles painfully clashing with the seven-year-old mouth of a name-caller. Since then I had avoided violence like a naked dwarf avoids nettles.

Within moments of Elaine leaving, the double doors swung open and in walked a doctor holding a serious expression and a clipboard. His face displayed more hair than skin. An interesting mix of Indian and West Midlands was evident in his accent as he introduced himself and asked how I was feeling.

'Groggy,' I replied. Then: 'What's the damage?'

'There is a fracture to your nose. It's difficult to say how badly broken it is at this stage because of the swelling but we'll do an x-ray in a few days. For medico-legal reasons if nothing else.'

I cocked an eyebrow. 'Medico-legal?'

'With assaults it is often necessary for the true extent of damage to be ascertained, for the purposes of any legal action brought against the accused. In your situation I would expect this to be the case.'

'In my situation? Do you know what happened to me?'

Swerving my question, Dr Patel shone a light into my eyes. 'There's cotton packing with a splint to protect your nose. It will probably heal itself. If there is any deformity surgery's an option. But that's the future, just relax for now.'

For some reason the words deformity and surgery weren't relaxing me.

Walking the curtain around the bed, Dr Patel closed off the rest of the ward. 'A nurse will be along later to give you a tetanus injection.' He slowed his speech, 'And there are a few further tests that we need to do.'

'Tests?' Didn't sound good.

'I just passed your fiancée. She tells me that you have no memory of what happened to you?'

'That's right.'

'When you arrived here you were unconscious despite paramedic attempts to bring you round.' He put down the clipboard, pressed his palms together as though arm-wrestling himself. Whatever he had to say wasn't coming easily. 'A blood test revealed a chemical in your system.'

What? My heart thumped at my ribs.

Dr Patel looked stern, all beard and disapproval. 'Firstly, I have to ask. Have you recently injected yourself, Mr Taylor, with any substance at all?'

'Absolutely not.'

'I feared as much.' He sighed. 'I have some rather worrying news. We found Ketalar in your blood stream, an extremely powerful anaesthetic. I'm afraid that you have been drugged.'

CHAPTER TWO

The curtain parted. Sam ducked under the railing, his face shining with sweat; his dyed black hair slicked back over his thinning crown. Elaine followed, parking herself on the bed. Sensing something was wrong they turned to the Doctor.

He frowned back. 'Last night, prior to Mr Taylor's arrival, I believe that he was forcibly anaesthetised.'

Elaine gripped my arm, looked at me, then at Sam. Palming sweat from forehead to hair, his dark eyes narrowed. 'You sure he wasn't anaesthetised here?'

'Positive,' said the Doctor. 'We don't even use Ketalar at this hospital.'

Still stunned, I finally managed to speak, 'I remember being alone, under the oak tree. This means I was conscious, after being attacked.' I looked at Dr Patel for an explanation.

'You arrived here with high levels of anaesthetic present in your system, but people do come round prematurely. A subconscious response could have been triggered. I suppose it's also possible that the anaesthetic was injected after you regained consciousness.'

'For Christssake, Quincy.' Sam shook his head and began pacing the room. 'Whoever did this would be long gone before Ed woke up.' He stared at the wall, speaking to himself: 'But something weird's going on.' He faced me. 'After Elaine called to let me know you weren't home, I went looking for you. The first place I tried was the park but there was no sign of you. I searched the area well. You weren't there, Ed.'

'But I was found there?'

'Yeah. A shift worker saw you near the path, and noticing the blood, he called an ambulance. But I swear to you mate, you weren't there when I looked.'

My body froze as a memory flashed by, not staying long enough to be recalled. There was something else. Something my brain was holding back.

Something bad.

Why had I been drugged? Why couldn't I remember being injected? And where the hell had I been?

A shiver. 'Doctor, has anything else been done to me?'

'We will know more after the tests but there is no evidence of major injury or any sign of a sexual assault.'

I exhaled my relief, noticing Sam deep in thought. I asked him if he'd any idea what had happened to me.

He replied, 'Normally, with an unprovoked assault on a pedestrian, I'd suspect a mugging. Some junkie needing a fix. If like you the victim is of mixed-race, then I'd have to include the possibility of a racially aggravated crime. But the anaesthetisation?' He shook his head. 'That changes everything.'

We spotted a stringy man in an ill-fitted suit. He was out in the corridor, jumping impatiently, like a kangaroo needing a piss.

'Well,' said Dr Patel, hurrying his speech, 'The effects of the anaesthetic will wear off, and I will be back to see you soon.' He motioned to Sam. 'If you could see to it that Mr Taylor does get some rest.'

'Of course.' Sam accompanied Dr Patel to the exit.

As the Doctor left, Skippy entered.

'Detective Inspector Brian Firwell, Thames Valley Police. I need to speak with Edson Taylor. It's about last night.'

CHAPTER THREE

Sam stepped in front of the Detective Inspector. 'Sergeant Sam Chapman, Northampton PD.'

Showing his identification, the DI led Sam to the corner of the ward. Puffing out his chest, Sam stretched to six-foot-five and looked down at the Inspector's overly large head. During a minute of discussion I listened hard but couldn't hear a thing until Sam turned back, dejected. 'I'll just be outside.'

With his head bobbing like a car toy, DI Firwell paced up to the bed. His huge stubbly chin came to rest on his sparrow chest.

Elaine sat up. 'Do you know who drugged Ed?'

'No. And you are?'

'Elaine. I'm Ed's fiancée.'

'Good for you.' He took out a pencil. 'Mr Taylor. Firstly, I'd like to clear up a few details. You left the *Shoehorn* at half past ten having been there for the previous two hours?'

'Yes. It was their quiz night. Sam's our captain.' Nodding towards the corridor I saw Sam flouting the "no mobile phone" rule. 'We tour the local pub quizzes. You know the place?'

He shook his superhero-sized jaw.

'It's a bit rough. The quizmaster has tattooed eyelids.' I sneered. 'Question one: Are you looking at me?' A nervous smile left my lips as the unmoved detective began to write.

'And between then and ten past two, nobody saw you. You were out cold.' He tightened his eyes. 'Anaesthetised, I understand?'

'Yes, although at one point I did briefly regain consciousness. I was in the park. There was blood on my face and hands.'

As his note-taking picked up pace I recalled an image: long, white hair.

Before I could make any sense of it the Detective's voice cut in, 'And what time was this?'

'I really don't know. I was dazed, could barely breathe.'

'Did you see anyone, hear anything?'

'Nothing. No one was around so I tried to get back to the path. I only managed a few steps before passing out.'

'Talk me through what happened when you left the pub.'

'I left alone, decided to go through the park. The path is always well lit and it cuts about five minutes off my journey home. I entered through the main gates, walked about thirty yards. Then I remember being knocked forward. Someone must have come up behind me.'

He waited a beat. 'And that's the last thing you recall, before losing consciousness?'

I nodded, adding, 'It felt like a huge hand was over my face. Then nothing.'

'Had you had much to drink?'

'Three, maybe four pints.'

'I'm told that anaesthetic has been injected into your blood stream. Are you telling me that you don't recall how it got there?'

I shrugged. 'Whoever attacked me must have injected me.'

'Why would anybody want to anaesthetise you?'

'I have no idea.'

The chin finally lifted. 'When is the last time you saw Gary Jasper?'

Gary Jasper? 'What does he have to do with this?'

'Just try to answer the questions please, Sir. Gary Jasper is your father?'

'Yes, but I haven't spoken to him for over ten years.'

'I see.' He scratched his head with the pencil. 'Do you have any enemies, anyone who'd want to hurt you?'

'None. Nobody.'

My tongue stuck to my gums as the questions kept firing.

'What about your father?'

'What?' I exchanged confused glances with Elaine. 'You think Gary Jasper could have attacked me?'

'Sorry, when I asked *what about your father?* I meant does *he* have any enemies?'

'Maybe, I really wouldn't know. Like I said, we don't speak. Inspector, why are you asking about him?'

'Please,' Elaine pleaded. 'Tell us what's going on?'

The DI locked his eyes on mine. 'In the early hours of the morning your father was found at his home in Buckinghamshire. At the time you were unconscious, he was assaulted.' Firwell's eyes filled with assumed sympathy. 'I'm sorry, Mr Taylor. He died from his injuries.'

CHAPTER FOUR

Numbness took over my body.

I was staring at space when DI Firwell's pencil came into focus. It was jutting towards me accusingly. 'His home is only a half hour drive from here, and yet you haven't spoken in over ten years. Some problem between the two of you?'

'I'm adopted,' I said. 'Gary Jasper's my biological father.' The DI's hostility was putting me on the defensive. 'The fact we live separate lives was his decision. I didn't even know who he was until I was in my twenties. I can count on one hand the times we actually met.'

I was raised by white parents, in middle-class Wycombe. Very few black or mixed-race people lived there in those days. Whenever I saw a tall, black man, I'd wonder if he was my biological father. Often I'd play out different scenarios in my mind; the jobs he might have; the music he liked. Sometimes I'd simply wonder if he was even alive. Or what difference it would make if he wasn't.

'We were strangers,' I said.

With a huff and a scribble, Firwell ended his questioning, saying he'd be in touch. A period of time passed before I realised Sam had rejoined Elaine at my bedside.

'Gary Jasper's dead,' I announced. 'Do you think they were trying to kill me?'

'No, Ed,' said Sam. 'You mustn't think that. Both cases are completely different.'

He seems sure of himself. I recalled his conversation with Firwell. 'You know something, don't you?'

'Like the DI said, Gary Jasper died from his injuries. Your assault is totally different. You have a broken nose.'

From his guarded expression I could see that he was holding back on me.

He sensed this. 'Your father was gagged and tied to his bed. What happened to you was—'

'What injuries?' I pushed Sam for an answer. 'How did he die?'

He relented, reluctantly pulling up his chair. 'Gary Jasper bled to death.' Drawing breath, he added, 'he was dismembered.'

My body sank. *Dismembered?*

'Something they are calling cross-amputation.'

* * *

Driving from the hospital, her heart heavy with dread, Elaine sank slowly into reality. Since the age of 17 she had been on the run; waiting for her past to catch up with her.

Last night, it looked like it finally had.

Her fears turned to Ed, her mind filling with his battered face. Heading home to fetch him something less revealing than a hospital gown, she felt his pain like a knife in her gut. What had she brought on him? Violence and murder: words synonymous with the world she'd left behind.

But cross-amputation? Sam had said that Gary Jasper had been alive when they severed his hand and foot. Elaine had witnessed unspeakable violence in her time but nothing quite so brutal.

Slipping her Peugeot into third, she passed the columns of the town hall, recalled the day Ed had proposed; on one knee in the middle of the bustling market. Making a scene never bothered him. He was used to drawing stares – being so tall, and having a smile that could stop traffic. She pictured his grin as she had screamed yes! How he had whisked her up and swung her round as onlookers clapped and cheered.

But even then, she had known this day might come. The day her past caught up with her.

Falling in love had never been part of the plan. She had always functioned better alone, with no one else to consider or worry about. But finding Ed was like finding her true self. He completed her and she him; they provided each other with the love they had both craved all their lives.

A headache crept up like a cat-burglar. As the traffic lights turned red, she applied the handbrake, rooted for a Paracetamol and closed her eyes. Was last night for her benefit? Were they warning her to stick to her side of the bargain? *To hurt the tough, you hurt the one they love.* She didn't know for sure, but last night had certain parallels with the man who had dogged her life for as long as she could remember.

She gagged on the Paracetamol; a car honked, the lights were green. Elaine raised an apologetic hand and made her way through the centre of Northampton: the place she now thought of as home. The day was bright and biting. The streets busy. People were going about their business. How she envied their freedom.

Since Ed became her life, Elaine had known she had to stop running. Like him, she had found her place in the world. It was why she had made her deal with the Devil and, for just one last time, had agreed to become the person she used to be. The thought of that alone reaped almost as much fear as the thought at what awaited her.

Leaving Ed at the hospital was bad enough. Abandoning him completely was too hard to comprehend. But what choice did she have?

Elaine was determined that the time she had left would be spent with Ed. She couldn't leave at this time. But her date with destiny was looming ever closer. And she had no choice but to comply: *The time is coming; you know what you must do.* Revisiting those words brought on palpitations. Her breath coming in short gasps, she lowered the window, felt the cold snap of air on her face.

The possibility that in some way she was responsible for Gary Jasper's murder felt like a weight pressing down on her chest. However much she didn't want to believe it, Elaine had to accept that she was no longer in control.

She had tried to talk to Ed, to explain. But the words lodged in her throat. To spare him, she would have to deceive him. It was the only way. If she survived she would return, tell him everything. But her decision was made. Her penance would be taken. And after spending nearly half her life on the run, she'd be free at last.

People warm to Ed, she told herself. They will want to help. But the timing of his father's murder could not be worse. Not when the date she had to leave was only weeks away – the date when she would have to break his heart.

SIX WEEKS LATER

CHAPTER FIVE

Friday. 9.30am
Westwood, Los Angeles, CA.

Special Agent Donnie Guzan was first to spot the CIA officials. Through a glass partition, he recognised the two of them, strolling down the corridor which lined the office making up the thirteenth floor of the Los Angeles Headquarters of the FBI.

Both men held their gaze on the door in front of them, neither one risking a sideways glance at the agents that lay in wait. Local relations between the FBI and CIA were at an all time low, with no sign of improvement.

Felix Proudlock was first to enter. His purposeful arrival was followed by the flapping tie of the shorter, yet heavier, Ethan Knight. Both men were experienced at dealing with the FBI and would be anticipating the cold reception.

Knight had the look of a blushing alcoholic, on account of the many blood vessels attempting to break through his cheeks. The red face came with a side order of grey, wispy hair and blue lips. Verging on ill – at best stressed – his demeanour was softened only by his *Donald Duck* tie. Guzan viewed it as Knight's attempt to portray a sense of humour. It had the opposite effect.

The other official, Proudlock, had on his *Men in Black* suit and sunglasses. They, together with his goatee beard, suggested that he was aiming for cool. But, like Knight, he was approaching 50 and his efforts were hampered by his overly shiny head. 20 years ago, Proudlock's wife had left him and his hair had quickly followed – many unsuccessful attempts at replacing both ensued.

The cynical FBI agents offered the courtesy of their attention as Knight took up position, coughed twice and addressed the room. 'The MEK or Mujahideen-e Khalq are an Iranian opposition group. The current consensus is that they are not considered a threat to the West.'

Clearing his throat, Proudlock took over. 'There are over six-hundred-thousand Iranians living in LA. That's more than any other city outside Iran. A large number of them would like to see the Iranian regime removed. As a result, many of these residents have donated generously to the MEK. The last thing they want is America declaring war with their mother country over nuclear policy.'

Images appeared on the whiteboard behind Proudlock, depicting two men. 'Currently residing in Omaha Heights, Ali Afshari and Syrus Meybodi exploit this generosity. Both ex-MEK members, they collect donations, but not a dime has made its way to the MEK.'

A veteran of the bureau, Guzan had heard enough. 'Let me get a handle on this. You want access to our resources to investigate money meant for an anti-Iranian group?'

'Coalition military commanders have been working with MEK members for information on Iranian mullahs' agents in Iraq. What we have on our hands is a terrorist US ally and we want it to stay that way. So yes, we need the FBI to help them recover this money.'

Guzan asked, 'What is this really about?'

Proudlock raised a palm. 'Give me just a little more time.'

'And our love will surely grow,' responded an agent with a General Johnson impression.

Knight struck a table. 'From now on, Ali Afshari and Syrus Meybodi are to be under your full surveillance. You need to act quickly and covertly. We need to know everything about them. And quite frankly I'm sick of the attitude. The fact is *we* now own your priorities. As my daughter would say, deal with it.' He glared at the room, pocketed his hands. 'Any further interruptions?'

'Just the one.' It was Guzan's partner, Special Agent Tyler Derego. 'Didn't *Donald Duck* wear bow ties?'

'This money is funding extremists,' snapped Proudlock, cutting short the sniggers. A sweat bead ran from head to goatee. 'During the conflict in Iraq a number of MEK bases were demilitarised. Splinter groups were formed. Afshari and Meybodi have been linked to such a group. Your involvement is critical.'

'You're holding back on us,' said Guzan. 'Why can't we bring these men in?'

Taking his time, Proudlock filled two cups from the cooler. 'Our source suggests that something is going down. Afshari and Meybodi are our best lead. Now, you have all the information you need.'

'Unless you give us more it'll be difficult to work this,' called a voice from the back. 'Our own priorities will have to take precedence.'

'Be forewarned,' said Knight, checking with Proudlock before continuing. 'Every cent could be destined for terrorist use.' He took a sip of water, looked like he was preparing to divulge information he'd rather not share. 'We have uncovered a connection between this money and the chemical breach in Arizona,' his weighty voice curtailed. 'So get out and do your fucking jobs.'

CHAPTER SIX

The Newman Clinic, Northampton.

In the six weeks since DI Firwell first visited my sickbed he had interviewed me several times in connection with Gary Jasper's murder. Given the circumstances of that night, their spotlight had fallen on me. My memory loss and subsequent lack of alibi aroused their interest, and coupling that with the colour of my skin I became the prime suspect. This was because of the nature of his death. Cross-amputation, I went on to discover, was still carried out in Northern Sudan and parts of Saudi Arabia. It was seen as fitting punishment for the charge of haraba – armed robbery, and was in relation to their government's interpretation of Islamic Law – Sharia. Fingers were pointed at the Muslim community of which I was deemed a part, based entirely on the fact that I did some volunteer work for a charity that happened to be run by a Muslim family. Oh, and that a friend of mine was Muslim. It was ridiculous but Gary Jasper's murder made no sense to anybody. He was a white Christian with no link to armed robbery.

Eventually the police lowered their suspicions, reluctantly accepting Dr Patel's evidence to discount me. Given the drugs in my body, he vowed that it would have been impossible for me to have done anything to anyone.

Cross-amputation usually involves dismemberment of the right hand and left foot and this was the case in the murder of Gary Jasper. First a hand is severed, then the foot, usually by a skilled surgeon with a special knife. Normally, cauterization of the wounds prevents the victim from dying. With my father, this did not take place. He was tied up. He was meant to bleed to death. The question was: why?

Mentally I was a complete mess, spending time avoiding life, fearing sleep and grasping at a memory that wouldn't materialise. According to my highly persuasive friend, Sergeant Sam Chapman, this was the place to tackle my 'psychological damage' and psychotherapist Bobby was the man to do it. So here I was – the Newman Clinic. For me to discuss my mental problems with anyone other than Elaine was tantamount to admitting to an outbreak of bum boils – only sitting here I was more uncomfortable.

A window separated the waiting room from a sour-faced receptionist. She squinted at me with undisguised suspicion as I caught my reflection. Superficially, all that remained from my attack was a little swelling around the eyes and a bump on my nose.

Thumbing through a huge stack of magazines that adorned a glass table, I discovered enough home improvement titles to suggest a link between DIY and mental illness.

Finally, a door opened. Out strode an imposing, sharply-dressed man. More soldier than shrink.

'Edson Taylor?' he announced my name with the easy smile of a salesman. 'Would you like to come in? I'm Bobby.'

No going back now.

I held out my hand. 'Call me Ed.'

His room was office-like; one desk, three chairs and a couple of framed certificates.

It's not that I was expecting straightjackets hanging off padded walls but there wasn't even a couch.

As we got underway I found myself engaged in chit-chat, happily skirting around my problems. It took Bobby to cut to the chase, 'So how long have you been having these bad dreams?'

Here we go.

'For the past six weeks,' I said. 'But I prefer to call them nightmares.'

The small talk and formalities were over. Resting two fingers on his bottom lip, Bobby asked, 'Do you have any idea why you're having these nightmares?'

Smiling nervously: 'I have a couple of theories.'

'Please, go on, Ed,' he waved encouragingly.

'Six weeks ago, I suffered a double trauma. The nightmares stem from that date, the night my father was murdered.' I watched his reaction as closely as he watched me. Where I was expecting shock, a sympathetic look appeared, his tanned forehead displaying a concerned frown.

What exactly had Sam told him?

'That same evening I was beaten and left unconscious in a park. When I woke up in hospital I was told that I had been drugged. Anaesthetised. By my attacker.'

Shifting forward, Bobby carefully tented his fingers. He was one of those big guys where it's hard to decide if they're muscular or fat. A clean-shaven head and pinstriped suit gave him the look of a nightclub bouncer. It was a look that didn't match his smooth *Classic FM* voice. 'Let's start with your father,' he said. 'He was murdered?'

I nodded. 'You probably heard about it on the news. *Gary Jasper?*'

Bobby's eyebrows nearly reached the top of his head. 'Yes of course, he was your father?'

Every section of the media had embraced his unsolved, grisly death. The cross-amputation angle had caused endless conjecture and so far, my existence had been kept out of it. It wasn't public knowledge that Gary Jasper had a son and it wasn't like anyone would see a resemblance.

I nodded. It felt weird acknowledging that he was my father. And it wasn't just that I had kept this quiet for so long; I felt like I was betraying my real dad, the man who'd brought me up.

Reaching for a pad and pen, Bobby asked, 'How was your relationship with your father?'

'There wasn't one. He gave me away when I was a baby. When I reached 21 I tracked him down. My adoptive parents had passed away so I began to look for my biological ones. I had always been curious to know who they were but it hadn't felt right to look whilst my parents were still alive. They had always been so wonderful to me and hated me referring to my biological parents. When I finally met Gary Jasper it came as a surprise that he was white. We shook hands and he talked about his job at the Football Association. Apart from his height all we had in common was a love of football. He named me after his favourite player – Edson was Pele's first name. There was no immediate bond. His reason – or should I say excuse – for giving me away, was that my mother had died giving birth to me and he thought it impossible to bring me up alone.'

Scribbling on his pad, Bobby held a pause, pondered his next question. Then: 'Tell me about your attack?'

Telling Bobby everything it became evident that much remained a mystery. Investigations had led the police to believe that whilst unconscious I had been moved – possibly from the park – and later returned. The conclusion was that I had been targeted but they didn't know why. Other than the date, the only link between my attack and Gary

Jasper's murder was in the skill of the perpetrators. Firstly, at neither site had a shred of evidence been found. This suggested a good knowledge of forensics. Secondly, my father's cross-amputation and my anaesthetisation pointed towards a degree of medical expertise.

Unable to make any progress on the events of that evening, Bobby changed tack. 'Tell me about these nightmares you have been having?'

Earlier I had glossed over them, unsure how either of us would react. I began, 'A man appears. Just his face. He doesn't seem to do anything but every nightmare this same face.' No question followed so I continued. 'And I'm always on edge. Like he's haunting me.'

Bobby's eyes narrowed. 'You mean, when you are awake?'

'Right.' Fear outweighed embarrassment, my limbs started quivering.

Keep it together, Ed. I folded my arms. 'Everything scares me at the moment. I constantly feel as though something bad is about to happen.'

My foot tapping called Bobby's pen into action. 'Tell me about this man who appears?'

Exhaling slowly, I squirmed my way to the back of my chair. If it were not for Elaine I would have avoided this but I had her to consider. The last six weeks had been tough on us both and it was time to face things. 'He's in his sixties, wears glasses and has long, white hair. Look at me, I'm shaking, scared of a pensioner.' I grinned weakly, thinking, tell him about the note.

'I've known people to be scared of all sorts of things,' smiled Bobby. 'What does the man do, in your nightmare?'

'Sometimes he speaks but the words never make sense.'

As Bobby waited for me to explain I noticed him glance up at the clock. His spine straightened. 'Your attack will take a while to get over and losing a parent, however distant, often brings about thoughts of one's own mortality.'

I wasn't thinking about dying. Something was frightening me but it wasn't that.

He put away his pad. 'You need time to learn how to deal with your grief. Six weeks is not long, and as for the sleep, there are things we can do to help with that.'

'I just have this fear that there's more to come.'

Tell him now.

Reaching into my pocket I pulled out a red envelope. 'And only this morning I received this.' I passed it to Bobby.

He unfolded the note:

Gary Jasper
Edson Taylor
Third time lucky?
Start counting…

Carefully he placed it back into the envelope. 'Has Sam Chapman seen this?'

'Not yet,' I said.

'I'm sure it's nothing to worry about. Still, better show it to Sam.'

CHAPTER SEVEN

Saturday. 10.12am
Omaha Heights, Los Angeles.

Parked a mere thirty yards from the craftsman-style bungalow sat a silver van, "SPRINGer's CLEANer's" inscribed down its sides. Through heavily tinted windows, FBI Special Agents, Guzan and Derego, were observing the building that housed the suspected terrorists, Syrus Meybodi and Ali Afshari. It was a modest home painted in immodest colours – a facade of deep orange with patches of brown where paint had faded. In contrast, the shiny Pontiac standing out front looked more befitting of men who'd fraudulently acquired over one million dollars.

Sat in the van's passenger seat – his saggy face almost as brown and leathery as his jacket – was Guzan. He flicked the remains of a fillet-o'-fish from his molars before re-thumbing a file on the two Iranians. Derego preferred to re-check his hair in the visor's mirror whilst popping a mint into his mouth. He lowered his shades back onto his nose and checked his shirt for creases. For Derego, going undercover meant looking like a movie star. 'So what's the deal with these guys?' he asked, mid-suck.

'Fled Iran when the Shah was overthrown,' said Guzan adding, 'now got dual nationality and, as American citizens, the usual surveillance restrictions apply.'

'Officially American and Iranian, huh? That's kinda like supporting the Lakers and the Knicks.' Derego squinted at the house. 'I'm betting they prefer the Knicks, you get me?'

He did. He and Derego differed in many ways but after nine years of working together they got each other; had learned to use their differences to their advantage. Guzan played the respectable face of the bureau. An agent for nearing 20 years, his face displayed a line for every case he'd worked on. Ten years his junior, Derego possessed none of Guzan's tired looks. Regular trips to the gym, combining body-building with fake tan, had given him a carefully sculpted image that was both intimidating to men and attractive to woman.

'What else does it tell us?' asked Derego.

Guzan drummed his fingers on the file. 'That they live and work together, supposedly selling books and collecting for the MEK. Meybodi owns the house and get this, he's a former lawyer.'

'Former lawyer, now suspected terrorist, must have seen the error of his ways,' said Derego.

'And he's fond of suing authorities for racism,' warned Guzan. 'As for Afshari, he's had a string of clerical jobs working for Iranian businessmen.' Guzan dropped the file to his feet. 'In summary, their records are cleaner than the Pope's bed sheets.'

'But according to the CIA the money trace stops with these guys.'

'They're sitting on well over a million.' Guzan let his green eyes focus on the house. 'You know what I don't get?'

'Laid?'

'Apart from that. If these men are linked to a chemical threat, arresting them might be enough to quash it. The CIA is waiting for us to uncover something before moving in for the glory, but we could finish this.'

'Here,' Derego reached across. 'You can finish my coke.'

Guzan screwed up his face. 'I can't believe you drink that. Only fat people drink *Diet Coke.*'

'Great slogan.' Derego lifted the plastic lid. 'Last chance?'

'Do me a favour.'

'Jeez, Don, you're in a pissy mood?'

Guzan ran a hand through his rusty mop of hair. 'I don't do pissy.'

'Right,' nodded Derego. 'What about when that psycho stalker mistook you for Gene Wilder.'

'Hackman. And I'm not in a mood. Just sick of CIA dirt landing in my lap. And on a weekend.'

'There must be more to this than we know.'

'Ethan Knight's meeting me later, he'd better have some answers,' warned Guzan, eyes glued to the house. 'How long is it since we heard anything?'

'Nearly an hour. You don't think Elvis has left the building?'

'We'd have seen them. They don't know they're being watched.'

'But things are a bit quiet. Do Iranians take siesta?' Derego didn't wait for an answer. 'I might just knock on the door. Tell them I'm collecting for the MEK.'

'And land a harassment charge? A dog peeing up their gate would get sued for discrimination.'

'I definitely am detecting pissy. You sure there's nothing else bothering you?'

'Your constant questions.'

Derego thought he knew what was bothering him. But he didn't know how to broach the subject. He settled on, 'I hate to bring this up but, well, I guess you heard about Kester Hardwick's release?'

Guzan froze, his blood heading south. Kester Hardwick's impending release from prison had been the talk of the bureau but previously nobody had dared discuss it with him.

'Apparently he gets out today.'

CHAPTER EIGHT

Northampton, England.

The man in his sixties appeared – the stranger's face hovering inches above my own. His pointed nose and piggy eyes sandwiching a pair of John Lennon spectacles. As he spoke, I was engulfed with the usual mix of fear and helplessness. I could feel his breath and thin white hair touching me and my own breathing became difficult. He was doing something to me.

What?

At 9.08am it ended. Only this time there was no relief upon awakening. As I bolted into consciousness a greater nightmare faced me.

My fiancée was missing.

Elaine McAdler, the love of my live. Vanished. The pain of sheer terror had me in its grip.

The previous evening I had returned to an empty house. No message. No call. No indication that she would not be there. Not like Elaine.

Dropping into an exhausted sleep – my first since she'd gone – filled me with horror. How could I snooze amidst such fear, such worry? The panic I felt in my recurring nightmare and the grief at my father's murder suddenly took a backseat. The fear of losing Elaine was all consuming.

And that letter: "Gary Jasper. Edson Taylor. Third time lucky? Start counting."

Third time lucky? It taunted me.

Despite my acquaintance with Sam Chapman, the police were unhelpful in the extreme. Granted, Elaine had only been missing for one night, and accepted, she was thirty-three, but there was a frustrating lack of concern. Not that it would've helped. I wanted action. They were going through the motions. *Have you tried her friends, family? You had an argument?* Their questions weren't helping. The police were playing the percentages, which were apparently on my side. They were sure she'd show up. Only we were not like the majority of cases. Not like most couples.

The red envelope. The letter. Third time lucky? Elaine was in trouble. Why could they not see that?

Under severe pressure the mind excels or explodes. Mine was on fire; processing memories and possible outcomes. I was overheating. It had been 39 hours since I returned to our empty home and my mind was at the point of breaking. Having exhausted all possibilities I now doubted my sanity. Was I missing something? Had she told me she was staying at friends? Were the police right: was she 'probably fine'? No. We hadn't had a fight. We didn't argue. She didn't stay away at friends. We didn't spend nights apart.

The evening we met was when my life began. Sam introduced us. He was hosting a party to celebrate a promotion in the force and Elaine had just started working for his wife, Janice. He changed my life with the words: 'Edson Taylor, meet Elaine McAdler'. As I saw a smile ignite her soft face I felt an incredible desire to make her happy. To protect her. To love her. Elaine was *everything* to me and I needed everything back.

I knew little of her past. She avoided my questions, saying: 'The past is too hurtful', or 'It's our future that counts.' I assumed she must've come out of a bad relationship and left it at that. Now suddenly everything I didn't know about her was worrying the hell out of me. All I knew was that at some stage she'd left America for Spain and later, Spain for England. Could she have left me? She had a history, and I'd not been myself recently. What with my nerves on edge and my sleep problems, I'd not been easy to live with. Was I perhaps avoiding the most logical outcome? I'd heard the stories of men being left out of the blue; there were no signs, she just upped and left. As quickly as the thought entered my mind it had disappeared. This was not an option for me. As much as I didn't want to believe that scenario, I couldn't. What I *did* know about Elaine was worrying me the most. I knew how much she loved me and that she would have called.

When my adoptive parents died they left me with a house, no mortgage and a healthy bank balance. For much of the week I would work freelance as an advertising consultant. The hours worked well with Elaine's telesales work meaning I'd arrive home just before she did. But, like most Fridays, I had been helping out at the community centre. That meant a later finish and that Elaine should have been home by the time I walked in. If she ever needed to stay late she'd leave a message. Her boss, Janice had noticed nothing unusual; Elaine had left at the regular time. Between her leaving work and my arriving home something happened. *What?* There was no evidence that she'd been home. None of her things were gone. The neighbours saw nothing, likewise her friends. There were no hospital records or car accidents reported. *Nothing*: she was gone without a trace.

Revisiting the past was proving futile so I focused on the note.

After Gary Jasper's murder and my attack, was this the third time lucky?

I was experiencing the fear and helplessness that flooded my nightmares. And this was real. *I can't wake up.*

The letterbox squawked like a dying parrot.

Startled, I was on my way to the front porch before the post landed.

My heart raced.

A second red envelope was lying on the floor.

CHAPTER NINE

As moods go, Agent Guzan had graduated past pissy and was now on edge. The mentioning of Kester Hardwick had left him feeling as awkward as a monk with Tourette's.

Shaking his peeved expression, he turned to his partner. 'What do you want me to say?'

Agent Derego was expecting a reaction, he just didn't know what. 'Wanna pay Kester Hardwick a visit?'

'Only when it involves putting him back in jail.'

Derego nodded. 'You expect he'll be a problem?'

'Can we talk about something else?' Cracking a neck muscle, Guzan turned to look out of a side window, away from the Iranians' house.

'Sure,' said Derego. 'Just that we've been here an hour and I'm running out of conversation.'

Law enforcement hadn't been Derego's business until 1997, but he was aware of Kester Hardwick. The tales of this all-knowing monster continued to do the rounds despite Kester's incarceration. In some quarters his legend had grown stronger. 'Look, I can see that you don't want to talk about it but maybe it'd help. It must bring it all back, huh?' Noting Guzan's distress he trod carefully: 'I'll shut up now but if you want to talk about Cliff, I'd be interested. What with their sponsored silence we've plenty of time on our hands.'

'Leave it alone, Tyler,' Guzan ferociously rubbed his face as though trying to scrub away wrinkles.

A minute of tension passed, both agents staring at the house.

On his first day at the bureau, Guzan had been paired with Cliff Donachie. It was a friendship that ended with his death. Cliff had been instrumental in Kester Hardwick's conviction. But at a price. Kester knew how to destroy people and in Cliff's case, it was through his family.

Feeling his stomach tighten, Guzan lowered his eyes to the dashboard. 'Cliff was a good man, brave as they come. What happened will always be with me.'

Waiting for his partner to elaborate Derego stayed silent.

'And you want to pay Kester a visit?' Guzan jabbed him angrily. 'You know what happened to Cliff and you think— What do you think?'

'That we're FBI,' said Derego.

'Don't be naive.'

Even though suicide was the most common cause of death amongst FBI agents, Derego couldn't ever imagine taking that route. He knew Guzan blamed Kester Hardwick for Cliff's death but for Derego, suicide was a cop out.

Cliff Donachie had injected himself with liquid barbiturate pentobarbital. Well known in the bureau as the preferred method of suicide. Easy enough for agents to get their hands on, it slowly paralyses the body before slipping it into unconsciousness. The result: a relatively pain-free death with no hanging body to find or missing corpse to look for.

Derego knew how badly Guzan had been hit by Cliff's suicide. It made him angry for his partner, believing he would have coped better had Cliff been killed in the line of duty.

'I know what you're thinking,' Guzan spoke sharply. 'You think Kester can't touch you? The fearless Tyler Derego, right? Wrong. Everyone has a weakness, Tyler, even you.'

Derego knew not to argue. Another minute passed.

Guzan drew breath. 'Cliff came over. The night the trial began. It looked like he had finally achieved the impossible. Put Kester Hardwick away. But there was no celebration. It was the first night Kester had been locked in a cell. The perfect alibi. Then came the call. Cliff was told there'd been a house fire. That his family hadn't got out. It looked like a tragic accident. Until the fire report came back.' Guzan started to rock forward and back. 'The fire started in a pan. The kitchen went first. Cliff's family had been sat at the table. The carcasses of his wife and three children were found facing one another. Each had been tied to a chair to keep them upright.' Guzan composed himself. 'The remains of breathing apparatus were found. Cliff knew his family had watched each other die. Burned alive.'

Horror on his face, Derego cautiously placed a sympathetic hand on Guzan's shoulder. 'We can take him, Don.'

'Maybe,' said Guzan. 'But knowing what he's capable of, are you prepared to pay the price?'

'All I know is that Kester Hardwick should not be back walking the streets.'

Guzan blinked. 'The saddest day in a man's life is the day he realises there's no justice.'

CHAPTER TEN

Northampton, England.

Mustering up courage, I dropped down and peeled the envelope off the draughty porch floor.

My stomach called out to me. I was unsure if it needed filling or was about to empty. The latter felt more likely.

The envelope looked exactly like the first one. The same blood red. But this had arrived by airmail. The first letter had been postmarked Bedford. This had come from the USA – postmarked Los Angeles. Dated a week *before* Elaine went missing. Carefully, I opened the envelope. Then I unfolded the small piece of white paper. Slowly. Allowing my nerves to settle.

Third time lucky?
Want your Angel back?
Now, Go Seek.

My heart thumped. Now I was convinced that whoever sent the note had Elaine. Like kicks to the gut, each line confirmed my suspicion. It wasn't a prank. I often referred to Elaine as my Angel – she even had it tattooed on the small of her back.

Now, Go Seek.

I took in a deep breath before calling Sam.

'It's me,' I said. 'There's another letter.'

'I'm on my way.'

'You don't have to come round strai—'

'No,' he interrupted. 'I'm literally on my way. Be with you in five.'

* * *

Through the net curtain I saw Sam's tall silhouette. Picking up the note, I answered the door.

'Thanks for coming.'

He looked past me, transferring his gaze to my feet. Something was wrong. I held back on handing him the note. He had his own news. 'Let's sit down, Ed.'

Neither of us spoke as we moved through to the lounge. Once there, Sam took an intake of breath. 'An Elaine McAdler was booked on a flight from Heathrow—'

'To Los Angeles?' I said.

'How—?'

'Look!' I showed him the second letter. 'It came from Los Angeles.'

He frowned, confusion in his eyes. He wasn't about to dismiss this one.

'I'll need to take this with me,' he stressed. 'For analysis.'

'This has to be good,' I said. 'Want your Angel back? Now, go seek. She has to be alive.'

He smiled encouragingly. 'It looks like Elaine flew out on flight AA77, Heathrow to Los Angeles International.'

'Are you sure it's her?' I asked. 'I mean, there could be other Elaine McAdlers.'

'Her Peugeot was found at Heathrow. Parked illegally.'

I tried not to focus on what this meant. We were at last getting somewhere. This had to be good. America or not, somehow she seemed a lot closer.

Sam wasn't sharing my optimism. He was slouched. His face carried despair. 'She was not alone Ed. Two men were with her.'

My heart sank but I fought to stay positive. This made more sense. It wasn't bad. It couldn't be—

Sam continued, 'Both American citizens. Their names—' – he looked at his hand – 'Faustino Ricard and Fernando Sanchez.' He waited for my reaction.

'Never heard of them. How do you know they were with Elaine?'

'Ten days ago three tickets were bought over the Internet, all under Sanchez's name. The LAPD have been contacted, they are trying to find him. In the meantime we're hoping to get photos of these two men. Maybe you will recognise one of them?'

An image passed by on a wave of panic – of the face in my nightmare. Could the white-haired man be Faustino Ricard? Or Fernando Sanchez? Both letters stated, *"Third time lucky?"* Could these men have killed my father and attacked me? I brought up the idea with Sam.

He shook his head. 'Other than you, nothing links the incidents.'

'The letters link them,' I fired back. 'And we don't know what has happened to Elaine. Like me she could have been drugged. Abducted.' I waved the note. 'Want your Angel back? How do they know I call her Angel?' My voice was jumpy, my hands animated. 'This note came from her abductors, these two men. This Ricard and Sanchez.'

His eyebrows raised a scowl. 'You're saying she's been kidnapped?'

'Yes, think about it. I'm the extent of Gary Jasper's surviving family. Someone finds that out and so they kidnap Elaine.' The more I thought about it the more obvious it became. Gary Jasper was well-known and wealthy. 'That's it,' I announced, now frantically pacing. 'I bet the next letter is a ransom note.'

'Ed. Listen to me. You have to pull yourself together man.'

I was undeterred. 'Think Sam. Look at the postmark, City of Angels – Los Angeles. They want us to know she's there. They've got her and they want me to find her. Want your Angel back? Now, Go Seek. They probably want money for a map.'

'Enough, Ed.' He raised a hand. 'Granted these notes could be from someone who knows where Elaine is but, well the most likely scenario is that she left of her own free will. For Christssake, you don't kidnap someone and walk through Heathrow Airport with them.'

'You still think she's left me? After this? You know her Sam. So you answer me this: Would she leave me?'

He paused. 'I wouldn't have thought so. But it happens.'

'Without telling me?' I cried. 'You saw us together, you know how we were.'

'I don't know, Ed. We're working on it. Just sit tight. The LAPD will find these men.' Drumming his chin with his fingers, 'we'll find her. But you might not like what we find.'

CHAPTER ELEVEN

After Sam left, I tried to access both airports via the internet. No relevant information was available. Once you could confirm bookings by name only but, as the site informed me, post-September 11 improvements in airport security had extended to the web. Their site boasted that Los Angeles International Airport (LAX) was the largest and busiest airport in America. It served California, America's most populated state. Not the encouragement I needed. Still the letter wouldn't let me give up, especially that third line.

Now, Go Seek.

If there was a clue on the web, I was going to find it. After all, there wasn't much else I could do.

The longer I explored the Internet the more depressing things became. Over 100,000 people were registered missing in Los Angeles alone. Dozens of companies claimed great success in finding them; no doubt cashing in on desperate loved ones. People like me. Prices ranged from a few dollars to thousands. Despite my misgivings I registered with two in LA County. Completed entirely online, they wanted her details and a picture:

Name: Elaine McAdler
D.O.B. 11.14.1975
Height: 1m 48cm

I attached a Jpeg of Elaine on holiday in Italy. For some reason she never liked having her photo taken, yet she was incredibly photogenic. Even in the red-eyed fuzzy shots she dazzled. As I sent the attachment, images of Elaine swamped my head. I became overcome with emotion that needed to spill out. But I didn't shed a tear. I couldn't. It was like a dam of hope was holding my tears at bay. Instead, I refocused my mind, returning to the two men. Could they really have forced her to go with them? Sure, they could have overpowered her; even drugged her, but Sam was right. Elaine wouldn't have simply walked through Heathrow and got on a flight without protest. Of the two of us, she was the tough one. It was one of the things that I loved about her.

The police believed that Elaine had left me. That much was clear. No doubt gone off with an ex-lover. It probably would have been tidier for them if she'd left with one man not two. But she hadn't. I wasn't in denial. The letters were my sanity: my lifeline.

I re-read them over and over in my mind.

Third time lucky.

The connection with six weeks ago screamed out to me. What had they done to her?

Cross-amputation?

As if a hand gripped my face, a claustrophobic pang crept up unannounced and overwhelmed me.

For the past six weeks I had been trying to live with the not-knowing. Suddenly it was all too much. The walls were closing in. My clothes felt tight, I was struggling to breath. It was like the night in the park.

I was reliving my fear and confusion. Only now I was imagining Elaine in my place.

I knew I had to get away. Adrenalin flowed through me as I sprinted to the front door and out to my car.

Speeding through traffic I was lost to fear. My imagination had become my greatest enemy.

Now, Go Seek.

My mind yelled. Get there! Save her!

Despite my erratic driving I somehow arrived outside my destination where I questioned my actions. What had seemed possible only a few minutes earlier was completely irrational. Elaine was not there. She was not in the park. She was never going to be in the park.

I lifted my forehead from the steering wheel and caught sight of my face in the rear view mirror. Tears cascaded down my cheeks.

The dam had burst.

CHAPTER TWELVE

11.20am
Lincoln Heights, Los Angeles.

Kester Hardwick reclined into his old chair. Leather welcomed his contours like a long lost dog. The last fifteen years hadn't been so kind to his office. Gone were his inscribed autographs and boxing memorabilia to be replaced by what he would describe as 'dreck'. His office now felt like a museum of bad taste: décor so desperate to impress that Kester was surprised not to see 100-dollar bills adorning the walls. Only in Vegas had he seen so much gold look so cheap.

The office needed checking for bugs, but he didn't know where to start. Methods of surveillance had advanced beyond him and there were plenty interested in his next move – and not just the authorities. His murder conviction had proved he was no longer infallible. Many of the influential people who owed Kester would be hoping to orchestrate his quick return to prison. Powerful people; people who achieved through bending the rules, and all with weaknesses they would be desperate to protect. Kester didn't so much have a finger in every pie as know each ingredient.

* * *

Bruno Meyer was not easily intimidated but, as he entered the *Flesh* club, he was as anxious as a mail order bride on her wedding night. Despite being the manager, Bruno felt like an intruder, his usual arrogant swagger replaced by the careful steps of trepidation. Knocking on the office door he wondered what awaited him. The last time he was with Kester Hardwick was 1993, a fuck awful year for both men.

Bruno's image bothered him. He imagined what Kester would make of the red band of hair that snaked across his otherwise shaven skull, his pierced eyebrows. Hardly the look of a manager, he thought.

On entering the office, he was eyeballed by his boss. Sat in the manager's chair, Kester's stare challenged Bruno to talk.

Just about returning eye contact and trying too hard not to show fear, finally, Bruno broke the silence. 'You look well, Kester,' he said, his German accent now banished.

'It's good to get away.' Kester's voice hadn't altered. He still talked disturbingly slowly, never a rush to cram words in. When he spoke, people listened. 'Prison,' he scoffed. 'Full of weak minds in there, Bruno.' Kester maintained the stare, his blue, stony irises unnerving Bruno. 'How strong is your mind?'

'Strong enough,' grunted Bruno, puffing out his pectorals.

'How do you know?'

Forcing a smile, Bruno displayed gold teeth. 'I'm still around. Still kicking ass.' The smile never reached his eyes.

'Won't you sit down,' said Kester. 'You must be tired, what with all that ass-kicking.'

Bruno awkwardly pulled out a seat, scooted it backwards and sat down. Now level with Kester, he couldn't avoid the strength still evident in those eyes. A look of control. The stare of death. It was easier looking down a loaded barrel. Bruno took in the physical changes that a fifteen year stretch had made to his boss. For one thing, Kester was thinner; his bones seemed to have shrunk whilst his skin had expanded. A yellowy film lay over sunken cheeks. Short grey hair was combed forward. Either he was receding or his forehead was getting bigger.

Bruno watched Kester eyeing the room, probably wondering what had happened to his *Rat Pack* autograph.

'I'll be honest, Bruno. I don't like what you've done to my office.'

'I was under the impression, well, I kinda thought that this was my office.'

'Not Auric Goldfinger's?' mocked Kester. 'What's with all the gold? You should have stopped at the teeth.'

Nodding sheepishly, Bruno looked like a brat on a naughty step.

'And I noticed you changed the name of my establishment. *Flesh*? Bit crude don't you think?' Kester had named the club *Flesh Dance* in the eighties.

'Just dropped the *Dance* part,' defended Bruno, thinking: what's the big deal?

Everyone called it *Flesh* anyway.

'Well there's certainly plenty of flesh around. Tell me, Bruno. Doesn't it frustrate you working with all this pussy. Given your *problem*?' It was Kester's turn to smile.

Bruno was taken aback. He took trouble to keep his problem secret. In mentioning it, Kester was asserting his authority. He could talk about whatever he wanted and there was nothing Bruno Meyer could do about it. No longer was he the big fish. Digging his heels into the carpet, Bruno said, 'There is no problem.' Thinking: not if people keep their big mouths shut. Bruno had gotten used to a life of celibacy. He no longer desired women. Still, it did his image no harm surrounding himself with strippers.

'Glad to hear it,' said Kester. 'And how is our flesh – you looking after the girls?'

'It's all good. So, do I keep running the show?'

Kester laughed. It wasn't the sort of infectious laugh you wanted to join in with. When Kester laughed it was like hearing: I'm afraid we removed the wrong lung.

'No disrespect Kester but I've been managing this place since '93.'

'As far as this club is concerned, I see no reason to change things.'

Bruno could hide neither his surprise nor delight. 'So, we're cool?'

'Cooling. But it troubles me that you have enlisted the help of one or two unsavoury characters in my absence.'

'One or two,' acknowledged Bruno. They might as well have spoken freely he thought, the LAPD knew of his association with Surgeon, the character Kester was undoubtedly referring to. With his boss in prison, Surgeon had replaced Kester as Bruno's protector. Surgeon was currently the most feared man in North East LA. Hardly anyone – not least the police – knew what he looked like. People usually met Surgeon only once.

'You will end your dealings with this psycho for hire – this *Surgeon*.'

'Fine,' Bruno lied, unable to say otherwise.

'Good.' Kester pushed himself up from the desk. 'We have one more matter to discuss.' He inspected his tie, looked at Bruno. 'The girl.'

Bruno's heart raced. 'Claire?'

Kester nodded. 'She is here. In LA.'

Shocked, Bruno quickly stood; his lungs filling with hatred and revenge.

'I tracked her down,' boasted Kester. 'She's on her way as we speak.'

'How? Where?' Bruno's arms waved randomly. He had wasted thousands of dollars trying to locate Claire Needlam. Yet Kester, within a few days of his release had not only found her, she was on her way. Amazed, he added, 'I came close but—'

'Contacts,' crowed Kester. 'But it's immaterial. Never doubt my influence.'

Bruno was shaken. 'You should have told me you'd found her.'

'And let you have all the fun. My need for revenge is even greater than yours. I found her, this will be my party.'

'You gotta let me see her,' pleaded Bruno.

'Sooner than you think.'

'What are you going to do?' Bruno's eyes bulged with excitement.

Silent for a moment, Kester stretched out his index finger and dragged it across his neck. 'We are going to kill her.'

CHAPTER THIRTEEN

12.40pm
Lincoln Heights, Los Angeles.

Bound-up and gagged, with her head between her knees, Elaine dug deep. Summoning up courage, she reminded herself why she was doing this. Freedom has a price, she told herself. Her mind repeated the mantra every time the car jolted pain into her spine. It was a welcome pain, taking her away from what lay ahead. The arrangement hadn't included riding in the trunk of a car, but the blackness befitted her situation.

Never show weakness she had been taught by her father, *especially fear*. Reflecting on this, she worked on her breathing, and slowly fell back into a time before love had entered her life. A time before Ed had softened her, allowed her true self to open up.

She couldn't be that person now. Not here. If she was going to survive the next 24 hours she would have to go back in time, to seize on the anger and pluck out the cocksureness of old. She had the rest of this journey to become the woman they were expecting. And she would give them what they wanted, with all the bravado she could muster.

By the time the BMW came to a stop, Elaine's transformation was complete. She just prayed that she was ready.

* * *

As the trunk popped open, Claire Needlam emerged, blinking hard as sunlight invaded.

Sweat stung her dilating eyes as she peeked up at the neon light. The letters coming into focus sent a chill through her aching body: *Flesh* club. She had tried to desensitise herself, visualising this moment many times. It had never seemed quite this bad.

The huge frame of Tino leaned over her, blocking off the sun. Reaching down into the trunk he untied her hands and feet, ripping the duct-tape apart with forceful ease, his gold bracelet leaving a scratch as he tore the tape from her mouth.

Claire sucked in air. 'There was no need to tie me up,' she said. 'Trunk doesn't unlock from the inside.'

'Get out!' barked Tino. He had the look of a heavyweight champion gone to seed, a latter-day

George Foreman – minus the smile and grilling machine. He gestured at a gun poking out from his brown shirt. 'Lessgo.'

Hiding her fear, Claire straightened her spine and yawned; she could feel her old defences resurfacing.

The passenger's door banged shut and Skid joined them. A foot smaller than Tino, Skid was a Hispanic man with patchy facial hair and a bumpy face that shone more than his cheap jacket. *Seriously ugly.* Claire couldn't quite decide which rodent he most resembled. She favoured a rat.

Claire's adopted attitude was merely a rehearsal for what awaited inside. She had seen men like Tino and Skid before. They had no axe to grind, as far as they were concerned they were doing a job. They wouldn't be permitted to hurt her.

Skid peered over the trunk, offering Claire an eyeful of nasal hairs bound together by snot. 'Inside,' he snorted.

Fighting against cramp, she swung her legs out with all the grace of a drunken elephant. Puffing, 'That's the last time I travel economy.' Humour had always been her mask, and she relied on it now, more than ever.

Now free of tape, she fleetingly considered running, but there was no point in delaying the inevitable. She'd come this far, there was no turning back. One way or the other it was time to end things.

A giant hand grabbed down onto her nape. Tino picked her up like a cub, almost swinging her into the repulsive Skid.

'So, Skid,' she asked, 'who the hell conceived you?'

He smirked, revealing himself as a dentist dodger. 'Satan.'

Flanked by both men, Claire was led to the *Flesh* club entrance. The place was even tackier than she remembered. Lining the walls were large monitors showing bouncing breasts. At the end of the entrance stood an old doorman in a new suit, his jacket was open, his shirt hugged his pot belly. Smiling creepily he leered at her. 'Like the tits?'

Claire winked. 'Muscles is a little quiet but Skid's growing on me.' The man's tired face creased into a smile.

Standing in the club, Claire's heart was in her throat as she came face to face with a man who wanted nothing more than to kill her: Bruno Mayer.

Waving away the reluctant Tino and Skid, Bruno stepped back. Eyed Claire up like a vulture. She crossed her aching arms, felt her legs weaken. An hour of being folded inside the trunk and she'd forgotten how to stand still. She released a breath; let her anxiety out like a slow puncture. Flicking back her hair, she forced herself to look at Bruno, determined not to let her turbulent insides permeate her icy exterior. She noticed that his boyish good looks had evolved into a more appropriate appearance. Years of over-indulgence: nose candy, sun and God knows what else, had taken their toll. Some men age like a fine wine;

Bruno, Claire thought, had aged like a banana milkshake.

'Welcome to hell.' Bruno revealed his gold teeth.

Immediately, Claire knew that she'd made a mistake coming here. He wasn't going to let her survive this. She thought of Ed, what she must have put him through. And for what?

Never show weakness. 'Hell?' she said, her mouth as dry as the Sahara. 'I heard you changed the name.'

Slowly, Bruno's face turned the same dark red as his hair – a stripe of spikes that reached for the sky like a class of infants holding an answer. 'I've waited a long time for this reunion.'

Claire swallowed the fright rising inside. 'And this is all the welcome I get? No bunting?'

'Saving it for your wake.'

'Hair like a rooster and humour. My, you have been busy.' Her body was destabilized by fear but her voice refused to show it.

'So where were you?' Bruno was visibly struggling for control. 'Spain?'

'Does it matter?' She shrugged. 'Let me guess, you dropped dollars trying to find me and you're wondering if you came close.'

Things were going wrong. She sensed the anger build up inside him, every muscle tensed with the effort of holding in his frustration. The fact that he hadn't already killed her told Claire that he would be expecting to soon enough.

Bruno made a fist, but relented. 'How do you know I didn't find you?'

'You've no patience. If you'd found me I'd be dead already.'

'So Kester found you.' He reproduced the gold-plated smile: 'Either way you are about to die a painful death.'

CHAPTER FOURTEEN

Northampton, England.

After my blubbering episode in the park I felt better, latching on to the hope brought by the second envelope. Both letters were inexplicably linked and had to hold the key to Elaine's whereabouts. Together with the flight details and postmark there was now a strong link between Elaine and Los Angeles.

Now, Go Seek.

My efforts were focusing on Los Angeles and those Spanish sounding names – Fernando Sanchez and Faustino Ricard – when my PC announced: You have mail.

Without thinking I clicked open the message.

From: replies-ginas69@hotmail.com
Message: Elaine
Mr Taylor,
I have recently seen Elaine in Lincoln Heights, Los
Angeles.
Unfortunately, I can't be of any more help. I missed
the chance to catch up and I've no idea where she's
at. Find attached a picture of her from the old days.
Thought you might like it.
Good luck.
Gina Sipple xxx

Stay calm. The message could be a prank, the attached jpeg a virus or pornographic image.

Only one way to find out.

The attachment was slow to open.

By the time the image appeared my heart felt like it was breaking free of my rib cage.

Three females emerged in what looked like a bar. A thin girl and a busty blonde were brushed aside as my eyes honed in on the woman in the centre. *Can this be Elaine?* Possibly, but the image was too small. All three women were dressed in a uniform and I made out the words *Flesh Dance* printed in red across stretched white tops. The woman in the middle had on a name badge. Unclear if it could be Elaine, I copied and pasted the image into Adobe Photoplus. Still unable to read the tag, I enlarged the image.

The badge read *Elaine.*

My breathing became short. I felt dizzy. Confused.

The resemblance was strong but inconsistent with the email message accompanying it.

Gina Sipple described it as a picture from the old days – the hairstyles suggested the eighties – but on closer inspection this Elaine looked older.

As I searched my confused brain for an explanation, the thin girl on the left caught my attention. I blinked hard. It felt like my brain was playing tricks on me. She looked no older than 16 but—*Can it really be?*

Her legs were too thin, her nose a little wide but—those eyes—that smile. The face of an angel that makes you want to sin. It was *my* Elaine. I gripped onto the desk, my body shaking. *This* was whom Gina had meant.

Think like Sam. Maybe it's a trick. The name *Flesh Dance* now jumped out at me.

Elaine must have worked there, despite being so young. Following up the lead, I Googled, '*Flesh Dance* Los Angeles', and came upon a nightclub called '*Flesh*'. It was located in Lincoln Heights, where Gina Sipple had claimed to have seen Elaine. An address was listed along with other nightclubs in North East LA. It occurred to me that I should reply to the message. Gina might not know where Elaine is but she could answer a few questions. Maybe she'd heard of Faustino Ricard or Fernando Sanchez? I thought about offering a reward for information but my course of action changed. As my excitement grew, a different train of thought landed on my track. I had only just entered Elaine's details into the Missing Persons site and yet this message came from somebody *already* in possession of my e-mail address. I started to believe that the e-mail might have come from Elaine herself, posing as this Gina Sipple. The postmark, the flight, now the message – all pointed me toward Lincoln Heights.

Now, Go Seek.

Feeling restless and alone, I decided to make my move and typed out a reply to the e-mail. In addition, I sent a further message to Elaine's personal e-mail address. If Elaine/Gina had not responded in the next 24 hours I was going to Los Angeles. If Elaine was able to read my message then news of my flying to LA might just persuade her to respond.

It felt egotistical, and given the circumstances a little crazy, but my relationship was strong. Whatever was happening was totally out of character for Elaine and there must be a reason for it. One thing was for sure, I couldn't escape the links with Los Angeles, and now I had a starting point.

Want your Angel back?

I wanted nothing more. The only question: *Will time be on my side?*

CHAPTER FIFTEEN

12.49pm
Lincoln Heights, Los Angeles.

'We all die,' said Claire, feeling the evil spilling from Bruno Meyer and threatening to submerge her. 'What's important is that we live a good and productive life.'

Bruno's bulky muscles raised their veins. He made a fist, pushing his jaw menacingly towards her. A loud cough caught his attention. He swung his head and glared.

It was Skid, lurking in the entrance.

'What do you want?' fumed Bruno.

'The boss won't like it if you start the party without him.'

Skid's words hung in the air, causing Bruno to back away, to rein in his anger.

Claire shut her eyes. Returning to LA was looking like a tragic mistake. She tried to hold onto the image of her perfect life back in England; yearned for a chance to return to the man she loved; pictured his face. Ed would have understood, joined her life on the run. It wouldn't have been so bad, said the treacherous voice in her head. Only, one day they would have been found. And it had been made clear to her what would happen to them when they were. Why was she torturing herself? It was too late now; she was here and must go through with it. *Never show fear.* Her eyes snapped open. 'As I said, a good and productive life. How is the drug dealing business?'

'Who are you kidding?' said Bruno. 'Making out you're Sister Teresa.'

'Mother,' Claire murmured.

'What?'

'It's *Mother* Teresa,' she corrected, holding her ground as his studded eyebrows performed a confused jig.

She was pumped up with adrenalin. But with Bruno on the brink of a violent tantrum, Claire eased off. Careful not to push too far. Skid was still milling around, pretending to give a wide birth, but she knew what Bruno was capable of, and that Skid couldn't stop him even if he wanted to.

Steadying himself, Bruno flashed his gold teeth. 'Think you're smart don't you. Even now. I've thought a lot about killing you, about the different ways I could hurt you. I'm gonna make you pay. Bitch!' Drops of spittle sprayed out of his mouth as he spat out the word.

Claire's stomach churned. Every second felt like thirty. She just wanted to crumble. To run. But whatever the outcome, she had to endure it.

It was the only way.

Bruno stepped closer, took a deep breath that seemed to suck the hope from her paralysed body.

The entrance yawned. Skid was holding open the door, looking at his watch. 'It's time, Mr Meyer. The boss'll be waiting. You ready?'

'Been ready fifteen years,' said Bruno. 'What about you, Claire Needlam? You ready to die?'

He hadn't expected an answer. She gave him none as she was bundled into the rear of the black BMW.

* * *

Watching through a window, Kester Hardwick saw the car pull around to the rear of his club. He set off towards it, noticed Claire on the back seat next to Skid, her head hung like a beaten dog.

It had been a long time, but he wasn't about to forgive what she'd done to him. There was a lot at stake here: his image for one thing; that of a cruel, unforgiving man. And so he was. Whatever had existed between them, this woman had crossed him. He was not a man to be crossed. Her punishment was expected. Even had it not been, he wanted her to feel regret for what she had done.

Tino got out, opened a door for Kester. He ducked inside, slid up to Claire. Her hands were bound and in her lap, shaking – her eyes flickering wildly, anywhere but at him.

Skid leaned in next to her, close enough to diagnose his halitosis. His gun pointed casually at her midriff.

'You've done a good job, gentlemen,' announced Kester, unable to remove his gaze from Claire's pale face. He focused on her frightened eyes, her taut mouth; examining each feature before moving on to the next. 'And it was good of you to come, Claire,' he added softly, almost tenderly. He squeezed her cold, trembling hands, felt her pulse rising. 'But alas, I have some bad news. The resolution you were hoping for, I'm afraid it's not possible, even for your pretty face.' Kester removed his hands, watched her suck in her cheeks, scrunch shut her blue eyes. 'What did you expect? You took away fifteen years of my life, a commendable achievement. Only now I get to exact my revenge. Personally.'

Kester noticed Bruno craning his neck, displaying unrestrained joy. 'I see Bruno is curious to know what I have planned. What about you Claire? Wondering how you're going to die?' He spoke conversationally, almost as though he was discussing the weather.

She gulped. Her voice unsteady, 'Are you getting Skid to breathe on me?'

Kester choked a rare laugh. Tino's shoulders danced.

A period of silence passed as they travelled through Lincoln Heights. Removing his gaze from Claire, Kester took in his surroundings. It saddened him to see the changes that had been wrought: the place showed more resemblance to the prison he'd just left than the neighbourhood he remembered. Seemingly every public and private space was now enclosed in the metal protection bars, gates and fences that started to be put up after the riots of '92. They covered the housing, dominating life. He had heard how they alienated people, destroying his community.

'Take the second entrance,' he urged.

The BMW swung through the wide-open gates of the Metal Treating Company.

They were heading for the furnace house.

'Not long now,' said Kester. 'Mr Sanchez, would you pass me the duct-tape?'

* * *

Lenny put the flask to his lips and tasted. Vegetable – made with love, and too much onion. As much as Lenny disliked the soup he loved the fact that his wife took so long to make it. He could actually taste the effort. Since his heart attack, Lenny's lunches had become leaner and greener. His dog, Samson, no longer watched him eat.

Returning to his crossword, Lenny was staring into space for inspiration when something broke his thought. A shadow appeared, over near the furnace house. *Strange*, he thought, *no one worked there on a Saturday*. Lenny checked the timetable. Nothing. He removed his reading glasses and focused on the window. Had he really seen someone? Should he call it in? As far as he knew there was nothing in there worth stealing.

He spun on his chair and checked the closed circuit TV. Nothing unusual. The furnace-house was closed up. There were no lights on. He pressed rewind but nothing happened. Not for the first time, Raul had forgotten to replace the tapes. The cameras worked but were not recording. *Oh well, probably nothing untoward*, thought Lenny, *anyhow, you can't get into the building without the code*. But never one to turn a blind eye, he headed out to take a look.

Amongst the handful of company vans, sat a Black Mercedes M-class SUV. Lenny returned to his hut and reached for Samson's lead. He had decided to check it out.

CHAPTER SIXTEEN

While Tino heavy-handedly dragged Claire from the car, Bruno Meyer stood back, his head going from side to side as he searched the site. The place looked deserted but sounds of industry were coming from buildings up ahead.

Watching his boss lead the way along a hedge-lined pathway, it began to dawn on Bruno just what Kester had planned for Claire. It was every bit as good as he had imagined.

Continuing past a sign that warned *Authorised Personnel Only*, the deep hum of machinery became a heavy groan. A similar noise was coming from Claire as Tino marched her towards the furnace house; his sausage fingers wrapped around her thin wrists.

Skid, his breath whistling in his chest, nudged alongside Tino, and said in an undertone, 'Ease off, big man.'

Bruno overheard. With an enraged stare at Skid, he made a point of taking Claire's arm, pinching it tightly as they reached a steel entrance.

Skid shrugged, dropped back, his finger busy with his nose.

Whilst Kester entered a code into a panel, Bruno increased his grip on Claire's arm.

She was rolling her head, frantically looking for help when he shoved her inside the furnace-house. Then he followed her in.

Hot, noxious fumes greeted them. Sweating profusely, the men were soon inhaling from under their sticky clothes. Bruno, gleefully watching Claire, saw that she had no such luxury – the duct-tape over her mouth was forcing her to breathe in the toxic air. He revelled in her desperation, the rage in her bulging eyes.

The temperature rose further as they moved deeper through the lifeless building.

Blinking away the heat, Bruno noticed Tino release his grip on Claire as their route narrowed. Not taking any chances, he whipped out his gun, dug it firmly into Claire's back. She began to lose balance. It seemed the combination of the fumes and heat was leaving her close to passing out.

'Stay on your fucking feet,' ordered Bruno.

Swaying, Claire shortened her steps.

Kester turned back and spotted the gun. 'If she tries anything you have my permission to shoot. Just make sure the bullet misses me.'

Bruno's eyes lit up. 'Come on, Claire,' he goaded, wanting desperately to squeeze the trigger. 'Surely you're not going down without a fight.'

They came to rest outside a furnace the size of an average garage. Kester parted a wooden door and entered a small zone immediately outside the furnace itself. Bruno bludgeoned Claire into the area then hung back. He didn't trust Kester enough to step in there voluntarily.

The heat was stifling and they hadn't yet entered the actual furnace. Pointing to a dial on the wall, Kester gazed stony-faced at Claire: 'It'll fire up in precisely ten minutes and will reach 1500 degrees. Ten minutes for you to think about what you did to me,' slowly he smiled, 'and then it will all be over.'

Ten more minutes of life, thought Bruno, barely able to believe it. After fifteen years of searching, of imagining her death, he was about to witness it first hand. His hand drifted to his groin as he listened to Claire's muffled pleas. Watched her beetroot face, her wide, panicked eyes. She was going to suffer. Know the kind of pain she'd inflicted on him all those years ago.

Kester offered a run down of the furnace's capabilities. 'It will act much like a cremation,' he explained, 'only it uses dry heat as opposed to flames. She will be consumed and vaporised, but for a few bone fragments and the ring on her finger.' Kester winked at Bruno. 'I thought you might like her engagement ring as a souvenir. I know how you like your gold.'

Engaged! Bruno thought of the poor sap, noticed Claire leaning away from Kester as he slowly ran a hand through her damp hair. She was sobbing and Bruno couldn't get enough of it.

She was bent over; trying to be sick, but her gag repelled it.

As Kester stepped away she fell back onto a wall. Then Kester left the furnace, looked again at the timer, turned to Bruno. 'In about seven minutes' time her insides will explode and her—'

A bang on the steel door.

Bruno felt uneasy – he didn't like surprises. He looked anxiously at the timer. *Six minutes.* Blood pressure built up inside his head as if he was blowing up a stubborn balloon. He said to Claire, 'Try anything and I'll shoot you.'

Seemingly unconcerned by the interruption, Kester called for Skid. 'Get rid of them. If whoever it is wishes to come inside, well, *let them,*' he nodded slowly, making it clear that if they insisted on entering it would be the last thing they would do.

Skid walked back past the furnaces, taking Tino with him. For every one of Tino's strides, Skid took two.

There was another knock. And barking; growing ever louder as they reached the steel entrance.

Skid opened the door, just enough to fill the gap.

A security guard of considerable age squinted down at him, struggling to keep hold of a barking Rottweiler. Acting nonplussed, Skid waited for the guard to speak.

CHAPTER SEVENTEEN

'What's going on?' asked Lenny.

Gripping tightly onto his dog's collar, he looked at the squat man standing in the doorway. Lenny didn't recognise the fellow and yet this man had a face even he would have remembered. A squashed face; sort of half-man, half-vermin. What's more, the hybrid had on black denim jeans, a dirty shirt, and no safety mask.

'Delivery,' snorted the runt in a Hispanic dialect. He lifted his sunken chin and gave Lenny an eyeful of escaping nasal hair. 'Four-inch-Frank. He Okayed it.'

'*Frank?*' Lenny couldn't get near the door. He had it all on to hold back Samson. 'I didn't think Frank was attached to the furnace house,' he wheezed.

'Just dropping something off for him. He wanted it putting in here.'

The Rottweiler's nose was a foot from his crotch. Spittle sprayed denim. The barking was so loud Lenny swore the man legs were vibrating.

'We won't be long,' said the diminutive freak. 'If you want, you can come inside, check it out.'

Lenny nodded an OK, tried to peer through the gap above the stranger. He could hear a furnace starting up.

Two minutes.

'Would you mind?'

The man shrugged. '*Seero problayma.*' He seemed to signal to someone else inside the building before applying a feral stare.

Lenny was wary. His dog was going berserk but the man had barely acknowledged him. It was this that unnerved Lenny. He had never seen anyone react that way to Samson before. Lenny pulled back on the collar. 'Think I'll just give Frank a call.'

'*Si*, your call *meesta*. Let him know his delivery is here.'

'Will do.' Lenny dragged Samson away.

The steel door slammed. Tino lowered his gun. 'Should I kill him?'

Skid shook his head. 'Frank will cover us.'

One minute.

'Not long now,' said Kester, but even his calm was slipping. He looked jittery as he reopened the furnace. 'I want to hear her scream,' he shouted over the roar of the furnace. Bending down he removed Claire's gag.

Bruno watched her breathe in the hot fumes, her lungs pounding like his uncle's concertina. He expected her to plead for her life but she just sat there, twiddling her engagement ring. When she refused to look at Kester he pushed her down off her concrete ledge, into the actual furnace. Bruno shared his frustration; he wanted her to beg for mercy, to cry for help.

He peered in, saw her spit ash. She was up on her knees, shivering, in spite of the heat.

Kester tugged Bruno back, and as the steel door closed they watched Claire lunge forward.

In a desperate attempt at freedom she threw herself at the narrowing gap. But it was too late. Her skull crashed against the inside of the door as a light came on.

The furnace growled into action.

Kester called out, 'Cover your eyes, Claire, might just stop them popping out of your skull.'

The heat intensified. Bruno backed away, victorious.

Returning his ear to the door, they finally got their wish. They heard Claire scream.

Both men listened as her screams died. For Bruno Meyer, revenge was sweet. For Kester Hardwick, it was expected.

CHAPTER EIGHTEEN

7.30pm
South Carthay, Los Angeles.

Sparks Bar boasted enough televisions to double as an electrical superstore. The screens had a hypnotic effect, with patrons staring for hours. Special Agent Donnie Guzan liked that about the place. It meant he could visit without being noticed, even take in several ball games at once.

CIA Officer, Ethan Knight, hadn't frequented Sparks since the days when smoking and conversation were permitted. Scanning the glazed faces for eye contact he noticed Guzan's tight ginger curls rising from the end of a long bar. With his brown, scuffed leather jacket, *Ray-Bans* and lonely beer bottle, he looked a little too much at home.

'Ethan,' Guzan reached out his hand, 'right on time as ever.'

'So, Don,' Knight pumped Guzan's hand, 'this is where you get your culture.'

The baseball-capped barman threw them a look of disdain. Guzan perched back on his stool, studied Knight. At 47, they were the same age and, as usual, Guzan compared looks, concluding that Knight looked younger, but only on account of his fatter face.

Aware of the scrutiny, Knight smiled. 'Tell me, Don, how are you?'

'Better than I look,' said Guzan. 'Mandy well?'

'Demandingly so.'

Two beers were ordered and paid for and the men retired to the corner table. It was the empty part of the bar, featuring the news channels.

Knight began, 'I take it you heard about Kester Hardwick?'

Giving a weary frown, Guzan downed what was left of his first beer. 'That's over with, Ethan.'

'Glad to hear it. Guess you've moved on, huh?'

Guzan said nothing.

Pulling up a stool, Knight lowered his backside and voice in unison. 'So, Don, this is where you tell me you have some information on our Iranian friends.'

'At the moment, zilch, but you'll be the first to know. If you tell me what the hell's going on?'

Knight feigned innocence, 'What do you mean?'

'Come on Ethan! The security threat?'

Falling silent, Knight looked both ways, and slid

up to Guzan. 'We are expecting Meybodi or Afshari to reveal something.'

Guzan removed his shades. 'Carry on.'

'Or what, you'll withhold information?'

'If I know what we're up against, I will be able to interpret any information properly. Our organisations might not be tight right now, but we trust each other, right? And anyway, I never said I had any information; you called this meeting.'

'I trust you.' Knight held up his hands. 'Man, everybody trusts you. But in the current climate I can't be too careful.'

'Whatever you tell me won't go any further,' vowed Guzan.

Knight rolled his eyes. 'You and Derego are closer than Mandy and my credit card.'

He checked again that they couldn't be overheard.

A moment passed.

'All right, all right, you win.' sighed Knight, lowering his voice still further, 'They are our best link to a terrorist. That extremist group we mentioned. Really we were referring to just one man. His name is Sadiq al-Barabi. It has come to light that he is the beneficiary of the money the two Iranians have been soliciting.'

Guzan pointed his empty bottle at Knight. 'Go on.'

'Intelligence has only just alerted us to his presence in LA. Sadiq al-Barabi controlled one of the largest MEK bases in Iraq. But he's not a military man, he's a mercenary: follows violence around like a war correspondent.' Knight shuffled his fingers. 'But I don't want the FBI concerned with him, only the two Iranians. We suspect that he intends to use their money to fund a chemical attack on a major Californian city.'

The men sat in silence as a flabby man in a referee's uniform ambled over, delivered their beers, stumbled away.

'How do you know this?' Guzan took a big gulp.

'The Patriot Act,' said Knight, pleased with himself. 'Amongst the recruited foreign nationals living in the US are a number of Iranians working for us. As you know, Iran is a denied area, and the only way to get relevant information out has been with the use of these expatriates. The man at the top of our wage bill had links with Al Qaeda.'

Guzan gave a low whistle. 'So you want Afshari and Meybodi to lead you to this guy?'

'Not exactly.' Knight folded a beer-mat. 'We already have him.'

'What?'

'You really think we would have kept him from the FBI? No, we got lucky. Sadiq al-Barabi had already been arrested. Three years ago. Shortly after he entered the country he was picked up for speeding. His face was enough to get his car searched. In the trunk LAPD found several metal bullets, imported from Russia and capable of piercing armour. He remains in the County Jail under a false ID.'

'And the Iranians, Afshari and Meybodi, they know this?'

'Of course, they have waited patiently for his release, which they anticipate to be on Monday. He meets with a parole council at which he's due to be freed. Of course, that's not going to happen. Sadiq al-Barabi is going straight to a unit for interrogation. But by our detaining him past his release date, Afshari and Meybodi will suspect we're onto them. We have until Monday. After that time, gleaning any information from the Iranians will be all the more difficult.'

'I still don't get why the bureau has been frozen out?'

'Certain information has been leaking,' said Knight. 'We can't take any chances with this.' He inspected his beer-mat origami, discarded it. 'They have fraudulently amassed a fortune collecting for the MEK, but finding that money is only half the story.' Knight hunched forward his shoulders. 'Remember the chemical breach we referred to? The one at AWS?'

Guzan put down his drink then patted his chin as he recalled seeing the crime report from Arizona Waste Solutions. According to the report, a large amount of chemical waste had become unaccounted for. The missing chemicals were categorised as safe by the Environmental Protection Agency, but doubts had been raised when a lab explosion killed four engineers; all of the men had been working on new ways to dispose of the waste. 'Yeah.' Guzan nodded. 'I remember.'

Knight locked his hands. 'Our intel suggests that at least one of those men was developing a formula to turn obtainable waste into a chemical weapon.'

'What intel?' questioned Guzan.

'Can't say. And let me remind you, this information is classified.'

Guzan smiled ruefully.

'We are conducting a thorough investigation into what happened in Arizona. It is my understanding that the formula had already been developed. The lab explosion wasn't an accident; it was to destroy evidence. If we can identify who killed the scientists it might lead us to whoever has the formula.'

'Any luck?'

'Not exactly. A short man, dressed from head to toe in protective gear, was seen fleeing the scene.' Knight gave him a look that said: don't get too excited. 'On the day of the explosion, a computer glitch wiped the security system. It could only have come from a hacker with high level government access.'

'An inside job?'

Knight didn't need to answer.

Guzan reached for his beer. 'So why involve me?'

A desperate look befell Knight. 'Because I need your help.'

CHAPTER NINETEEN

Typical CIA, thought Guzan, always an ulterior motive. When he was asked to meet Knight he should have known better. 'You need my help,' he repeated. 'This should be good.'

Knight tore the label from his beer bottle. 'I haven't been completely honest with you.'

'I'm all ears,' said Guzan, noticing that Avengers' fans were starting to fill the section of the bar screening the football.

'We believe that Sadiq al-Barabi is intending to use the Iranians' money to acquire the formula. We need to know who is selling it to him, and what he plans to do with it. By putting Afshari and Meybodi under surveillance we hope to learn something.' Knight loosened his tie, licked dry lips. 'There is another person who might know what Sadiq al-Barabi has planned.'

Guzan frowned. 'Oh?'

Knight shuffled uncomfortably. 'Kester Hardwick.'

Dread crashed over Guzan. His mind travelled back to the time of Cliff Donachie's suicide, a time when Kester seemed to know everything. But that was then. 'Get real, Ethan,' he dismissed. 'Kester Hardwick's spent the past fifteen years in prison.'

Knight looked up. 'Exactly.'

'What?' Guzan shook his head, 'He on Sadiq's wing or something?'

'They shared a cell.'

A chill froze Guzan's spine. The image of Cliff's wife and children burning to their deaths filled his head – the same image that had driven his partner to suicide. With sickening certainty, Guzan knew that Kester was back in his life and this time there was no Cliff Donachie to bring him down.

Covering his mouth with his bottle, Knight explained all. 'Five years ago, Hardwick was moved to the County Jail. Officially, his sentence was winding down. Unofficially, he had become too influential at the Fed Pen, so his transfer was arranged. He found himself on a black majority wing, but he soon bought, threatened, and bribed enough respect to call the shots. Then Sadiq al-Barabi walks in. Also wealthy, he made friends the more traditional way. Violence. Might have got him killed in a prison full of lifers but, in the County Jail, it earned him a year on his sentence and a couple of trips to the medical room. That extra year was a token gesture. There's been a cover up. Most of his actions have been swept under the carpet. It's said that his hands are like weapons. Apparently, he practically decapitated a man with one strike of his hand.'

'Apparently?'

'Another prisoner squealed for it. But there are other incidents. Established gangs tried to recruit him, but he wasn't having any of it. Having no gang affiliation helped him. What's more, he appeared to be fearless.'

The conversation halted as a shapely cheerleader walked up to the table, lowered her come-hither cleavage.

'Get you boys anything?' she smiled widely.

With a sweep of his bottle, Knight dismissed her.

'We're fine, thanks,' smiled Guzan, her satin mini-skirt waved him goodbye as she pivoted away. He shook his face, asked, 'How did he wind up in the same cell as Kester?'

'Rumours were circulating that Hardwick enjoyed certain privileges,' said Knight, 'the latest tunes on his I-pod, what-have-you. The Warden claimed that by making him share with an unhinged brawler like Sadiq al-Barabi, he was showing everyone who the real boss was. We don't believe it for a second. Either Hardwick, or Sadiq, bribed the Warden. He refutes this, but we know that forty thousand dollars went into his account. It was clear to us that one of them wanted the other's company pretty badly. But we don't know which, or why. They shared a cell until Sadiq was given keep-away status. He's been kept in isolation for the past six months of his sentence.'

Guzan rubbed his puffy eyes. 'I don't see what I can do.'

'My guess is that Hardwick arranged their bunk up and I want you to find out why.'

'Can't The Unit do it?'

Within the FBI there were many units: Crime Scene Unit, DNA Analysis Unit, Intelligence Unit, Foreign-language Translation Unit, Behavioural Science Unit, Cyber-crime Unit, Hate Crimes Unit, to name a few, but it was the Terrorist Unit to which Guzan referred. It was known by Field Agents as *The* Unit, reflecting the workload they devoted to terrorism.

'The threat isn't active,' said Knight. 'And it would take too long for them to get inside Hardwick's head. You know him already. Better than anyone. Look, Don, I know you have reservations after what happened to Cliff and his family, but getting hold of this formula could pre-empt a chemical attack. You're the best man for the job.'

Accepting that he had no choice, Guzan reluctantly agreed. Averting a chemical attack wasn't his only motivation – a friend's honour was at stake.

'Any thoughts?' asked Knight.

'First off, I doubt very much that Kester would ever trust Sadiq al-Barabi with his plans. He made a point of hiring non-Caucasians but never dealing with them. What he feels goes beyond racism. That means if he arranged their hook-up it was to use the terrorist for his own end. What else do we know about him?'

'He's a Kaffir. A non-believer. Speaks a number of languages, but we believe him to be of Sudanese origin. He is suspected of genocide but even that's open to conjecture. I would focus on the money. Sadiq al-Barabi has reputed wealth, but we only know of the fortune the two Iranians have collected. We have also to assume that Hardwick knows about this money.'

'That would make sense,' agreed Guzan. 'Kester may have influenced the parole board, manipulated his own release to occur days before Sadiq's. That can't be coincidental. Kester must have designs on this money.'

Loud cheers erupted at the bar, a profusion of black and red bouncing to the news that their team were up on Chicago Rush. When it came to football, Guzan was a Raiders man, but he spoke through smiling teeth, 'What is the CIA doing?'

'Our priority remains uncovering the formula. Hardwick may or may not have anything to do with this, but we have to assume he knows everything: Sadiq al-Barabi's past, the fact that he isn't going to be released. Everything. Commit what resources you can to Hardwick, but in the meantime keep your focus on the Iranians. And keep me in the loop.'

CHAPTER TWENTY

Sunday.
Northampton, England.

Having spent a third long night without Elaine, I was
barely functioning. Sleep deprivation had ensured
the absence of my nightmare but I had become
encased in visions of her death. Struggling to shake
off the belief that something terrible had happened
to her, I pushed myself under the shower, bumbled
into the kitchen and forced down some cereal.

The phone rang. My heart stopped as I heard
Elaine inform the caller they had reached the home
of Ed and Elaine. Each word tugged at my soul.
She sounded distant. Like a voice from the grave.
The message that followed was left by a reporter
wanting to ask me a few questions concerning the

murder of Gary Jasper. That was *all* I needed. I put him off until Monday. By then I'd be in Los Angeles. It was time to reclaim my soul.

It was time to Go Seek.

* * *

Sam called by with his son George on their way to his Taekwando class. He was desperate for his son to learn a martial art before attending big school. Carrying a packet of chews and a mischievous grin, the seven-year-old headed straight for the TV.

Unfolding a scanned photo, Sam showed me a mug-shot of Faustino Ricard. The upshot was: I didn't recognise him. Given that, it didn't really matter what he looked like. For the record, he was black and from the width of his neck, a big bruiser of a guy.

'He's a chauffeur.' Sam added, 'Columbian. Forty-three years old and lives in Lincoln Heights.'

His words winded me. Lincoln Heights again.

Folding like a deckchair, I dropped onto the couch, mug-shot in hand. Holding up the black and white image, many questions prodded my brain.

Sam sat down, perching himself on the edge of the leather recliner. 'There are no available pictures of the other guy, Sanchez. He isn't in the system.'

'So what's *he* in the system for?' I jabbed the photo.

'GBH. Faustino Ricard has a fondness for fighting,' Sam sighed regretfully. 'LAPD will bring him in for questioning, but they are reluctant to do so until they have more information.'

'We can't wait for that.' I lowered the mug-shot. 'How does *he* know Elaine? And what the hell is *she* doing flying to Los Angeles with him?'

My only clarity was that waiting for news was getting me nowhere fast. We talked more about the letters and Gina's e-mail. I told Sam of my plans to fly to America.

His response was predictable. 'That's a bad idea, Ed.'

'And what if Elaine's in Lincoln Heights?' I protested. 'She might not be there long. Think about it, Sam. We know she flew to LA. The e-mail included a picture of Elaine that gave us *Flesh Dance* – which is in Lincoln Heights; which is where Faustino Ricard resides.' I was aware my frustration was showing and that it wasn't fair to take it out on Sam, but I couldn't help myself.

He shook his head. 'So what's your plan? To fly to LA and what, go to this club?'

'Exactly. I'm booked on a 4pm flight.'

His hand shot up to his mouth, slid to his head, patting down his dark, shiny hair.

'And what if she's not there?'

'Someone there will know her, I'm sure of it. *I'll* find Faustino Ricard. Watch me!'

Sam wagged a finger. 'I have told you the LAPD will —'

I cut him off: 'Their cops aren't bothered about a woman missing from England. You don't understand what it's like here. I have to do something to stop myself going insane.'

'I know it's tough buddy.' Sam paused, his dark jittery eyes finally settling on his son. 'But it's best you leave it to the professionals. In the meantime, if Elaine wants to contact you, she will. You don't want to be out when she rings.'

'She has my mobile number and I can access e-mail via my phone.'

Losing the argument, Sam rose to his feet, establishing authority. 'Edson, my advice as a friend and a policeman is not to go.'

'Somebody wants me there, maybe Elaine, maybe not. But the letters; Start counting, Go Seek. Everything is pulling me to Los Angeles.'

He sucked on a lip, closed his eyes. 'Promise me you won't go anywhere until I get back.'

I looked away. Said nothing.

* * *

After two hours of planning and packing the phone rang. Once again I waited for Elaine's message to kick in.

'Alright you win,' conceded Sam. 'I could do with a tan.'

Diving for the phone, I grabbed it up. 'What?'

'I'm booked on your flight,' he sounded strangely upbeat.

Amazed by his sudden change of heart, I said, 'I'm grateful but there's no need.'

'I've sorted it at the station. I can come out for a few days. After that you're on your own.'

'What about Janice? The kids?'

'They'll be fine. She understands. She's worried about the both of you.'

'But two hours ago you were totally against the idea!'

Stumbling for words, 'We just got the phone records back from Betta- Mobility.'

Betta-Mobility? Has Elaine called someone from work?

Sam answered my unspoken question: 'A call was made from her office, to Los Angeles, a week ago.'

The line went quiet. Then: 'I still think this trip's a bad idea but someone's got to look after you.'

'Are you sure about this?'

'No, but if you are, I'm going with you.'

CHAPTER TWENTY-ONE

9.43am
Santa Monica, Los Angeles.

The Palm House Nursing Home was just as Donnie Guzan remembered it. Clean, clinical, as homely as hell. Glass walls and ceilings flooded the place with sun, making it as hot as it was bright.

He was pleased to see his favourite nurse greet him in reception. Ah, Nurse Garcia: genuine smile, mischievous eyes, no wedding ring. Maybe she fancied him – he could never tell. As she praised the weather and bemoaned the air-conditioning, he smiled nervously. Serial killers scared him less than attractive women. Not that nurse Garcia should be attractive. Her nose was bumpy, her mouth a little lopsided, but when it came to the sum of all parts, her face just worked. Perfectly. Afraid of flirting, Guzan asked after Mrs Donachie, the resident he was there to see.

'She's about the same as your last visit,' said nurse lovely, in a voice as clear and smooth as her skin. 'You're just in time for morning tea,' she added, gliding into the main lounge.

Following like a duckling, Guzan admired how her tight, lemon uniform complemented her dark olive body.

Why have I only ever dated one Hispanic woman? He asked himself, bringing to mind the athletic Cuban from Anaheim, a pitcher for the local baseball team. Guzan didn't know if she was any good but he never got past second base.

Spotting Mrs Donachie in her usual seat, Guzan walked over. A heavy-set woman with a gentle face, she was sitting in one of forty wipe-able recliners positioned in a circle. The seating plan was how he imagined an AA meeting to look. It reminded him of his LAPD days; being reliant on the juice. Back then alcoholism was rife in the force and in an attempt to clamp down, it was decided that all heavy drinkers would be referred to AA. One morning the Captain had reported this back, pulled Guzan to one side and asked, 'What would you say if I ordered you to go to Alcoholics Anonymous?' With a slow smile, Guzan had slurred, 'Huh? Which one of you two said that?' The Captain had just laughed; he was the department's biggest drinker. Nothing more had been said and over time, Guzan had got the juice under control.

When Mrs Donachie saw Donnie Guzan, she stared blankly for a few seconds before her face lit up. Cliff's mother had always been fond of Guzan and after her son's suicide they had kept in touch: partly to aid his own grieving process, but mainly because she had no one else. The house fire hadn't just taken Cliff's family, it had taken hers too. The timing of Guzan's visit was no coincidence. Like him, Mrs Donachie blamed Kester Hardwick for her loss. He wondered if she had heard the news of Kester's release. If not, he wanted to be the one to tell her. It was principally why he had come today.

For some time she had suffered from Alzheimer's. Guzan took this as a blessing. It was as though her mind was protecting her, often allowing her to recall only the time before tragedy struck.

'Clifford,' Mrs Donachie exclaimed in her loud Irish voice. 'How are you son? Let me look at you.' She loved to rub Guzan's cheeks with her palms. Bending down, he obliged. 'Your eyes look all sleepy, so they do, and your face all crinkled.'

Guzan cringed. Thankfully, Nurse Garcia was out of earshot.

'You need more kip,' Mrs Donachie went on, 'and sleep on your back. It'll help with your crinkly face, so it will.' She noticed his presence was gaining an audience. 'This is my son,' she proudly announced to the world. 'He's a policeman.' She was wrong on both counts but Guzan played along, offering a goofy smile back at the residents, not all of whom were staring at him, just the awake ones.

Now sweating profusely, Guzan slid off his

leather jacket and hung it on his seat, inadvertently catching the attention of a dosing resident. *Big mistake.* The frail lady was suddenly wide-awake and gazing up at him. Oh no, he thought. Somehow she had beaten off the effects of chronic osteoporosis to make enough eye contact to invite conversation.

She gripped his arm. 'Don't mind me, I'm 82,' her lopsided face read *Gotcha!* 'Would you like a mug of coffee?' she asked in a weak voice. 'Second one of the day.'

Declining the drink, Guzan sat between the two women. The fragile old lady seemed sweet but he didn't have long to chat. After seeing Mrs Donachie he had a busy day ahead.

'Haven't you lovely red hair?' complimented the 82 year-old, grasping unsuccessfully for a handful of Guzan's curls.

Better than crinkly, he thought as he thanked her and switched attention to Cliff's mother.

'Don't talk to Mrs Donachie,' moaned the old dear, pulling him back towards her make-up-splotched face. 'She'll probably complain about her Alzheimer's. She never forgets to tell people that. I'm more fun, have a drink with me.' She winked and jerked his arm. 'See him in the white fleece? We call him Mister T 'cos he sneakily pours extra tea into his flask. *Everybody* knows it.'

Unable to quieten the lady up, Guzan gestured apologetically at Mrs Donachie who had drifted elsewhere.

'Hey! Mister T,' the lady belted out across the room, forgetting to be weak and fragile. 'This man is a policeman. He's here to arrest you. Seize your flask.' She laughed so hard her teeth danced.

Looking daggers at Guzan, Mister T frantically opened his flask. In his rush to hide the evidence, scalding tea dripped down his front.

She now pointed at a man in glasses so thick they could be bulletproof. 'See him there. His name's Charles. He's the only man in here that's any good in bed. And do you know why?'

Trying to slip free his arm, Guzan winced, 'No.'

She gripped tighter, pulled down on him. 'He's the only one who can keep his bed sheets dry.' She bellowed out a laugh that ended in a coughing fit.

Taking the opportunity to free himself, Guzan shook off the old girl to face Cliff's mother.

Mrs Donachie frowned. 'I know you, don't I?'

Before Guzan could explain a voice piped up from behind. 'It's your *son*.'

'Clifford!' Mrs Donachie gleamed, life back in her eyes. For the next few minutes she talked freely, blissfully unaware of the past. It was as though fifteen years had been wiped from her mind. Then she clammed up. Her eyes sharpened. 'Have you caught your man yet?' she asked.

'My man?'

'Oh, he's a bad man, Clifford. A big wide face so he has. I detest him.'

'Who?'

'*Who?*' She screwed up her mouth. 'That Kester.' Hatred filled her dry eyes. 'I have been thinking son. Remember what I told you about not dropping the case.'

'Remind me.'

'I said you should stick to your guns. Despite the threats, you go after him.' She paused, pulled on her fingers. 'Well I was wrong, you should drop the case. Protect your family.'

'I don't follow,' said Guzan thinking: *what threats?*

Mrs Donachie's stare was serious. Focused. Her face shook with anger as she strained her words, 'And so help me God, I think you should have him killed.'

Standing to compose himself, Guzan knew his visit had been a mistake. He wanted to reassure her, even brighten her day, but instead he'd awoken old feelings and confusion. Kissing her cheek, he slowly backed away from his chair.

On reaching the door he heard her call out, 'You finish that big-faced bastard!'

Turning back, Guzan saw shock on her face and her hand to her mouth. The room fell silent, Mrs Donachie flushed with embarrassment. Saddened by her outburst, Guzan decided it was best to make his retreat, regretful that his visit had upset her. Maybe she did remember, he thought. Maybe she sat there feeling nothing but hatred.

On leaving the nursing home, Guzan felt a tap on his back. It was Nurse Garcia. 'Everything okay?' she asked.

'Yep. Sorry about back there, I guess you heard it.'

'Everyone did. Mister T thought she was talking about him. Nearly spat tea on his fleece. And I'd only just wiped it.'

Immediately her smile put Guzan at ease. She had a warm, caring nature – just the sort of company he needed in his life. The timing was weird but he bit the bullet. Defying years of social conditioning, Guzan asked her out.

CHAPTER TWENTY-TWO

Guseppi Biani felt the weight of the 1966 M40 sniper rifle lean against his leg. Wrapped in a refuge sack, the weapon looked at home behind the large recycling dumpster that hid Guseppi from the *Flesh* club's car lot.

The 67 year-old Italian was peaceful, God-fearing. But like everybody else, the former military man had a limit. A breaking point. His was reached the day his son went missing. Fifteen years ago, Franco Biani was happy. Then his path had crossed Kester Hardwick's.

In court, Guseppi had sworn that he'd be waiting for Kester. His desire for vengeance – an eye for an eye – had kept him alive. It meant battling cancer and the death of his wife, but Guseppi was still standing. He had survived for a reason: he meant to honour that promise. The grey coat on his back camouflaged his lean body, and the charcoal boonie hat tied under his chin shielded his eyes from the sun. Yanking his belt up to his naval he knelt down.

Then he waited.

A powerful adrenal rush filled Guseppi with strength the moment he sighted that murderer, Kester Hardwick, walking out of the strip club. He'd bided his time long enough. Finally his chance for justice had arrived. Grinding his teeth, he pawed for the rifle; his gaze remained locked on his target as he tore away plastic and brought the scope to his eye. A respected shooter in the army, Guseppi had honed his skills.

Damn it. Someone was blocking the sight. Lifting his eyes, Guseppi saw a large, black man, striding alongside Kester. Accompanying them was a stubby, weird looking man in a black jacket, sleeves down to his knuckles. Looked like a Mexican; probably the hired henchmen thought Guseppi, fixing his glare back through the scope. Still no clear shot. He'd have to get closer.

The men stopped at a BMW. The black man's huge frame covered Kester as he motioned him into the back of the automobile. The ugly Mexican joined them. Before their doors were shut, Guseppi was pounding towards his Honda.

The BMW turned right onto Parkside Avenue. Flooring the accelerator, Guseppi followed. His engine and heart raced in unison. Recently, his doctor gave him the green light to keep driving, with a proviso that he avoided high speeds. Within a minute, Guseppi was only one car from the BMW. In the rear window he recognised a small Columbian flag next to a bumper sticker: it read, FAT PEOPLE ARE HARDER TO KIDNAP!

Following the BMW was proving too easy; to avoid suspicion he hung back. By the time they were on the North Mission Road all thoughts of sticking too close seemed immaterial. The traffic busied, cars cutting in and out like dodgems. He struggled to stay with them, but Guseppi was focused. He was hyped up on revenge.

* * *

After battling the Sunday traffic, the BMW passed what used to be the old jail – now real estate – then entered Boyle Heights. Looking for the Newby office, Tino was directed into an industrial area. Barred up warehouses were present on both sides of the street, only a handful showing signs of activity. The further in they drove, the quieter it became.

'Here we are,' said Skid. 'The Newby Company.'

The car slowed, Tino pulling up outside the only new building on the street. It looked almost apologetic. Kester wondered how long it would be before it became infected with the decay of its neighbours.

Tino was ordered to stay with the car whilst Skid joined Kester. As they walked up to the narrow, three-story office, Kester felt a little uneasy, as he often did away from Lincoln Heights. People thought it strange that a man of his wealth lived amongst such paucity, but Kester felt safe in Lincoln Heights: untouchable, and the king of his domain.

At least the office was suitably remote, he thought, perfectly inconspicuous for such a meeting. A security camera picked them up as they approached the entrance. Kester smoothed forward his grey hair, buttoned his jacket and buzzed the intercom.

'Do come in,' replied the deputy mayor in an overfriendly voice.

The small reception area smelt new, meaning less dust filled air that was air-conditioned cold. Masquerading as furniture was a cheap coffee table which parted two plastic chairs.

Deputy Mayor, Howard Francis, complete with politician's smile and professional hairpiece, stepped out of a room. 'Kester; how the hell are you?' Francis stuck out a hand.

Both influential and corruptible; Francis held the two qualities Kester looked for in a mayor. 'Surviving,' he replied as the men exchanged power handshakes.

Glancing in a southeasterly direction, Francis performed a double take at Skid. 'I thought you might like to meet alone but I see you've brought a friend.'

Without breaking eye contact, Kester held out a

palm. 'Skid, this is what your deputy mayor looks like.'

Skid looked unimpressed.

Turning to face him, Francis spoke in a patronising tone as if addressing the retarded, 'Pleased to meet you, Sir.'

Kester hid a smile. It was clear from the deputy mayor's expression that he was anything but pleased. People always took an instant dislike to Skid. They couldn't help it. With his dark, oily skin, low forehead and reaching nostrils, he looked distinctly rat-like; not helped by the fact that he appeared to have shaved with a blunt penknife. Nobody liked a visit from Skid. His own mother would sooner open her door to a debt collector.

Skid nodded; smiled thinly. 'Call me Mr Sanchez,' he snarled, waiting by the entrance.

'Own a few offices myself,' said Kester, as his eyes ate up the room. 'You just moved in?'

Francis grinned. 'I assume you are alluding to the lack of furniture?'

Kester nodded politely.

'The developer calls it minimalist, but I take it you're not here to sample the interior décor.'

'Actually, I am here to do you a favour,' fabricated Kester.

'Oh?' mouthed Francis, wearily, 'maybe we should sit down.'

A door was opened. The deputy mayor led Kester into a back room. Once again the furniture – what there was of it – looked cheap and fake. Quite fitting for a potential mayor of LA, thought Kester.

Preferring to stand, he closed the door behind him and waited while the man lowered himself into a plastic seat.

'I'm sure you'll agree the last thing LA needs is another investigation into a corrupt and prejudiced force,' said Kester.

'What've you got?'

'Tomorrow, a prisoner is due to be taken to the appeals court at City Terrace for the formality of his release. Only he's not going to be released.'

'I'm sorry, I don't follow.' Francis lightly scratched his head, careful not to disturb his $1500 toupee; a lightweight model specially made for the summer.

'The authorities are planning to take him to a secure unit and fit him up. What they are planning is off radar and therefore illegal.'

Francis flapped his hands. 'I'm sure due process will be followed.'

Kester glanced away in disgust. 'When you cross racism with paranoia you get these situations. Under the banner of suspected terrorist they think they have *carte blanche* to treat people as they like, regardless of evidence. Only this prisoner is important, a former political leader of sorts. In today's climate it could turn nasty if he is treated anything other than fairly. This man is known as Sadiq al-Barabi. He may well be guilty of something, but this is about fairness.' Kester paused, added, 'And avoiding embarrassing protests, or worse.'

Francis held out his hands then clapped them together. 'I don't see how I can interfere, but if anything untoward occurs I can assure you tha—'

'I'll start again,' said Kester, his voice slow. Menacing. 'What we are talking about here is *me* doing *you* another favour. You know what that means, Howard?'

'I'm the deputy mayor now, Kester,' he rebuked, trying to dismiss the threat, 'I've moved on.'

'And I'm sure you don't need reminding how you came into office.' His eyes delivered a warning. 'I am not being unreasonable. All I am asking is that you uphold the law.'

Sinking his shoulders, Francis squirmed in his squeaky seat. 'What can I do?'

'Insist that things are done properly. When Sadiq al-Barabi leaves prison he must be arrested officially, then taken to the appeals court at City Terrace for the formality of his release. His treatment should be above board; his journey from prison routine. Once they have him there I couldn't give a shit if they want to charge him with treason, but there is to be no secret location. Understand?'

Francis leant back. Nodded. 'Fairness.'

'Good. There might be surprise at your request. Tell them it came from the Iranian Embassy. That will protect us both.'

* * *

As Kester ended the meeting, Francis felt confused but relieved. As favours went, this was a cinch. He didn't even have to break the law. Just ensure that a prisoner is taken to the City Terrace Appeals Court. Easy peasy.

Glad to see the back of them, he showed Kester and his freak show out of the building and returned to his office. Which was when he heard the blast of gunfire. Through a window he looked on in disbelief as Kester Hardwick crashed to the ground.

CHAPTER TWENTY-THREE

Witnessing his boss take the hit, Tino jerked up. The bottle of Pepsi-Max clutched in his fist sprayed the inside of the BMW. Discarding it, he reached under his seat, grabbed his Heckler and Koch MP5 machine gun and cautiously scuttled from the car. Kester was on his back, Skid's hands pressing down on him. Staying low, Tino searched for the sniper amidst the abandoned lots. In the mirrored windows of a building he caught a break; the reflection of a man carrying a rifle. Cradling his machine gun, Tino set off in pursuit. A stranger to running, by the time he turned the corner his lungs felt like they were on fire. The gunman was getting away. About to lose him and on the verge of a heart attack, Tino stopped – kneeled to steady himself – and prepared his firearm.

* * *

With no time for a second shot – or to admire his first – Guseppi Biani had bolted from the site. His determination not to miss left him too far from his waiting car. It was behind the next corner – tantalisingly close – but the end of the alley wasn't coming quickly enough. He discarded his rifle. Pumped his arms. No use. His arthritic joints had inflamed, slowing him down. *Keep going!* His mind yelled, fearing that he had been seen. Which he had.

As Guseppi reached the mouth of the alleyway, it turned into a war zone. A series of gunshots blasted out. Guseppi didn't look back. He couldn't. His left leg collapsed on him, causing him to roll forward as blood spurted out from what remained of his knee. A bullet had torn straight through. Despite the sheering pain, he had no alternative but to go on; to scramble for the corner. He managed to get his body weight back onto his good leg and with a monumental effort he snapped it straight, flinging himself around the corner just as another round of bullets whizzed by. But the corner would not shield him for long. Tears flowed as he thought of his son and pleaded to the sky. *Help me my boy.*

Manoeuvring himself up onto his feet, Guseppi hopped toward his car. Three hops later he felt his chest tighten, his legs go weak. Overwhelming agony informed him death was impending. Collapsing onto the sidewalk he became numb with pain. As time stood still his awareness turned inward. Life didn't pass before his eyes: instead, in a mixture of rage and sadness he thought longingly of how everything might have been, were it not for Kester Hardwick. He didn't just blame him for his son's disappearance but for its impact; his wife's death, his own tumour. In that moment of agony all the things that had gone wrong in his life he laid at Kester Harwick's door. Keeping Guseppi alive through it all had been his drive for justice. Having been consumed with purpose he could now die content that he had taken that monster with him. Friends had been killed in combat for less; at least he would die with equanimity. Holding his chest he rolled his body around. His hat slipped down the back of his head, its strap falling to his neck. A machine gun was pointing down at him. Beyond it stood the thick-necked driver, panting hard and scowling over at him.

Weeping, Guseppi braced himself.

'Wait!' a voice called out. Both men turned to it.

Guseppi's red eyes bulged with horror.

The voice had come from Kester Hardwick.

* * *

Kester lumbered towards them, a grimace to his face. His shirt was open revealing the bulletproof vest he'd worn since leaving the slammer. Toting the old man's rifle was Skid.

Despite the gunshots the place was silent; an industrial estate devoid of industry, its only business was in offices to let. They were standing at the end of an alley that opened out onto a car lot, on which stood a burnt out Ford and a Honda that Kester assumed belonged to the crumpled mess before him. He stared down quizzically. This was no hit-man, determined Kester, neither was he anyone he recognised.

'So, who the fuck are you?' Kester punched out every word despite his difficulty in breathing.

No reply. The injured gunman had curled into a ball, his shoulders vibrating. Losing patience, Kester knelt, rifled through his pockets, but found only car keys. Grabbing onto clumps of hair at the back of the man's head, Kester dragged his motionless body like a rag doll. Checking for life, he delivered a hard kick to the kidneys.

The assassin let out a groan.

'I said, who the fuck are you?'

Again no answer.

The man omitted a hollow scream of agony as Kester trod on his gaping knee. His mouth pointed skyward with an expression Kester had seen many times before. It was the look of a man broken beyond repair.

Kester motioned to Tino. 'Get him up.'

Bending down, Tino whisked him up like a toddler. The man didn't fight. He was indeed broken.

Having travelled across to the Honda, Kester beckoned his men to follow. Using the gunman's car keys, Kester opened the boot. 'Stick him in there.'

The man was dropped into the compartment, his limbs hanging over the sides.

Taking the vintage rifle off Skid, Kester held it over the man. 'First you shoot me then you disrespect me. I'll ask once more, for curiosity's sake. Who are you?'

Slowly opening his eyes, the old man spat out a mixture of blood and tears. Gasped, 'Fuck you... *asshole.*'

All eyes were now on Kester and the rifle.

He shrugged, forced a smile at Skid and Tino, and in one fluid motion smashed the gun's butt end down onto the man's throat, breaking his neck. A loud sucking noise followed as his last breath escaped him.

Kester summoned up phlegm and spat at the dead man. 'Fetch the car,' he called. 'And dispose of this mess.'

CHAPTER TWENTY-FOUR

Looking out of the plane I saw England sprawling below me, the evening sun providing a carpet of light. Three nights earlier, Elaine had travelled the same route and I couldn't help but picture her at every stage of the journey, imagining her emotions and wondering why the hell she was with Faustino Ricard and Fernando Sanchez.

Satisfying myself with the knowledge that I was at last moving in the right direction, I nearly forgot my dislike of flying. Sam had managed to get us upgraded to business class without even flashing his badge. Apparently, being six foot five classed us as disabled. Even so, he complained crassly to anyone in earshot that there was barely enough legroom for a landmine victim. He made do with muscling in on the two first-come-first-served armrests that parted our row of three. With Sam guarding them with his life I settled happily for the window seat. On Sam's left sat an Oriental man who retained his dolphin grin despite Sam's elbow digging into his ribs. The Oriental man soon got his own back. Comically swatting air away with his tie, he griped, 'Sorry 'bout that one, must have been the skunk I had for breakfast.'

I liked him instantly and we exchanged introductions. His name was John Yeung – a journalist from Los Angeles whose hobbies included conversation. He had spent a short weekend in London reviewing our capital's merits as a city break. He wrote for the largest Chinese publication in LA. His take on London: History At A Price.

'Are you two on holiday or business trip?' he enquired, scanning Sam's khaki walking shorts and striped short-sleeved shirt.

'Neither/Business,' I/Sam replied simultaneously.

'We're looking for someone,' I said. 'My fiancée,' I added, figuring he'd overhear us anyway. 'She's missing and might be in LA.'

John Yeung tilted his head. He hesitated. I sensed he had so many questions he couldn't decide which to ask, or how to ask them.

I got in first. 'She could be in Lincoln Heights, do you know the area?'

His smile momentarily slipped. 'Don't much go Lincoln Heights.'

I tried again. 'What's it like?'

'Small neighbourhood. Near downtown,' his

singsong voice halted mid-sentence. After the brief pause he smiled. 'Surrounded by freeways.'

'Is it a nice place?' asked Sam.

John Yeung ran a thumb down his tie. 'Urban. Mainly working class, mostly Latino. Some Chinese but they don't buy newspaper' – he looked up apologetically – 'Lincoln Heights is how you say? Deprived.'

'Have you heard of a club called *Flesh?*'

'Flesh. No, sorry. Wish I could help you, Mr Edson.'

'I'll find her,' I replied firmly, liking Edson as a surname.

Smelling a story, John Yeung asked about Elaine. I filled him in. On everything: Gary Jasper's murder, the attack, the letters, the e-mails. Everything. I wasn't looking for sympathy, merely a fresh opinion.

He listened intently; a look of sadness grew on his face. I regretted burdening him with my problems. Probably wasn't the fluffy aeroplane chit-chat he was used to.

'So, John,' I asked, lightening the mood, 'you live in LA?'

'Yes, downtown, where I work. I like downtown because all tall buildings there. Like Hong Kong, where I come from. If you get time I show you best Chinese restaurants, I also food critic for newspaper. Call me. Chinese Daily News, extension 251, ask for John. Remember 251, ask for John.'

A thousand miles over the Atlantic Ocean I actually managed to relax a little. The combination of John's bright outlook and Sam's familiar pessimism had a balancing effect on me; on my ying and yang.

'You enjoy your job, don't you John,' said Sam.

'Of course, but I prefer Chief Writer's job. Need big break, but I still happy.'

After the media interest in Gary Jasper's murder the last thing I needed was a hack giving me grief on the plane, but John Yeung didn't push. Just smiled.

'There is old Chinese saying about smile,' he recalled. 'A smile will gain you ten more years of life.'

Sam grinned. 'Then you should be welcoming in the next millennium, no trouble.'

John Yeung chuckled then turned his gaze on me. 'There are many Chinese sayings. I have one for you Mr Edson. About hope,' sympathy tempered his enthusiastic tones. 'Shed no tears until seeing coffin.'

I nodded slowly, preferring the one about the smile.

CHAPTER TWENTY-FIVE

1.01pm
Omaha Heights, Los Angles.

In forty hours of observation, suspects Syrus
Meybodi and Ali Afshari had not left their home.
No phone calls had been made, no Internet
accessed and most worryingly, they were bereft of
conversation. The obvious conclusion: somehow
they knew about the surveillance.

From the discomfort of their van, FBI Special
Agents Guzan and Derego had sat watching for the
past two hours. Food had run out and conversation
run thin.

'Favourite animal?' Derego asked.

'Geez, we are bored.' Guzan smiled thinly. 'I've
always wanted a pet monkey.'

'They're a nightmare to keep,' claimed Derego. 'You know the Mexican who owns the Pool Hall on Mullholland?'

'Popeye?'

'That's him. He once kept one of those little monkeys. Anyway, one night they were watching TV together – sharing a jar of pickled onions – when suddenly the furry fella pulls out his left eye. Squeezes it like a stress ball.'

'Sheesh.' Guzan winced. 'Unbelievable. *And* he's called Popeye.'

'It's true,' laughed Derego, 'but he used to be called Miguel.'

Guzan smirked. Derego was pleased to see his partner lighten up.

It didn't last long.

A black Honda pulled up in front of the Iranians' Pontiac. The agents watched in disbelief as uniformed men ambled to the front door. Fake cops; complete with super-sized visors, helmets and bushy moustaches.

What the hell?

Guzan placed a call to the Field Office. 'Approaching the house are two Caucasians dressed as police officers.'

'I don't understand,' queried Agent Cooper, accessing the images. 'Are they cops?'

'Negative.'

Holding a small camcorder to his window, Derego tracked the men up the path relaying his feed back to Cooper.

'We haven't enough to ID them,' complained Cooper.

Both men looked to be about five foot nine and 150 pounds but their faces were hidden. Their disguises did precisely that.

'What more can you give me?' he asked.

'They arrived in a black Honda, Arizona license plate HG67546—hold on,' Guzan quit talking as Syrus Meybodi answered the door, 'They're going inside.'

'Agents have been dispatched,' said Cooper, 'and LAPD have an ETA of five minutes.'

'Copy that.' Guzan dialled another number. *Keep me in the loop.* 'Something's happening.'

'Talk to me,' replied Ethan Knight.

With Derego straining to listen, Guzan briefed Knight on the situation: how two unidentified men – possibly armed and definitely fake LAPD – had entered the Iranians' house.

Knight, playing back the feed, responded: 'They look like two of the *Village People*. Okay, I have you on satellite – we can track the Honda from here. I'm connecting with FO – they can go through me.'

With all eyes and ears directed towards the house a period of time passed, silent but for the occasional rustle of movement.

What are they doing?

Guzan's long career hadn't dampened his need for the job and it was moments like these that he thrived on. Not the action, or reaction, but the need for quick planning; the thinking on his feet. There was nothing like it.

'I once saw the *Village People*,' said Derego, his own focus waning. For Derego, it was all about the action.

'Not now, Tyler.'

'They all had different jobs,' he whispered counting them on his fingers. 'There was the cop, a construction worker—'

'Later,' snapped Guzan, ears straining, keen to react to the strange goings on.

Derego mouthed, a sailor, Red Indian—

Shaking his head, Guzan smiled wryly at his partner's way of defusing the tension. Why not? He thought. The house was silent so he decided to play along. 'Since when is being American Indian a job?'

'Could be,' argued Derego. 'Now what did the fifth one do? Oh yeah; the cowboy.'

'There was a sixth,' said Guzan, never averting his gaze from the house.

'No kidding, what did he do?'

A sound interrupted Guzan. The noise demanded his complete attention. He listened closely to what sounded like fastening straps. 'What *is* that noise?'

They both listened intently, but the sound stopped.

'Help me out here, Don,' muttered Derego. 'The sixth village person?'

Guzan relented. 'It was the gay guy,' he whispered.

'*The* gay guy?'

'That was his job, a professional gay guy. He wore leather and had a giant moustache. You happy now?'

'As a sandboy.'

The front door opened.

Out stepped the pseudo cops. But behind the disguises were not the men who'd entered minutes ago. It was the suspects, Meybodi and Afshari.

Adrenalin fuelled Guzan's body. That noise. They had been swapping clothes. Realising the white men were the same build as the Iranians, Guzan recognised it as an attempt to evade surveillance.

With the men heading for the black Honda, the phone clicked. It was Knight. 'Talk to me, Don.'

'It's a switch. Either that or the cops have borrowed Tyler's fake tan. I know you wanted this to remain covert, Ethan, but they're onto us. Should we tail them?'

'Go one better. Bring them in. *Now!*'

CHAPTER TWENTY-SIX

Exploding out of the surveillance van, Guzan and Derego had the attention of the suspects who now ran for the Honda.

Unclipping his revolver, Derego yelled, 'Freeze, FBI!'

Ignoring his cry the suspects reached the car; within moments they would be mobile. Unable to get there in time, Guzan popped two bullets into a rear tyre as the Honda squealed away, leaving a swirl of smoke in its wake.

They raced back to the van.

Derego floored the accelerator as Guzan spoke with FO. 'Suspects on the move,' he panted, 'heading south along Palmetto Drive.'

'We have you on satellite,' replied Cooper,

watching with a ten second delay. 'Assistance is close.'

A click on Guzan's frequency. 'Don't lose them,' warned Ethan Knight.

Skidding round a tight corner, the Honda swung onto Southill Road, causing a truck to mount the sidewalk. Cars broke and beeped as the Honda struggled to control its blown tyre. The agent's van followed, groaning as they took the corner, brushing the centre divide. Through cautious traffic, Derego saw an opportunity. At the next junction the Honda would hit the stoplights where a retaining wall flanked the road. Providing the lights were red, the Honda wouldn't get through.

The lights obliged. The suspects were locked in traffic. Positioning the van behind the Iranians, Derego trapped them behind a line of motors. Now bumper-to-bumper, the van nudged the back of the Honda, wedging it in. Derego exited the van clutching his revolver, and placed himself alongside the suspects. 'Get out of the car and put your hands on your head!'

The lights changed.

Ducking down, Guzan scrambled past the Honda to the vehicle in front. It was crucial this car remained stationary. He flashed his badge, told the driver to employ the parking brake, get out and stay down. As Guzan eased him away, he spied the offside door of the Honda slowly open. Hands on their helmets, the two men stepped out. One pleaded 'Don't shoot!' in a peculiar accent as a squad car screeched up behind them.

Holy shit!

Alarmed and confused, Guzan ran closer to the men, horror on his face. *It wasn't the Iranians.* It was the men who'd entered the house. Meanwhile, two genuine cops had crouched in front of them, guns readied.

'Put down your weapon.' The order was in Derego's direction.

'FBI,' he replied, allowing his jacket to drop open and reveal his badge. 'We are in the process of detaining two suspects.'

Not bothering to introduce himself, Guzan shouted,

'*You* cuff 'em' – he pointed at the nearest cop – 'and *you*,' he gasped. 'I need your car.'

Rushing to the squad car, Guzan stopped as Derego removed the suspects' headwear, revealing them to be heavily made up. Tinted foundation filled the gap between visors and moustaches. The same build as Meybodi and Afshari, up close they were nothing like the Iranians: Eastern European was his guess.

Driven by the second cop, Guzan was soon on the road, turning into Palmetto Drive. Leaving his radio in the van allowed him a moment of reflection before facing the music. He felt like an idiot. He prided himself on his decision-making and yet he'd allowed the suspects to dupe him. As the black and white neared the suspects' house, Guzan's shoulders dropped, and he melted into his seat. Outside he saw Agent Beasley's silver Audi.

The Iranians' Pontiac was gone.

Beasley greeted him with a cell-phone. 'It's Ethan Knight. And he's seething.'

Guzan took the call. 'I'm sorry Ethan, what can I say? They looked like the Iranians, and not just their skin colour, their walk, their—'

'Enough,' scolded Knight. 'Your fake tan comment said it all. You screwed up.'

He's right, thought Guzan. His mind focused on finding the men. 'Satellite has the area covered and there's a tracker on the Pontiac.'

'The Pontiac's at the end of the street.'

Staring into the distance, Guzan put his hands to his head.

'The slippery fuckers used a "switch car,"' said Knight. 'Last seen driving off in a red Taurus, we're looking for them now. For your sake they'd better show.'

Chapter Twenty-Seven

After the debacle in Boyle Heights – which saw him shot – Kester Hardwick was back at his hillside retreat. Of his many buildings in Lincoln Heights this was his official residence. Referred to locally as Hardwick House, the pad was palatial compared to its neighbours. With this in mind, much of the valued art and furniture had been kept in storage during his prison stay. He needn't have bothered. Despite being left unoccupied there were no signs that anybody had dared to break in.

Enjoying a moment to himself he reclined into his leather chair and reached for a Cuban cigar. A stabbing pain momentarily winded him, coming from beneath the CD sized bruise that marked his chest. The vest had done its job; a suspected broken rib was acceptable damage given the bullet would have blasted his heart open. Kester's motto: always shoot for the head.

A cell-phone vibrated his thigh. Not his regular phone, the expensive one; costly because of its multiple-relay system that made calls impossible to trace, track or record.

Kester took the call. 'Speak.'

'Mr Hardwick? This is Ali Afshari. I acquired your number from Sadiq.'

Anger gripped Kester by the throat. Ali Afshari was one of the two Iranians Sadiq had told him about: The money-men. 'Contacting me is dangerous,' said Kester. 'I gather this is important.'

'I don't know what you have been told, but I know about your deal with Sadiq.' Afshari sounded agitated, with a threatening undertone: 'He is wealthy enough to fund his freedom, but it is the money we've secured that will pay for your formula. What I and my associate want to know is how this will work? We need assurances, Mr Hardwick, before we part with half a million dollars.'

Kester sat forward. 'Who are *we?*'

'My partner, Syrus Meybodi, is with me.'

Right, the other Iranian. Kester paused, twiddled the cigar, but decided not to light it. *The scrambler had better work.* 'How can you be certain your phone line is secure?'

'We are free from surveillance, at a safe location. It is just as much in our interest to keep this conversation two-way.'

Kester rocked back into leather. 'What do you want to know?'

'How our money will be spent. Frankly I don't envisage the Arizona chemicals ever being classed as poisonous. All we have is waste produce from the phosphate fertilizer industry – merely sodium fluoride.'

Having dealt only with Sadiq al-Barabi, Kester was reluctant to divulge information but – as Afshari had pointed out – he was the money-man. *So be it.* Kester explained, 'That waste produce is a deadly bi-product, almost as toxic as arsenic. The fertilizer industry has problems discarding fluoride without it killing fish, vegetation – even livestock – so it sells it to the Government under the claim that it is good for us. It costs taxpayers $12,000,000 to fluoridate LA's water supply.' Kester continued, 'But don't be fooled, Mr Afshari, fluoride is a corrosive compound. It is used to refine metals, as insecticide, pesticide, as rat poison—'

'But we have *sodium* fluoride,' grumbled Afshari, 'used to clean teeth.'

'Yes it cleans teeth, but in the same way it's used as rust remover. Sodium fluoride can do untold damage to the DNA repair enzyme system and our immune system. It accelerates tumour growth and is linked to many cancers. What's more, fluoride is tasteless, colourless and odourless.'

'Forgive my scepticism, but I don't see how your formula will turn this fluoride into a chemical weapon?'

'Maybe you haven't been listening,' considered Kester. 'Fluoride *is* poisonous, and in the right dosage, deadly. The plan is to follow the government's lead by adding it to water. At present, drinking water is prescribed at only eight tenths parts per million – much smaller amounts have caused cancer in test animals, but I digress. What the formula reveals is how to add the fluoride, and what casualties can be expected. Picture the widespread panic. The terror. Anyone drinking the water or even bathing in it will suffer serious health problems, but of course the extent of the damage will be up to you. Do you prefer to upset a million stomachs, or wipe out an entire water park?'

Afshari was quiet, as if he was unable to believe how simple it sounded. Then: 'Aren't fluoride levels checked?'

'Not once water has passed through the filtration system. Theoretically you could add as much as you want. Routine checks will show up unusually high levels, but by then it will be too late. You get one chance at this, a clear shot. My contact has the formula. I presume you are set for exchange.'

'With respect, talk is cheap, how will Sadiq know the formula works?'

'He understands the science as well as anyone. When he sees the formula it will be clear to him how to apply the fluoride.'

'Then the money is ready, *cash* as you require. When will we exchange?' asked Afshari, excitement now in his voice.

'When Sadiq delivers the money. Tuesday morning the people of LA could be waking up to carnage. You might want to leave town.'

CHAPTER TWENTY-EIGHT

1.43pm
LAX, Los Angeles.

Sam and I said our goodbyes to John Yeung in the arrivals queue. Customs officers made it seem like a police line-up: suspicious eyes fixing intimidating glares, making me feel about as welcome as a wet fart.

Eventually we left the cold, hard airport behind. Outside we were met by a deluge of noise and heat. Shouting and traffic competed for attention. I could taste the sun-melted pollution; the air so dense we not so much inhaled as swallowed it.

A short, scruffy man stood on a box preaching of the perils of a world obsessed by celebrity. Sam made a point of interrupting him to ask where he might get one of those maps that showed where the stars lived.

Once Sam had had his laugh, he wanted to set off and find a hotel but I convinced him otherwise. I couldn't wait any longer. Now I was here I had to head straight for the *Flesh* club.

As we queued for a taxi, Sam said, 'He had a weak handshake.'

'Who, John Yeung?'

Sam nodded. 'I don't trust limp-wristed men.' He caught my expression, shrugged. 'What? Doesn't make me homophobic.'

I rolled my eyes. 'I liked him. He's got some good sayings.'

Sam scoffed, 'So has Forrest Gump.'

We reached the end of the taxi line, the next one was ours. As I got in, Sam followed, muttering to himself. 'You say "paw" to my Aunt's poodle, it shakes with more grip.'

I ignored him.

If bacteria had a smell, this taxi was it. I gave our destination to a driver wearing a dirty yellow vest. Greasy black hair dropped dandruff onto his tattooed shoulders. I didn't think hair could grow through tattoos, but his back suggested otherwise. He pulled off, informing us that Lincoln Heights was 25 minutes away.

* * *

After half an hour we were still headed north on the 110 freeway: a wide road, busy yet fast-moving.

Billboards the size of stadiums told us the cheapest ways to spend our cash.

'Not much longer,' said Furry Tat.

As we exited the freeway we suddenly had a clear view of an LA skyline with fewer skyscrapers than I had envisioned. We then took the Broadway Bridge over a waterless concrete river before entering Lincoln Heights.

'Locals call this Broadway,' announced the driver.

Broadway was a six-lane High Street. Palm trees lined both sides; shops hid behind them with facades shabbier than a tramp's trousers. John Yeung had described Lincoln Heights as deprived; Sam preferred the words *shit* and *hole*. All of the shops were caged in. Not just the shop fronts, but the street vending machines too. Everything was behind bars. The streets were dotted with pedestrians, just stood around talking.

Furry Tat grinned. 'Where chain stores fear to tread,'

'There are a lot of florists,' observed Sam.

'Got that right.' We turned off into a quieter neighbourhood. This time it was the houses that were caged in. I exchanged concerned looks with Sam.

Furry Tat took a hand off the wheel, started pointing. ''Bout fifteen years ago these bars started going up. Soon they didn't know when to stop.' He pointed to a lone, fenced palm tree. 'They cage everything in here. Creates a siege mentality.' He gestured to a house with clay lion sculptures. 'Bars to protect lions from the people,' he winked into his rear view mirror; clearly enjoying that we were tourists.

Many of the homeowners had painted their metal bars in different colours. It was unlike anywhere I'd ever seen.

What was Elaine doing here?

'See that underpass,' he motioned, 'all those flowers and stuffed animals mark areas where gang members have been killed. Practically a daily occurrence.'

Sam and I looked at each other. *Explains the flower shops.*

'Nearly there.' He slowed down. 'You still sure you want this club?'

'I'm sure,' I said, not imagining Elaine could be here, at least not of her own free will.

As he announced *Flesh* club, I was pleasantly surprised to see a building free of metal bars. Sam agreed to wait with the taxi whilst I entered the club. The meter kept ticking.

An elderly doorman welcomed me with a nod and a wink straight out of the 1970s. The foyer was seedier than a watermelon. A sign inside the door read *Flesh* club: Distinction, Discretion, Big Tits. *Classy.*

What looked like two medicine balls in a satsuma bag approached me. *No false advertising here.* I lifted my eyes to the woman's face. Her skin was so tight you could play drums on it.

'Could I speak with Gina Nipple, sorry, Sipple,' I stuttered. 'Is she here, Gina Sipple?'

The woman didn't answer, unless open-mouthed chewing could be construed as a reply. She performed a three-point turn before an index finger beckoned me to follow. Disappearing through a mirrored door, we emerged in a large area, dimly lit blue. I followed her past half a dozen men sitting around; like a pack of starving wolves they were eyeballing an upside down dancer wrapped around a pole. She was bare-naked but for a g-string, whose sole purpose was to hold dollar bills. An aroma of testosterone and beer sat in the air above an eclectic mix of stages and tables, all gold and tinted blue. We stopped outside a row of booths curtained with golden silk. A confused looking woman appeared, walked up to me. Her make-up was displayed in clown-like proportions and her shoulder-length hair had seen more bleach than an OCD sufferer's toilet.

'I'm Gina, who wants to know?' she said whilst chewing. It was difficult to see what she looked like, a possible explanation for her cosmetic indulgence.

'It's about the e-mail you sent?'

'Huh?' Gina's pungent scent of perfume only partly masked stale sweat. 'What e-mail?'

'About seeing Elaine McAdler?'

More confusion: 'Who? Look Mister, I dunno no Elaine MacWhatever, and I ain't sent no e-mail, you get me?' Her chewing was vociferous, bordering on aggressive. Looking a decade past her sell by date, Gina no doubt had a great personality to fall back on.

'What about Vixen? She digs you mixed bloods. She'd be hot for you, big boy.'

'No thanks.' I looked around expecting to have created a scene. Thankfully the gawkers were too busy ogling to notice. 'So you didn't email me this picture?' I handed her the image of the three females and watched her reaction.

Her eyes tightened, she looked away before returning for a second look. 'I never sent you this.'

'Do you recognise anyone in the picture?'

'Nope,' she stressed, darting sideways glances.

Looking more closely at her bone structure, I pointed at the picture. 'Isn't that you on the left?'

Before she could reply, a STAFF ONLY mirror slid open and a stern looking man slid out. He had a half-shaven head parted with a wave of red hair; a look that only the seriously hard could pull off. His suit suggested that maybe he was a manager of sorts. One thing for sure, his presence distressed Gina and discouraged me. Stuffing the picture back into my hand she nervously edged away, her eyes manic. Whoever this man was, she wasn't willing to talk in front of him.

'Ah well,' I said. 'Guys must come here all the time asking for girls. Never mind, I'll try elsewhere.'

Sensing trouble I made for the exit. Before I could get past the doorman a threatening voice called me back, 'May I see that?' It was the man with the fiery hair. He stepped towards me. I noticed Gina was frozen upright, her eyes screaming *no*.

'Don't worry about it,' I said. 'I've got the wrong place.' I smiled. He looked like I'd just shat in his shoe.

I made a sharp exit. Maybe he could have helped me, but the message I was getting from Gina was that once away from the club – away from chuckles – she might talk.

Heading for the taxi I wasn't happy with the visit, but I was glad to be out of there. Next time, I would take Sam with me.

Clamping hold of Gina's arm, Bruno Meyer pulled her into his office and pinned her against a wall. 'Just the one question,' he said. 'Was *she* in that photo?'

Shaking with fear, Gina nodded.

Before she could defend herself Bruno yanked onto her arm. As he burst out of the club, Gina had to run alongside to prevent her arm leaving its socket. Bruno stuffed her into his Corvette before taking the wheel. With the stranger's taxi still in sight, he turned his attention to Gina. She was crying, protesting, 'I don't know him or where he got that picure, I swear on my mother's li—'

Bruno cut across her, 'I heard him say he got it from you. I warned you Gina, don't say I didn't.'

As she pleaded for mercy, Bruno called Surgeon.

Chapter Twenty-Nine

2.48pm
Naud Junction, Los Angeles.

Having followed the taxi the short journey to a hotel, Bruno Meyer parked his Corvette and watched as Gina's visitor emerged from the cab. Another man was with him, this one white. He paid the fare.

Bruno looked daggers at Gina. 'Well. You recognise his boyfriend?'

'No,' Gina shook her head fervently, 'Never seen him before.'

Whilst the men walked their suitcases into the hotel, Bruno brought his cell to his mouth. 'I'm outside the Hotel Angelino. Get here fast. I have something to deal with,' Bruno glanced at Gina, 'but it shouldn't take long. The target's well over six-foot, multiracial and speaks with an accent, maybe British. He's with another man, equally tall, but white, looks like a tourist,' Bruno shook his head, 'fucking socks and sandals. Make sure they don't leave, especially the dark one. I'll call back soon.'

* * *

The infamous Hotel Angelino was known for a gruesome murder on New Year's Day, 1999. A drug dealer had been strangled to death in his room. He was then sawn in half at the waist before being hung up in the wardrobe like a suit. The police were called when blood came through the ceiling below. Labelled 'the tailor', the perpetrator was never caught.

Surgeon arrived quickly as Bruno had requested. Worried that he might not have been fast enough; he was perturbed as to why Bruno hadn't waited for his arrival. He was fed up with his boss slipping up and making constant demands. The money was good but Surgeon knew that one day Bruno's mistakes might cost him. He was ready to jack the job in, especially now Bruno's boss had resurfaced; Surgeon couldn't work for Kester Hardwick.

On and off, Surgeon had been on Bruno's payroll nearly ten years. Often he was hired to put the fear of God into people but would kill if the situation demanded. His victims – or as Bruno called them, *targets* – were usually dealers who'd stepped on the wrong turf. Given Bruno's description of his latest target, he doubted that was the case here. Still, he hoped to inflict his brand of torture. His drug was sadism, and he tingled with excitement at the possibilities that awaited him. It was on account of his penchant for medical instruments that he'd become known as Surgeon.

Focusing on the task in hand, he tilted forward his black Zorro hat and entered the hotel lobby. It had been refurbished since his last visit. On that occasion the situation *had* demanded, and he took pride in the extra custom his work had gained the hotel. Where would it be without its notoriety? Mused Surgeon – the man they knew as 'the tailor'.

Bruno was expected back at any moment and Surgeon was yet to establish if the men were still here. He marched up to reception. Smoothing down his long black coat, he planted his bag on the end of the desk. Inside the black holdall were a variety of blades and cutters: his instruments. Carefully positioning his body at the corner of the counter, he called for service. A spotty young man with a neat, greasy parting pranced towards him. 'Good afternoon, Sir.'

Surgeon pursed his red lips, providing some colour to his snowy white face, and spoke softly, 'I wonder if you could help me. I just dropped off two tall gentlemen. They left this in my car.' Surgeon gestured to his bag.

'Oh right. Thank you, Sir. I'll keep it safe for them,' lisped the youth. No doubt aware that Surgeon was not exactly sporting the typical attire of a taxi driver, especially on a hot day like this. Usually, he preferred to disguise himself – as he had the last time he'd been at the hotel – but Bruno's call had demanded he come at short notice, meaning Surgeon was dressed as himself. His face – which usually acted as a canvas – was his own.

Before the youth could take the bag, Surgeon placed a hand on it. 'The trouble is I'm not sure if it's theirs. It was left behind a seat.'

'Ah. I'll place a call up to their room.'

Surgeon dipped his head. 'Good man.'

In under a minute the receptionist returned. 'We've spoken to the gentlemen and no, it's not their bag.'

Relief washed over Surgeon. *The men are still in their room.* 'Are you sure they're the men I described?'

'Well, they were the last guests to arrive.'

'Fine,' smiled Surgeon.

Thirty seconds earlier he had watched the interphone being accessed, seen the room number being dialled.

When the coast was clear he made his way to the second floor.

* * *

I had not given up on Gina or the *Flesh* club, but my only real lead had not been as fruitful as I'd hoped. With Sam off to get a menu I reached for my mobile phone. I was worried that it might not work here. Sam had belittled it, boasting that his was a suped-up version, but I managed to get online and send an e-mail. Anyone with access to Elaine's address now knew that I was at the Hotel Angelino: that I was coming for her.

Sitting in an immense city of eight million people, I ignored all thoughts of needles and haystacks and pondered my next move.

My thoughts were broken by a knock on the door.

CHAPTER THIRTY

Naud Junction, Los Angeles

Lisa Connelly cursed as she pulled up in front of the Hotel Angelino. She was too late.

She checked again, but her eyes hadn't deceived her. It was Tino she'd spotted jogging towards the entrance. Normally, the sight of a huge black man running would demand stares, but the area was quiet, shielded by trees. As Tino entered the hotel he was followed by a short man whom Lisa could only describe as looking like roadkill.

Cruising past the glass-fronted foyer she found a parking bay, looked back at the hotel, considered her position.

Barely ten seconds after he'd entered the hotel Tino came bursting out like a rhinoceros. Watching on in astonishment Lisa saw him duck behind a palm tree and crouch down as glass revolved and Edson Taylor walked out: taller than she'd expected and even better looking. She almost missed the man following in his shadow. Dressed only in black, he was on the small side, his face hidden under a wide hat. Part of his coat was hoisted up over his arm, which was stuffed into Edson's back. Now noticing the fright on Edson's face, Lisa predicted a gun to be under the cloth. The horror of the situation dawned on her. She felt fortunate that she *had* been late. It could have been her life in danger.

Cowering and slowly backing away, Tino was doing everything he could to avoid being seen. It seemed to work. Edson Taylor and company were heading away from him to the parking bay. They were, in fact, heading for Lisa's Mazda. She was in disguise – a blonde wig and dark sunglasses – but she hid her face as they approached, nonchalantly attending to her nails until they had passed. Slowly, she looked up, only to see Bruno Meyer's Corvette tearing up the drive. *What is this?* Her stomach made a fist. Averting her eyes she quickly slid down in her seat as he drove by.

Inching up steadily, Lisa manoeuvred a side mirror until she located Bruno abandoning his motor. A white bandana and mirrored sunglasses failed to disguise him. She wanted out of there but a mixture of fear, intrigue and a promise to her friend kept her rooted.

Coming from behind her, Lisa heard the sound of a van door sliding. Again she adjusted the mirror, this time to no avail. Craning upwards she saw the man with the gun guiding Edson Taylor into the back of a black GMC van. The gun wielder swept the door closed and looked furtively around, offering Lisa a glimpse of a milky face she didn't recognise.

Hoping to avoid detection she stayed down and waited, uncomfortably aware of her heartbeat. Above its thumping she caught the mutterings of a conversation moving across the parking bay. It was Bruno, talking with the gunman as they walked back to the van. Sliding further down in her seat, Lisa heard what sounded like a door close. Not the slider, a front door. Then the van started up. She heard somebody slap goodbye to the side as it crawled away. Holding her breath, she cautiously reached forward and turned the ignition key, trying not to think about the consequences. She risked being seen, but she had no choice. A promise was a promise. And that meant following the van.

* * *

I was in complete darkness, just a foul smell for company. With nothing to grab hold of, each deviation in speed or direction caused me to slide along the van's floor before crashing into the sides. Stretching out my limbs I managed to wedge myself in and walk my hands up the offside. With turns becoming infrequent I grappled at the door, feeling for a handle or lock. Oddly there was nothing, the van's insides consisted entirely of smooth surfaces. In addition, there was an unusual lack of light or sound; despite feeling the van's every move I could barely hear an engine.

How could I have been so stupid? Why the hell had I opened the door? The thin, white-skinned man had looked harmless enough: an effeminate Goth with narrow shoulders and just a bag for company. He had stood there motionless in the corridor. Arms by his sides. Vacant eyes looking up at me. I had thought that maybe he had the wrong room. I had been about to close the door when he uttered two words, *Elaine McAdler*.

All rational thought had vacated my mind and I'd let him in. Almost methodically he'd placed his bag on my bed, carefully lining it up with the horizontal pattern on the sheets. Backing away, I had watched in morbid fascination as his black-gloved hands started unzipping the bag. He was creeping me out, but curiosity – and his mention of Elaine – had fixed my feet to the floor. With the door in sight I hesitated as he reached inside the bag. I should have known better. Delving in with both hands, he had pulled out a gun and was pointing it at my chest, instructing me to stay calm. He had then motioned me towards the door, in complete control of the situation. I had stopped, dug my heels in, drawn breath to speak. Then I had felt his hot breath on my neck as he leaned close, his reptilian lips caressing my ear, whispering her name: *Elaine*. Any impulse to resist had dissipated.

Coming to LA I should have expected trouble. My heart and head had been constantly yelling at me that Elaine was in danger and yet I had turned up at an overtly dodgy venue like the *Flesh* club and flashed her picture around. What was I thinking? Sam was expected back at any second, but part of me had been pleased not to see or hear from him. I hadn't wanted him walking into this and hoped to God this Goth hadn't already met with him.

The van stopped then set off again, jerking my body in the process. With bruises forming on aching muscles, I wished I'd at least had the wit to hang onto my mobile phone, but the Goth had snatched it from me along with my picture of Elaine. Fear was getting the better of me; the only thing holding off the blind terror was the hope that with every bump and turn I was getting closer to finding out what had happened to Elaine.

The van finally came to rest. As the door slid open, light flowed in, wrapping around a dark shadow that stood in front of me. Adjusting to the light I could see the Goth; his glazed eyes seemed to stare through me, as he looked me up and down. Behind him was a black door, on it the words FLESH CLUB printed in gold. It seemed that we were in a car park at the rear of the building.

Why had he brought me back here?

The Goth's bag lay on the ground. In one hand he held the gun close to his waist, in the other was the picture he'd swiped from me. He nodded three times at the image, as if in turn he was acknowledging the presence of Gina Sipple, the older looking Elaine and my fiancée.

'*Now* they are all dead,' he declared theatrically.

'What?'

'In your picture. *These* three' – he presented the picture, flashing a disarming smile. 'All are dead.'

Chapter Thirty-One

3.29pm
Lincoln Heights, Los Angeles.

The Goth was lying, trying to scare me, or at least mistaken. After all, I was sure that Gina Sipple was the woman on the left of the picture. *All are dead.* How could they be?

Ignoring the comment I demanded to know what I was doing here. His response was to spin the gun that hung off his thumb. He was waiting for something. A reaction from me? It was apparent that I was taller, heavier and younger but he didn't seem concerned. I may not have been restrained but I was unarmed and unable to reach him before a bullet reached me. Is that what he wanted, an excuse to shoot me?

A gold Corvette I had seen at the hotel took the space marked 'Manager'. Shuffling into sunlight, I dropped my feet out of the van, and turned the way of the car. The tough looking driver emerged. Biceps of a Serbian shot-putter, and a face of the possessed. His scowl brought his pierced eyebrows together. His red band of hair may have been hidden under a white bandana, but I still recognised him. It was the man who'd been at the *Flesh* club; the one taking an interest in my picture. The man Gina had seemed so afraid of.

If I was going to fight my way out of this I'd just missed my chance. 'What is this about?' I asked him.

There was no time for an answer. In one fast swoop the Goth snatched my hand, forcing it up between my shoulder blades. I jacknifed as excruciating pain shot through me. Working me like a puppet, he lifted me onto my feet and walked me to the back of the strip club. Using my head as a door opener, he guided me into a dimly lit corridor. As I staggered forward several women in varying degrees of nakedness scattered like bowling pins, disappearing off to find something or someone to do.

The bandana with the biceps spoke, 'My name is Bruno. I'm the manager here.' He motioned as if the club was the star prize on a game show. 'My pasty pal is known as Surgeon, but only a select few get to meet him.'

Surgeon? The Goth's knowing smirk sent my stomach into spasm. *My father's cross-amputation and my anaesthetisation pointed toward a good medical knowledge.*

I averted my eyes back to Bruno. Brushing a tan substance off his silk waistcoat he continued, 'The woman you were asking 'bout, *Elaine McAdler*. How d'ya know her?'

'I don't,' I protested, looking aimlessly for a friendly face. We were alone in the dark corridor, a splattering of spotlights in the floor lit up Bruno and Surgeon like characters from a horror movie. I decided to play down my relationship with Elaine, but their faces weren't buying it. 'It's true,' I insisted, 'I'm here on holiday. My friend, a workaholic cop, wanted to chase up a missing persons lead while we were here.'

Lifting his foot, Bruno placed the thick sole of his shoe against a wall next to me. Close enough for me to detect what smelt like burnt sugar emanating from his clothes.

'The white dude with the slick back hair, he's a cop? But he sends you in with her picture?' The scowl was back, he wasn't having it.

'My friend thought I might fare better. When we entered the area we didn't see many white faces.'

'What are we?' Surgeon beamed proudly. 'Ain't nobody whiter than me.'

Bruno slipped off his bandana, pocketed it. Flattened tufts of his red hair sporadically popped back into position. He stepped his foot down in front of me. 'You walk into my club, uninvited, with *this* picture, and start asking questions.' His gold teeth and chain took it in turns to glisten. 'You have a death wish?'

'Guilt by association,' added Surgeon, keenly.

Bruno nodded. 'Here's an example,' he said to me. 'When Gina sent you that picture she proved herself unloyal.'

'Disloyal,' corrected Surgeon.

Bruno flashed him a look, proceeded, 'Gina paid the price for it. That's how things are.'

Eyes wide with excitement, Surgeon rubbed his hands together and spoke to me. 'The nature of your association is irrelevant, your guilt is worthy of punishment.'

'Wait,' I said. 'I don—'

'Agreed.' Bruno slammed me against the wall. As I bounced off I felt my elbows rip together behind me. My spine was on the verge of snapping, breathing impossible. I was manhandled into a side room, completely helpless – as in my nightmare but with genuine pain. My pelvis met a table and I folded; my chest and face pushed down onto a wooden table top, releasing just enough for air and life to be sucked back into my body.

'We take our revenge seriously here,' said Bruno. 'Gina knew that.' He was bent over me, his weight pressing hard onto my back, fixing me to the table. My neck was twisted. Through bulging eyes I scanned the panelled room, empty but for a roulette wheel and card tables.

Bruno spoke directly into my ear, 'The women in your picture are dead.' His words vibrated my eardrum. 'There's nobody to find.'

Eying Surgeon, I squeezed out the words, 'You killed them?'

Removing his hat, Surgeon tilted his head, until

his pale face was horizontal with mine. 'Let me do my thing,' he said, disappearing below the table. I heard the slow unzipping of his bag, like a weight of dread being released. Surgeon rose up holding small steel loppers. With my arms clamped to my spine I was unable to move my upper body. I kicked hard but at nothing, my legs swinging beneath the table. Bruno had moved to the side, still holding me down. Any screams were halted by his bandana, which had been scrunched up and forced into my mouth. I could see Surgeon, gloved hands above me, loppers lowering to my arms. Metal was slipping off my sweat-drenched skin. I did my best to make a fist but the angle of my bones made it impossible to bend my fingers.

'Reminds me of this little piggy,' said Surgeon. 'This little piggy had roast beef,' he said, adding, 'Very British,' in a posh accent. Steel clicked against my ring before finding my little finger. As I struggled the loppers found their grip. I tried to call out but my gag wasn't having it. My cheeks were fit to burst.

'And this little piggy went—'

Crack. 'Ammhgh,' came through my gag as extreme pain shot to my hand, to a digit that was no longer there. I saw a gloved hand dangling my little finger in front of me. Surgeon flicked it away, moved closer. He was examining me, enjoying my suffering. On his white face sat a smile and droplets of my blood. 'Not all parts are as expendable as fingers,' he said bringing the cutters closer to my face. 'But we have two eyes for a reason.'

CHAPTER THIRTY-TWO

Like a wild cat, Surgeon inched closer. Sharp metal filled my view. I tightened my eyes, tried to roll my neck but a combination of my spine and the table locked my head in place. I kicked and I groaned and I thought of Elaine.

* * *

How the hell? Breathless with rage, Kester Hardwick snapped closed his cell phone in disbelief when Skid had informed him that Bruno and his enforcer – Surgeon – were with Edson Taylor. It had all been going so well, but now, suddenly, an unforeseen event was threatening everything.

Driven by fury, Kester was soon racing back to the club. He had made some calls and it hadn't taken long to locate them. He could only hope he would not be too late. Skid had driven; running stop signs and manoeuvring through traffic with the nonchalance of a local cab driver.

On arrival they piled inside. Ordering Skid to wait in the corridor, Kester crashed open the door of the seven-eleven room.

Startled, Bruno turned sharply towards him, blood covering his front. Metal struck wood as Surgeon, dropping the cutters, looked at the door.

Bruno stepped away enabling Kester to survey the scene. A man was face down on the table, writhing in pain, blood caking his back and dripping onto the floor. When he saw it was Edson Taylor, Kester let out mournful groan, put his hands out. 'What have you done?'

'Nothing much.' Bruno said. 'Just lopped off a finger.'

Horror eased a little when Kester registered that the blood was spilling from the hole in Edson Taylor's hand. He spotted the finger on the floor; a nasty injury – but that aside, Taylor appeared undamaged. No thanks to Bruno's enforcer. *You will end your dealings with this psycho for hire.*

Recognising Surgeon from his description, Kester engaged eye-contact with this slight man for the first time. Unable to read his soulless eyes and blank expression, Kester spoke, 'It's members only back here.'

Surgeon bowed his head in acknowledgement.

'Quite right, Kester,' he grinned through teeth the shade of his skin.

For a moment, Kester retreated to the door, calling for Skid to fetch plenty of ice, no water. Keeping his voice calm and cold he then switched attention to Bruno. 'Both of you will leave. Now!' Kester's eyes narrowed; he stood tall, puffing out his chest.

Eyeballing Edson Taylor, Kester saw a frightened man looking back at him; a man drained of everything but fear. It was a strange sight; Kester couldn't quite believe he was setting eyes on him for the first time; he looked so… so weak. And Bruno was responsible. His disobedience risked destroying everything. He was becoming a liability. The anger building inside Kester ignited to white heat. Controlling it, he snapped in Bruno's direction, 'Why can I still see you?'

Afraid of losing face in front of Surgeon, Bruno bravely stood his ground. 'We have business to finish. We'll clean up when we're done.'

'Business?' Kester nodded in Taylor's direction. 'What is he guilty of?'

Bruno reached into a pocket. 'He came here with this' – Kester took the picture from Bruno – 'Gina sent it to him.'

Kester nodded. Now it made sense.

* * *

On removing my gag, I brought my throbbing hand across my chest and up into my armpit, trapping my fingers in tightly and rolling onto my side in an effort to stop the oozing blood. Now I had a clear sight of the man Surgeon had called Kester. He had arrived in the nick of time; just as my eye had been about to go the way of my little finger. My head pounded in response to the anticipated pain.

This Kester seemed to hold authority over Bruno, who shuffled nervously, his back to me as they talked. After looking at the picture, Kester looked up. 'Where is Gina?'

Bruno almost melted into his heels. 'I had to let her go. She betrayed me.' His apologetic tone hardened as he muttered to himself, 'And when I think of the loyalty I'd shown that bitch.'

For the moment, it seemed I had been forgotten and all I could think of was making a break for it. Given my proximity to Surgeon and Bruno I didn't like my chances. I envied Sam; by hustle or muscle he would have found a way out of this. Instead, my hopes were pinned on Kester, this well dressed man in his late fifties. It seemed that he had some control over the thugs who'd set out to disfigure me.

'I ask again. Where is Gina?' Befitting his age, his hair was grey and receding, he had the yellowy skin of a chain smoker. Despite this, tough guy Bruno was on the defensive.

'You said *I* was the boss and she betrayed *me*.' He was shifting feet, intermittently glancing to Surgeon who looked on with interest.

'What have you done to her?' asked Kester.

'Took her to the furnace house,' said Bruno.

Kester rubbed the back of his head. 'What time?'

Bruno turned again to Surgeon, seemingly taking confidence from him. 'Set to fry at three,' he bragged, 'slow heat.'

Looking at his watch, Kester slumped, exhaling a drawn out sigh. He filled up again with rage, 'Get out of my sight.' The words were laden with threat.

What kind of animals are these people?

A new wave of pain – a different kind – rattled through my body. If Gina was dead, maybe they were telling the truth about the picture.

Bruno nodded at Surgeon then made for the exit. Following his cue, Surgeon pursued him, stopping short of the door. 'Can we take our friend with us?'

Kester answered with a hard stare that encouraged Surgeon on his way. He then walked over to me. I was in shock, shaking like a cornered animal. Vomit launched itself from my mouth and onto the floor. Coughing up bile, I used my good hand to push myself up. My head was thudding, my throat on fire. I exhaled a groan as I got steady on my feet. Blood had seeped into my shirt, my hand refusing to dry up. Getting to my feet the pain had intensified but it was nothing compared to the fear occupying my thoughts.

'I must apologise for your treatment, very unfortunate.' He shook his head. 'You can call me Kester. And you are?'

'Edson Taylor,' I strained.

'Apart from the obvious have you any other injuries?'

With the immediate danger seemingly over, my focus moved elsewhere. 'Sam,' I cried. 'They could be going back for him. I have to call my friend.'

He scratched his neck, pulled out his phone. 'What's your friend's number?'

Feeling dizzy, I spoke through shallow breaths. 'I don't know.'

'Well where is he?'

Could I trust this man? I wondered. *Do I have a choice?*

I spilled. 'He's at the Hotel Angelino.'

Flipping open his phone Kester dialled, asked for a number for the Hotel Angelino.

A short, malnourished-looking man with odd features stepped into the room, carrying a bucket. His head was unshapely; his spine hunched. Sporadic growths of hair clung to what barely constituted a jaw. Kester greeted the man and closed the phone, *before* getting the hotel's number. 'Ah, good. This man's finger is down there,' he pointed the way for the greaseball to put down his bucket and scuttle around on all fours. 'No Skid, beneath the roulette wheel. *There*, that's it, put it in the bucket,' said Kester. 'That's it – lay it on top of the ice. If it gets wet it will shrivel up.'

Kester turned to me. 'Skid knows what he's doing. This isn't the first time either of us has encountered an injury of this nature.'

The room started to spin.

Letting a table take my weight I recomposed my

breathing. 'Call the hotel,' I said. 'Please. Warn Sam. Then call me an ambulance.' I looked at Kester with pleading eyes.

He was inspecting the bucket. 'I will try to contact your friend but an ambulance is out of the question.' He picked up my finger. 'But with the cells dying as we speak, I'm afraid you do need to see a doctor. By keeping the finger cold and dry we have between six and twelve hours to get you and this little digit reacquainted.'

He placed my finger back onto the ice. 'It just so happens I know a specialist. Like I say, we have seen such injuries before.' He smiled, clicked his fingers. 'Skid, fetch some clingfilm, and see if we still have iodine in the first aid cupboard.'

Skid skipped away.

'Don't worry, Mr Taylor, I will arrange the specialist. And Skid is a dab hand at cleaning up wounds.'

CHAPTER THIRTY-THREE

I had to endure two minutes of excruciating pain as my hand was cleaned up and dressed. The iodine solution hurt like hell, as did the heavy bandage that compressed my wound, stopping the bleeding. The pain was out of all proportion to the size of the injury. The only thing keeping me from passing out was the relief that coursed through me when Kester announced that he could help me find Elaine.

He repeated that he would have a specialist at his home forthwith. With my finger wrapped in clingfilm and laying on ice, I agreed to go. But it wasn't the lure of a specialist that enticed me. It was the promise of finding my fiancée.

I was weary of Kester; I was weary of the whole business. I wanted to wake up from this nightmare and be back at home with Elaine in my arms. But the facts were he'd saved my skin, and at my behest, had called Sam. I heard Kester introduce himself and tell Sam not to worry, before handing me the phone. I asked Sam to check out of the hotel immediately and find somewhere more salubrious for us to stay. I didn't want to talk too much in front of Kester, so I explained that I had a lead on Elaine and would contact him later. I had expected a barrage of questions, but rather surprisingly, Sam appeared to accept my vague instructions, agreeing to wait for an update via his suped-up mobile.

Whoever this Kester was, he wasn't somebody to go against. Maybe he could find Elaine? I didn't know why I believed him, but I did; probably because I wanted to. It was for this reason that I had not alerted Sam to what had been going on; I knew instinctively that if I blew the whistle on Surgeon and his pal, Kester would drop me.

Soon I was sitting in the back of a BMW, my finger for company, being escorted by Skid. Kester had stayed behind; apparently he had an errand to run before meeting us at his home. I guessed it had something to do with Gina. He'd seemed shocked by Bruno's horrendous claim. Who wouldn't be?

Set to fry at three.

It sounded as though my turning up had had deadly repercussions for Gina. The thought of a furnace was too horrifying to entertain, but having experienced Bruno's wrath at first hand I feared for her. As I feared for Elaine.

All are dead.

From the moment I had opened my hotel door to Surgeon it was as if a whirlwind had blown in with him. I had been taken at gunpoint; my finger had been sheared off, I had nearly lost an eye; and now here I was, sitting behind a weirdo called Skid.

I leaned forward to ask him if he thought Bruno really could have put Gina in a furnace. Even as I said it, I could not bring myself to believe it. Skid's response was a noncommittal grimace; his teeth looked like they had been put in upside down. I shifted closer to the window to avoid seeing his face in the rear-view mirror. He was as repulsive as he was menacing. The top of his head wasn't much better, a bony skull covered with the patchy hair of a mange-ridden mongrel. As we motored along a freeway he barely spoke, once in fact; to grumble that the BMW was being followed. He didn't elaborate.

After fifteen minutes of freeway we arrived at Kester's home. It could have belonged to a Third World dictator. Sat on wooden stilts, the palatial building climbed high into the hillside, dwarfing the surrounding shacks. Unlike every other home on the street there were no metal bars in evidence.

Once inside I followed Skid to a long reception room where I was instructed to wait. The specialist was yet to arrive, and so was Kester.

The whole place screamed power and success. Modern art mingled with an eclectic mix of expensive furniture. I picked out a chaise longue to rest on; its rail back creaked under my weight.

After placing my finger in a freezer, Skid joined me, leaning against a cabinet and resting his elbows on his thighs. He looked like a gargoyle.

Lifting my inflated hand I felt it pulsating, counting down the seconds to the specialist's arrival.

The front door clacked. A side, panelled door opened.

'Not waited too long I hope,' said Kester, entering the room. An affable smile filled his gaunt face as he sank into an enormous leather chair. His smile emitted a strange *déjà vu* feeling, like I knew him from a past life.

His demeanour changed rapidly when I suggested we called the police on Bruno and Surgeon.

He dismissed it, changing the subject. 'My friend, the hand specialist, is out of town, but he's racing back as we speak. He said that we have done the right things, just make sure you keep that bandage on tightly.' At the sound of a door he waved Skid away, turned back to me. 'I will handle Bruno. You have more pressing matters, like finding your fiancée.'

'I didn't tell you Elaine's my fiancée,' my voice hardened. 'How do you know about us?'

'It is my job to know things, Edson,' he said. 'Like the fact that you hail from England and you are looking for a former employee of mine. I recognised Elaine from that picture of yours. Don't worry; she was just a waitress, too young for anything else. A summer job I think.'

Impressed and disconcerted in equal measure, I pushed for more information.

'I have a reputation for knowing things, and for getting things done.' He sat forward. 'I can find Elaine McAdler, but you have to help yourself.' Locked in thought, he protruded his jaw, revealing an under-bite. 'Your running around after her has put you in danger. I can ensure your safety, but it is important that you remain here, at my home. I'm afraid that Bruno and his sidekick will see you as unfinished business. You see, Bruno has a vendetta against your fiancée and he sees you as part of it.'

One half of my brain was screaming: *What vendetta? What has she done? How is she mixed up with these people?* The other half had got stuck on *remain here.* I didn't like the sound of that. 'For how long?'

'What's left of today and tonight. At least until your hand's been seen to. What d'you say?'

Did I have a choice? 'How will you find Elaine?'

'As I said, it is my job to know things. By tomorrow I'll have exhausted my sources. At least then you'll know if she's findable.'

'I don't mean to sound ungrateful, but why would you help me?'

'In my world, reputation and publicity are everything. As the owner of *Flesh* club I can't afford an investigation, especially one involving my manager. I was hoping that by helping you we could forgo any police involvement.'

My instinct was right: it explained why he denied me an ambulance.

'I help fix your hand, find Elaine, and we agree to ignore today's events. What d'you say?' he repeated.

So that was it. Even if I had insisted on calling the cops, I didn't think Kester would allow me to. Behind his charm and well-spoken persona was somebody with the influence to dismiss animals like Bruno and Surgeon. I saw the way Bruno had cowered out of the club; behind all the bravado and biceps he was shit-scared of this man. It seemed sensible to go along with him. For now. In my mind it was wrong not to involve the police – Bruno had practically admitted to murder – but I would have to do that later. Finding Elaine superseded everything – no matter what.

Deciding to broach the subject of Gina, I voiced my fears over Surgeon's disturbing revelation. 'The picture Gina sent me. Surgeon told me all of the women in that picture are dead. All of them: *both* Elaines, and Gina?'

As Kester entwined his fingers I detected a smile. He was about to speak when floorboards groaned. Skid re-entered the room. Behind him, a man stood in the doorway, a black man so tall and wide, all I could see was his pinstripe suit. He ducked down and squeezed into the room. Kester waved him away, but not before I had seen him, recognising him from his mug-shot. It was Faustino Ricard. One of the men who'd taken Elaine.

CHAPTER THIRTY-FOUR

Faustino Ricard – the giant chauffeur with a fondness for fighting – was staring curiously at me.

She was not alone, Ed. Two men were with her.

Kester stood. Flustered. 'What is it Tino?'

'The, er, thing's sealed and ready, boss.'

Boss?

Kester shooed him away. 'Yes, fine, give me a minute.' Tino went into reverse, squeezing backwards out of the doorway.

His appearance had thrown my breathing out of kilter. I was seething. Desperate to go after him, put a gun to his head – demand to know what he'd done with Elaine – but I had to hold it together. I couldn't let on that I recognised him. Averting my gaze, I tried to look blankly nonchalant.

Boss. This changed everything. Kester knew of Tino's involvement in Elaine's disappearance. He had to. *It is my job to know things, Edson.* But what was his role? My brain was working overtime. The way he rushed Tino away, it was like he didn't want me to see him. No wonder he wanted to forgo any police involvement.

But why did he want me to stay here? To fix my hand? Unlikely.

Having thought that Kester had saved my skin, I was now confused, vulnerable, but my decision was made. I would pretend to comply and then at the first opportunity I was out of here. I'd hook up with Sam and we'd go to the police. But my reaction to seeing Faustino Ricard could be telling. First off, I needed to win Kester over.

'Thanks again for your help,' I said. 'I will wait here while you look for Elaine. After all, I don't fancy bumping into Bruno or Surgeon again. And, as you say, the hand specialist will be here later?'

'Any moment now,' said Kester, looking quizzically at me. 'I will let you know if I get anywhere with Elaine, and Skid will see that you have a comfortable stay.'

The gargoyle nodded, following Kester out the room.

Creeping to the door, I held it ajar, waited, listened hard, heard muffled conversation and footsteps. Voices became clearer as the front door scraped open. I made out Kester's steady speech. He was talking to Skid. 'Make sure he doesn't leave.'

Slowly stepping out I watched Kester and Faustino Ricard take the steps down to the road as Skid closed the door and bolted it.

A thought struck me, is Skid, Fernando Sanchez?

When I was sure they'd driven away, I crept along the hallway. To the exit.

Skid intercepted me, his hand hovering over his right pocket.

'Problem *meesta?*' spat Skid. He had a knowing snarl, expecting trouble.

'Just wondering. The name Skid. Is that short for anything?'

'It's a nickname,' Skid whined. 'Ain't short for nothing.' He wobbled his knees, demonstrating the loose limbs of a drunk.

'I see. Your real name hard to pronounce?'

'What you sayin'?'

'Just chatting.'

'How 'bout chatting yourself back in there.'

Skid was small and spindly, but scary as hell. The thought of him with Elaine was too horrible to contemplate.

'Is there a phone I could use?'

'Nada,' he snorted, rolling his neck like he was limbering up.

I stared at him, weighed up my options. I wanted to wring his neck, to squeeze information out of him, but I couldn't give away my suspicions. Not when what I really needed was to get out of here and he was the only thing in my way. Anger inside me reached a crescendo. It needed a release.

I was ready for him, prepared to throw everything at him, but reading my intentions, Skid pulled his gun on me. It was getting to be a habit, one I wasn't getting used to.

'Mr Hardwick asked that you stay here. I think that's best.' Skid's eyes narrowed. 'So turn around now and go make yourself comfortable.'

Reluctantly, I did as he said.

'No.' I turned to see him point with the gun. 'Use that door.'

I pushed open the heavy wooden door, gave a quick scan of the room; a four-poster, thick curtains, a crystal chandelier.

The door slammed behind me. A key turned, locking me in.

CHAPTER THIRTY-FIVE

8.20pm
Westwood, Los Angeles.

'Please be there; please be there,' Donnie Guzan repeated to himself as he hot-footed it along Westwood Boulevard. The failure to locate Meybodi and Afshari that had blighted his day now threatened to ruin his first date with Nurse Lovely. Being forced to get ready at FBI headquarters wasn't the ideal preparation, but he had at least managed to duck under a shower and grab a fresh pair of pants from his locker. Derego had provided him with a flowery shirt and a whole lot of ribbing.

Finally, Guzan arrived outside *Evuna's*: the Spanish restaurant's front window was lit up like a beacon. He almost leapt with nervous excitement at the sight of his date sat alone in the corner. Ah, Nurse Maria Garcia; even her name sounded sexy. *Calm down, Don. Be cool.*

Catching his reflection, he decided to remove his tie and undo his top two buttons. After using the tie to wipe his wet forehead, he pocketed it and pushed open the door.

Wow, he mouthed as he held in his stomach and swaggered over to her table. Incredibly, she looked even better out of uniform. Her hair dropped down over a sexy, white lace V-neck that went in at all the right places. As she stood up he swallowed hard. A smile broke from her irresistible mouth, the candlelight illuminating her skin.

Bending awkwardly for the double-cheek kiss, Guzan apologised for his lateness. Then said: 'You look fantastic.' On noticing her silk skirt ride up her golden thigh, he repeated, 'Fantastic.' Quitting before his stare became a leer, Guzan floated back to his chair. Maria's sweet smell followed.

'Thanks,' she smiled. 'And it's nice to see you all scrubbed and smart.'

'It so happens I wash and shave religiously.' He winked, 'Every Sunday morning.' Lame Don... Wait, she just smiled.

'Then I timed this date well but you might find me busy Saturday,' said Maria.

'Wise,' nodded Guzan. The early hint of a second date cheered up his face.

She smiled back, shaking her head. 'Nice shirt.'

'Do I detect sarcasm?'

'No, really, it's just that it's not one I would've pictured you in: a pink floral scene?'

'I'm limited with what goes well with my hair.' Then: 'Mainly hats.'

Nice one, Romeo.

She tut-tutted. 'Enough of the self-deprecation, you're a handsome man.'

Patronizing? No…take it. 'Thanks.'

She smiled. 'And I like your chestnut curls.'

Chestnut? 'Really? My partner Tyler calls them my public pubes.'

Ah crap! Taxi for one!

She took a breath, glancing away. 'Don't date much do you?'

How could I retrieve this? 'My last date was… I don't know, maybe a year ago. Picture this, having earlier drunk me under the table, she proceeded to stand up and do her party piece; which consisted of belching to the tune of Puppy Love'.

Maria laughed.

'It's true – you could have heard a pin drop that night at the opera.'

More laughing.

'Ruined the Osmonds for me.'

As the date raced by, Guzan relaxed. It was hard not to with Maria Garcia's genuine smile beaming back across the table. He felt like a different person, as if the trepid Donnie Guzan was lost somewhere in her deep brown eyes. She appreciated his compliments, even his jokes, but it was when she spoke about her work that he felt the real connection. They shared the same attitude that was lacking in so many of their colleagues; they both cared about people. He didn't know why Maria liked his jowly mug, but by the time their plates were removed he was sure that she did. Funny how things turn out. Without Mrs Donachie's outburst he wouldn't be on the date, and now he couldn't believe his awful day was ending so well. He was already hoping the curse of the FBI wouldn't ruin their relationship. Of the sixteen agents on his floor, not one had a happy marriage. He had heard all the excuses about being married to their jobs, but for Guzan it was something else. He had seen – not least with Cliff – how an agent's family could be in the firing line. Agents could look after each other, but protecting their loved ones was more difficult. And it seemed that the closer, more loving an agent's family, the harder it was for them to accept the dangers of the job. Being a federal agent helped attract women, but it soon repelled them. That suited Tyler fine, he went through women like a transvestite goes through razor blades, but Guzan wanted much more than to just get laid.

'Trouble at work?' Maria asked, breaking in on his thoughts.

'I made a bad call, but it'll be okay.' He nodded hopefully, reached for a bud.

Maria flicked back her hair. Not flirtatiously, businesslike. 'I've been thinking about what Mrs Donachie said.'

'Her outburst?'

'The name she mentioned, Kester Hardwick?'

Hearing that name on Maria's lips just felt wrong;

Guzan shuffled uncomfortably as she continued, 'Mrs Donachie went to see him in prison, that's how I knew the name.'

Guzan's eyes widened. He put down his bud and listened.

'It would have been four, five years ago, just after I started work. In those days Mrs Donachie was allowed to take herself off places. Her church went on a coach trip to the county jail. It was called "a journey into forgiveness and light."' Maria shrugged. 'She took it as an opportunity to speak with Kester Hardwick. She told me that he had threatened her, saying he can get to anyone.' Maria shook her head. 'But that wasn't the worst thing. The way she grabbed my arm, her intensity, she was adamant that he was behind her family's murder. She told me all about her son Clifford and his untimely death.'

Guzan released a sigh. 'Cliff was a hero, his suicide affected us all.'

Maria's brow creased.

'What?' asked Guzan.

'Mrs Donachie never mentioned suicide.'

Chapter Thirty-Six

9.59pm
Lincoln Heights, Los Angeles.

Sunset had been and gone. Not surprisingly there was no sign of the hand specialist.

It was time to get out of here.

Not wanting to feed Skid's suspicions I had kept quiet – waited, just sitting on the bed, planning my exit. Ignoring my body clock.

Overpowering Skid wasn't an option. My best hope was to be long gone before he discovered I was missing. If I was going to escape it had to be without their knowledge and it had to be without my little finger.

As the cover of night came I got to work.

Now or never.

I unhooked the dusty curtains, spreading them out on the floor. Using the cotton lining to make them twice as long, I rolled them up, did the same with a sheet off the bed, and then tied the lot together. Using my right hand and left elbow, I fastened one end through a rocking chair and dragged it to the open window. The drop to the paving that ran alongside the house was over twenty feet.

I fed the thick line of fabric out of the window. It reached about half way. I'd have to jump the rest. I adjusted my bandage to allow my bad hand some degree of grip, then proceeded to climb out the window – at first hanging to the frame, then wrapping my body around my improvised rope. My hand protested. It was no use, I had to release it. But my body weight was ensuring my descent. My one-handed grip loosened. My shoes noisily scraped down wood until I reached a ledge. From there I still had a fifteen-foot drop, and I was out of fabric. I could see cars parked on the road, and soon I would be noticed – assuming Skid hadn't already heard me. I tried not to panic. There was a wooden stilt beneath the ledge. *If I can just get to it.*

The rocking chair creaked, the fabric was lengthening, about to come away. I started to rock, the chair creaking louder with each swing.

I had one chance.

As I swung towards the stilt I let go of the curtain. Falling. I reached out; smacked the thick wooden column, managed to wrap my arms around for a second before losing my grip. I landed in a heap, not on the path but under the house. In dirt. My body moaned with pain, but my bigger concern was the noise I'd just made.

I heard the front door open, a volley of footsteps pelting down the stairs.

Skid was coming.

I tried to get up, but my body wouldn't allow it. There was a security camera above me – tied beneath the ledge – but it was pointing away, to the front of house. I had to hide, but how? My legs had twisted under me, but it was my back that had taken the brunt of the fall.

Make sure he doesn't leave.

I stretched myself out and rolled beneath the house. Into darkness. From there I watched Skid appear, immediately noticing the curtain.

Snaking on my front, I slowly moved up the bank, my bandage unravelling behind me. Quietly crawling through weeds and dirt I continued up, heading for the dark, until I could go no higher. When the base of the house met the bank I hid. Waited. It was dark, wet; not a place I wanted to die.

I watched as Skid's bony silhouette moved under the house, his gun leading the way.

Keep low.

I dug my face into the mud.

Skid's footsteps became louder. He was back on the path. Slowly lifting my eyes, I caught sight of his face. He looked worried, scared even, violently scratching his bony skull. His limbs pointed in different directions, but he was looking up, beneath the house. He hopped forward, snapped his body into position, and headed along the path. Towards me.

With every step he got closer, slowly disappearing from the head down until all I could see were his legs. Skid was close. A yard away.

I was trapped, defenceless.

If he looks down now he'll see me.

I held my breath as Skid stopped walking. His knees parted. He was bending.

Chapter Thirty-Seven

A loud shriek came from the roadside. A woman wailed, 'Hey, you looking for that man?'

Skid jumped up, shot down the path towards the voice.

I rolled in dirt until I could see out from under the house. Skid reached the woman, his gun held behind his back. The blonde's arms were flapping, her voice high-pitched. It sounded like she'd seen me.

'I'm tellin' ya straight,' she cried hysterically, 'some tall brother.'

My only exit was via the path, in full view of Skid. And now she was pointing.

But not at me.

'Legging it through your neighbour's yard,' she pointed again, 'he was over there!'

Following her direction, Skid darted off.

Looking up at me, the woman waved, held a finger to her lips. I crawled out, scrambled to my feet as she beckoned me urgently towards her. Crouching in an effort to hold back pain, I headed down the path. Gravity kept my legs pumping to a cumbersome stagger.

Skid was out of sight. But for how long?

I reached the road, scanned the well-lit street; looked in vain for the mystery blonde.

What now? Where's she gone?

The lifeline she'd handed me was running out.

The pain in my back was killing. Barely able to move, I was a sitting duck, nowhere to hide.

Three ramshackle homes up from me, Skid burst out into the road. His eyes found mine.

He started to run.

Out of nowhere a red Mazda screeched up to me, passenger window down. The blonde leant over. 'Get in. I'm a friend of Elaine's.'

Elaine's? Without hesitation I flung open the door, got in.

'Get down,' she ordered.

I turned back; I couldn't help myself. Skid was standing in the road. He'd put away his gun and was speaking into a phone.

My heart pounded with hope as we raced away from him. Who was this woman? *A friend of Elaine's!* Was she taking me to her? My breath couldn't come quickly enough.

The hyped-up driver pulled off her pinned blonde wig and shrugged out of her beige coat as she tore up the empty streets. She was driving her Mazda like an accident was imminent; wide-eyed, constantly checking mirrors for company. Under the wig, her hair was dark, cropped; she looked like Demi Moore in *Ghost*.

With the traffic lights obliging, several neighbourhoods flew by, disparate but for their depression. I clutched the dashboard as she cornered; my hand hurting almost as much as my spine. I gingerly dragged a seat belt across my body, clicked it in place. I desperately wanted to know where she was taking me, but I was afraid to break into her concentration.

Demi checked her mirrors again as we entered a quiet estate. Trailers sat on square flat plots of land bordered by chain-link fencing. Lighting was a rarity here, as even moonlight avoided the area. She switched off the headlights, eased off the accelerator, and carefully navigated the dark, neglected street. We made a left, up a gravelled drive. Pitch black.

I released the question that had lodged in my throat: 'Are you taking me to Elaine?'

She glanced across for the first time. 'Not unless you know where she is.'

My gut tightened. 'Don't *you?*'

'Ed, I can call you Ed, right?'

I nodded.

'Stay easy, Ed.' She stopped the vehicle, got out, wig and coat in hand. Could I trust her? There was no sign of life, and no keys in the ignition. I began to wonder if I'd have been better off with Skid. At the mention of Elaine, I had trusted this mystery woman. Had I not learned from my mistake with Surgeon?

She moved behind the car, opened the boot. I waited, once again helpless.

I heard the boot slam down, saw her walk to the front of the car carrying something under her arm. She bent down by the radiator grill.

I reached for the door handle but before I could get it open, she was back, sliding into the driver's seat.

'Had to change the plates,' she mentioned as if it was an everyday occurrence.

Confused and relieved, I tried to think: who carries spare number plates?

She reversed back out of the drive, took a boiled sweet from her handbag, flicked on the headlights and pulled away.

'You know my name. Do I get to know yours?' I asked.

'Lisa Connelly, friends call me Magnum.' Her mood and driving had relaxed a little.

'Magnum?'

'I'm a PI.'

Within a minute we hit a freeway, started to cruise a long bend that hugged the base of a hill.

'You're a Private Investigator, *and* Elaine's friend?'

She nodded. 'Your lucky day.' Her demeanour was friendly, calm; unrecognisable from the shrieking passerby outside Kester's house.

I curled my arms around my chest. 'Do you know if she's okay?'

Her boiled sweet cracked. 'I've not heard from her in over a week.'

What? I *had seen her more recently.* It was as if I had been booted in the stomach; like I was losing Elaine all over again.

What had I done? Kester had been clear; *I can find Elaine, but you have to help yourself.*

In one breath, words sped frantically from my mouth, 'The owner of that house said he could find her, I think he knows where she is, she came here with men called Faustino Ricard and Fernando Sanchez, they work for him and were ther—'

'Look Ed,' Lisa interjected, fishing for another sweet. 'I have a place, not far from here. We can talk there.'

As I inhaled, I felt my back spasm, but the pain was nothing compared to my hand. I unravelled my dishevelled bandage, starting to reapply it. Lisa caught sight of my wound and sucked in air. My hand was now a nasty plum colour. What remained of my bandage was covered in muck, so was the inside of the Mazda.

'Tell me,' I winced. 'How did you know where I was?'

'Your e-mail.'

'*E-mail?*'

'About arriving at the hotel. I tried to warn you off. I went there to ask you to leave LA, for your own safety. But when I saw Bruno Meyer I knew to keep my distance. After you were forced into the back of that van I decided to follow.'

'*You* were at the *Flesh* club?'

'Doing my thing. Then Kester Hardwick arrived.' She whistled. 'Man you attract quite an entourage. I followed you to Hardwick House, parked up and waited.'

I remembered Skid grumbling that the BMW was being followed.

Lisa checked the rearview mirror. 'When you didn't leave I thought it was going to be an all-nighter. I don't normally put my life at risk but, I don't know, your botched escape drew my pity.' I could hear the smile in her voice.

'I'm grateful for that.'

'You're welcome, just helping a friend.'

'I still don't understand. Did Elaine give you access to her e-mails?'

Lisa clammed up, her tone stiffened. 'Before we talk properly you gotta make me a promise. Without it we go our separate ways.'

'Go on.'

'You don't contact anyone, or ever mention me. You trust nobody, and I'm not just talking about Kester Hardwick. I mean nobody. Not the police. Sam. *Nobody.*'

'How do you know about Sam?'

'I'm a PI,' she shrugged, 'and you named him in your e-mail.'

I didn't like Lisa's demands; Gina Sipple could have been murdered. And what of Sam? I had to call him. 'You expect me not to trust my best friend?'

She shook her head. 'You think I need this heat? You can call your buddy when you're out of my hair. But even then you don't mention me.' Lisa glanced over. 'Agreed?'

'Fine, we have a deal. Tell me what you know and I'll take it from there. I promise to keep you out of it.'

She slowed the Mazda, indicated to come off the freeway and looked across at me as though assessing my sincerity. 'I showed up at the hotel and followed you because of what you meant to my friend.'

'What I *meant* to her? You mean what I mean to her, right?'

Lisa kept her eyes on the road. LA's high-rise buildings were now ahead of us. 'She gave me her e-mail access months ago. Wanted me to keep track of everything. She'd come to accept that her past would catch up with her, but when she met you she became more and more concerned about it; mainly about Bruno Meyer finding her.' She paused, took a breath. 'I know you're here to find Elaine, but…' her voice tailed off.

'But what?'

The streets suddenly busied; people of all ages out for a Sunday night stroll. Befitting my confusion, signs no longer appeared in English.

'Your first mistake is that you're looking for Elaine McAdler.'

What? Things were surreal. It was like I'd just entered the twilight zone, been teleported to Asia.

'Your fiancée's name isn't Elaine.'

'Of course it is,' I protested, even more confused, 'what do you mean?' For a brief moment I wondered if this whole thing was a case of mistaken identity. But it couldn't be.

Lisa explained, 'Elaine McAdler is an anagram of her real name: Claire Needlam.'

Chapter Thirty-Eight

Elaine McAdler/Claire Needlam; I worked out the anagram in my mind. 'Why did she change her name?' I demanded to know.

'Hold on a minute,' replied Lisa Connelly, turning the Mazda left at an impressive Art Deco theatre and on past a bus station. 'We're here,' she said, edging the car up to a four-story apartment block. A swipe card raised huge metal doors and lit up a car park. Lisa drove under and parked up.

I asked again, this time pleading with my eyes.

'Once we're inside,' she said, getting out the car.

Carefully reaching across, I released my seat belt, tried to angle my body back towards the door. Lisa held it open, waited as I slid my feet out. My spine protesting, I let out a groan. Lisa took my arm and with a sharp exhale I climbed to my feet.

She locked the car - *beep-beep* - and keeping hold of my arm, guided me towards the entrance. The smell of her perfume soon became lost to disinfectant as we entered a lobby. Crossing over a sticky floor, we reached the lift just as its doors parted, frightening the bejesus out of an elderly Oriental.

Lisa's open-plan apartment was on the third floor. Cream walls, pine furniture, everything modern. There was nothing personal, not a photo in sight. More showroom than lived-in, it had the smell of a DIY store and overlooked a tiny communal garden, the type that offers no privacy or ball games.

She lowered me into a hard-backed chair, and sympathetically helped me off with my blooded shirt. I felt my back tighten as she headed into the kitchenette.

'Nice place,' I said automatically.

'I live in the hills. This is more of a second home. It's not even in my name. I can leave in a flash.'

'Where are we?'

'Hampshire Place, on the western edge of Koreatown; Korea as in location not vocation,' she said, handing me a wet flannel, 'but I guess you already worked that out.'

I grimaced as I wiped my left side. 'Had my money on Chinatown,' I said.

'It doesn't go after the tourists like Chinatown or Little Tokyo. The food's too spicy for them.'

Lisa was clearly stalling. She was going to tell me why my Elaine was really Claire Needlam but in her own time.

'Stay easy; I'll see if I have anything for your hand. You must avoid hospitals right now.'

'You sound like Kester.'

Lisa reappeared with a small, green first-aid kit, which she opened, removing its contents one by one. She grouped together a roll of bandage, cotton gauze and a pack of antiseptic wipes. 'To be honest, I live in K-town 'cos it's cheap. Believe it or not the community is still recovering from the riots of '92 in the aftermath of the Rodney King verdicts. Half the total citywide loss occurred here.' – I fought back pain as she wiped the edge of my wound – 'Many of the businesses have still not reopened. Koreans refer to it as sa-i-ki or April-29, in much the same way as we refer to 9-11.'

As Lisa applied the gauze to my hand I bit down hard, trying to counter the pain. She asked me to hold up my hand whilst she wrapped a bandage around the gauze. I felt sick and noticed my bare chest drenched with sweat. I wanted to yell out but couldn't. I realised that I was holding my breath.

Lisa kept talking, keeping my mind distracted. 'Hampshire Place was built to attract the wealthier Koreans, but if there are such people they don't live here!'

I exhaled slowly. My hand had developed its own pulse.

'All done,' she smiled. 'Let me get you something to drink.'

I had barely nodded when she returned with an OJ poured from a tap on the fridge.

Before taking a sip I waited for eye contact. Then pleaded: 'Tell me about Elaine?'

Her face became still, as though she was thinking up an excuse. 'But you're barely dressed.'

This time she disappeared into a side room, and came back holding up a t-shirt with *Green Day* on the front. 'It's a concert shirt, they only had large.' She gestured for me to lift up my arms and carefully fed my bandaged hand through a sleeve.

'Please Lisa.' I repeated, 'Tell me about Elaine. What's happened to her?'

She swung a leg over a stool and sat up at the breakfast bar. Folding her arms, she looked down at me. 'LA thrives on gossip and rumours, but they mean nothing to me, Ed. I deal with facts. Much of my work is investigating men whose wives suspect them of cheating. If they are, I prove it. These women are suspicious. In most cases if I gave them the nod they'd head straight for divorce court, but *I* need evidence. Not a compromising photo that could be interpreted a hundred ways, *real* evidence, like a video of his hand in the cookie jar, so to speak.'

'Evidence, I get it, but what has this got to do with Elaine?'

'You're right about the men she arrived with. They work for Kester Hardwick, but that's where the facts end.'

'But there are rumours?'

'Sure, but they don't add up. It is best we deal in facts; there's no point worrying about conjecture.'

Worrying. 'Please, Lisa. These past few days I've considered all possibilities. I have a PhD in worry.'

'You sure you wanna know?'

'I *need* to know,' I pleaded. Maybe ignorance is bliss but for me bliss was history.

Lisa sighed, sucked on a lip. 'The story doing the rounds is that Claire—Elaine, was taken by Kester and Bruno and—' – her words dried up, she looked solemn – 'Look, it doesn't make sense.' She shook her head dismissively.

My heart was heavy, and I was choking up. 'Please—Why would Kester and Bruno have taken her?'

'Because they both want her dead.'

CHAPTER THIRTY-NINE

Bruno *and* Kester want her dead.

I had seen Bruno fuelled with anger, violently out of control. After what he and Surgeon had done to me, and said they'd done to Gina, I had major alarm bells ringing where Elaine was concerned. I was not surprised about Bruno, but Kester had given me hope. *I can find your fiancée.* News that *he* wanted her dead was a hammer blow. Elaine had travelled to LA with two of his employees for heaven's sake, and that knowledge left my fragile emotions in tatters.

Sitting forward in the pine chair, Lisa's t-shirt rode up my aching spine, leaving cold sweat on my lower back. I rested my head on my palms and thought; *Elaine was taken by Kester and Bruno. They wanted her dead. Why? My Angel; the most caring,* loving, sensitive soul anyone could wish to meet. 'Why would they want her dead?' I asked aloud, my voice full of despair.

Lisa sat down in front of me, cross-legged. 'Fifteen years ago, Kester went to prison for murder. He found out that his partner was cheating on him, so he shot her dead. He then tried to frame her lover – a man named Franco Biani – for the murder. Kester had planted strong evidence against Biani but it didn't fly. Biani's testimony was set to convict Kester, who was seen as untouchable at the time. The protection given to Biani was of presidential proportions, but Kester got to him before the trial. He had people on the inside, possibly still does. That's why you mustn't trust anybody, and why you can't risk going to hospital,' warned Lisa. 'With the case against Kester about to be thrown out, a witness came forward. Claire. When the murder was taking place, she was washing glasses in a back room. She saw it all on a security monitor. I told her it was suicide to testify, but she was adamant and went into hiding. Kester claimed temporary insanity – a crime of passion – then settled for second-degree murder. LA looked on with interest as he vowed his revenge.'

It all rang true. *This* was the real Elaine that I now recognised: caring and strong; a fighter for justice. It also explained why she was unwilling to talk about her past. She'd changed her name and left her life behind to protect herself. She'd had no choice. 'And Bruno?' I sighed. 'Does he also want her dead for witnessing the murder?'

'Bruno has his own grievance.' As Lisa continued her voice sank to a strained whisper. Her eyes were still, looking inward. 'The night of the sentencing, Claire resurfaced. She went back to her flat to collect a few things before leaving for good. Only when she got there she walked in on Bruno raping her flatmate.' Lisa drew breath, allowing her words to fall onto my heavy shoulders. 'Angry at seeing Claire, Bruno immediately turned on her. But Claire was ready. She grabbed up a bottle, smashed it, and as Bruno attacked, she dropped to one knee and drove the broken glass into his groin. Essentially, she castrated him; left him screaming in agony and rolling in his own blood while she got her flatmate out. After that, she took her things and disappeared. Apparently the Feds had already helped set her up with a new identity.'

I let out a silent cry; it explained Bruno's brutality towards me. *Guilty by association.* But had he already killed Elaine? God – how brave she was and what she must have suffered. I looked across at Lisa. She was sniffing, her brown eyes moist.

'What happened to her flatmate?' I asked.

Lisa took a slow, chest-expanding breath. 'Bruno left her alone in return for her silence. She eventually became a private investigator.' Lisa turned away. After a second or two her neck tightened and her chin lifted. Filled with pity, I let her speak.

'In '93 when Claire left LA she was just seventeen-years-old and alone. I had no contact with her until a year or so later. She wanted to know if, people were still trying to find her, particularly Bruno, and if so, how hard. I was able to tell her that he was spending a fortune trying and I promised I'd warn her if he got anywhere. That's when I started befriending people with access to information, private investigators and the like. Claire left Spain for England because I got wind that Bruno's net was closing in on her.'

She had been running away! 'But, say she was found in England. Why leave and get on the plane with Skid and Tino?' *You don't kidnap someone and walk through Heathrow Airport with them.* 'Say that she wasn't forced, what reason could she have to come back?'

Lisa shrugged. 'She called me nine days ago, said that she was coming to LA. I couldn't believe it. I tried to talk her out of it, but it was like telling her not to testify, her mind was made up. She claimed that she had no choice, that it was the only way. Her major concern was you. She was afraid of what Bruno might do to you to get at her.' Lisa glanced to an open laptop resting on a low coffee table. 'Since that phone call I've not heard a thing from her, and I've kept online at all times.'

Lifting my head, I stiffened up. 'Maybe if we can get to Tino or Skid, we can find out what they know.'

Lisa shook her head. 'You're out of your depth. You don't know what you're dealing with.'

'Then it's time I learned!'

'It's getting late, Ed. My advice is to get some rest and then in the morning, go back to England. Go home. Whatever Claire is up to she doesn't want you involved. I understand you wanting to stay in LA, but you're in too much danger. They may or may not be looking for Claire, but they will be looking for you.'

I felt a wave of irrational anger towards Elaine. Taking this out on Lisa, I snapped, 'Why didn't she tell me any of this? Whatever trouble she's in we should be facing together. If she wants me to leave she can tell me herself.' I knew it was not so much anger as fear. I also knew that I wasn't going anywhere, but I so desperately needed to hear from Elaine. I would do anything just to know she was alive.

Lisa looked to the floor. 'If there are things Claire didn't want you to know, believe me, it was for your own safety.'

* * *

Using a damp towel, I freshened up. It felt good to wipe the stink of dirt, sweat and blood from my body. Lisa kindly washed my clothes, spun them in a dryer and got the couch looking like a single bed.

I was soon curled up and uncomfortable. My hand had swollen up like a football and was throbbing like a generator. It had been a long day but I couldn't sleep. This had little to do with pain, the narrow sofa-bed or its slippery upholstery. Lisa's laptop was in the corner of the room, calling out to me, and at around 3am I succumbed to its advances. Pulling out the speakers, I got online and quietly typed in the name: 'Kester Hardwick'.

30 hits. One of which took me to the *LA Times* website. It contained all their reports for the past week. His name appeared in an article marking his release from prison. It used words like *notorious* and *kingpin* and pretty much backed up what Lisa had said. His name also appeared in their archive section. To access this I had to register to the site. I quickly did so and came upon a report of Kester's arrest for murder. Next to the story was a picture of the victim. Her name was Elaine and I recognised her immediately. It was the woman with the name-tag, the one standing in the centre of Gina's e-mail attachment. *This* was Kester's partner?

A chill swept down my spine. *All are dead.*

The image was branded on my brain: the older Elaine in the middle, with Gina to her right, and my Elaine to her left.

At that moment a horrible thought invaded my mind and I broke my promise to Lisa.

I e-mailed Sam's phone.

CHAPTER FORTY

Monday, 7.18am
Koreatown, Los Angeles.

Images of torment and menace posed as sleep. Finally shrugging them off, I sat up and unravelled my bandage. My hand was maroon coloured and painful as hell, but mercifully, no worse than last night.

I pulled my laundered shirt and trousers off the back of the sofa-bed and gingerly stood up. My back felt a little freer. I even managed to take advantage of Lisa's shower, before reapplying bandaging to my hand and getting dressed. When I emerged from the bathroom, Lisa was in the kitchenette; made up and smartly dressed; a hat or scarf away from an air hostess. A whiff of pancakes drifted from where she stood, carefully arched over maple syrup, trying not to mark her blue skirt-suit.

After a quick swallow of miniature pancakes and coffee, I felt it acceptable to make my way over to the Venetian blinds where I squinted through into the breaking sun.

Relief put a smile on my face. Sam had read my e-mail and, as instructed, was waiting outside the apartment block. I was so pleased to see him. And not only had he found Hampshire Place, the big guy had turned up in a hire car.

Lisa came over, opened the blinds. 'Gonna be a warm one.'

I nodded, hiding behind a smile my guilt at contacting Sam. She offered me a second cup of coffee. I declined, picking the moment to ask the question that had blighted my sleep: 'The woman Kester murdered. Was she related to Elaine?'

Ashen-faced, Lisa turned away. 'Why do you ask that?'

'I came to LA with a picture in my hand, from when Elaine was here before. One of the other women in that picture was called Elaine. She looked a lot like my Elaine, only older.' Lisa's eyes were distant, gazing down at the road. 'I have to ask. Did Kester murder Elaine's mother?'

'Oh my God!' she yelled. 'Look!'

'What?' I followed her eyes down to the street. How the hell? It was Skid. Four cars back from Sam's hire car sat the BMW. Vermin-features was leaning against it.

Lisa stepped back in horror. 'What have you done?'

'Nothing, I haven't mentioned you, or—' – I saw that Sam was walking towards the entrance – 'Shit.'

'What now?'

'I asked Sam to meet me outside this building.'

'You gave this address?'

'I never mentioned the apartment.'

'If you had, we'd be dead already.' She paced the floor. 'You stupid, *stupid*...' She collected herself, took control. 'All right, they're here for *you*. Take the back exit and—'

'Sam's coming in.'

We saw him waiting outside the entrance. 'He won't be able to get in,' said Lisa.

Watching a woman exit the lobby, I said, 'I think someone just let him.'

'Just great,' cried Lisa, circling the room.

I looked back at the BMW. Suddenly there was no sign of Skid.

Lisa scooped up a set of keys. 'Follow me!'

We left her apartment, heading for the underground car park.

The lift stopped prematurely at the ground floor. Doors parted revealing a tall, lone figure standing in the lobby. Sam's face struck with recognition and surprise. 'Ed, where the—'

I cut him off. 'Get in!'

The lobby was empty as the lift closed.

'What the hell's happened to you?' he said.

With the lift continuing south, I spilled. 'There's

a man outside. Look, I can't explain, but we have to get out of here, right away.'

The doors opened into a car park.

As Lisa jostled us out, Sam eyed my hand. 'What's going on, Ed?'

'There's no time!' chastised Lisa with a stare that made it clear if he asked again, she'd rip out his tongue. 'You need a car.'

Skid would recognise Lisa's Mazda so we had no choice but to *borrow* a motor. She gestured towards a silver Hyundai Tiburon. 'Take this bastard's,' she growled. We looked at her. 'He's a slimy letch.'

'Fair enough,' said Sam, hot-rodding the bastard's sports car. My eyes kept flicking back to the lift, looking for Skid.

The engine roared and dance music blared out. Sam rapidly slid back the seats, and I crammed myself in as quickly as my back allowed.

Lisa took out a swipe card and ran towards the huge metal doors.

Sam took the wheel. It touched his chest.

'You guys ready?' called Lisa.

'Ready.' I turned off the music and clicked in my seat belt. I had a feeling I was going to need it.

'Hurry up!' Lisa yelled, 'And stay low.'

The metal exit groaned, letting in an abundance of noise and light as it disappeared into the ceiling. Again, I looked for Skid.

Cranking the car into gear, Sam screeched us towards the exit. Tightly packed cars passed by. Forced to wait – the Hyundai's nose poked out into the daylight – we were sitting ducks.

Fighting the urge to look for the BMW, I stayed down and felt the car jerk forward. I glanced out, saw that a cyclist had slowed just enough for us to join the crawling traffic; two lanes taking it in turns to stop whilst the other caught up.

Rolling my head, I searched in vain for the BMW. Realising that it would have been quicker on foot I scanned the streetwalkers' faces. All Korean.

I called to Sam. 'Do you see a black BMW?'

He checked his mirrors. 'There's one three cars back. Who is it? What the hell's going on, Ed?'

I spotted it; blacked out windows. *Skid*. 'It's one of the men who took Elaine. Now he's after me. He's armed. And switching lanes!'

Our lane slowed to a stop; the BMW was now only two cars back.

Sam slammed his hand onto the horn, but our lane wouldn't budge. He was shouting, staying low as the BMW came into view.

It stopped alongside us. Car horns protested as the BMW blocked a lane.

The driver's window lowered ominously, revealing Tino; his dark eyes looking through me. Skid was in the passenger seat, giving a pin-toothed grin.

I screamed, 'Come on Sam, Go!'

But we were stuck behind a van.

Then Tino aimed his rifle.

CHAPTER FORTY-ONE

Ready to fire, Tino closed an eye. And I froze. My senses were on full alert, making every moment appear in slow motion, but I could do nothing. The van in front refused to shift. All I could do was brace myself, staring across at the gun trained on my window. There was no way Tino could miss me.

Screams and car horns cried out; people had seen the rifle. But for some reason, Tino delayed his shot; just long enough for a space to open up in front of him.

Sam pulled down the steering wheel. The corner of our Hyundai met the driver's side of the BMW. They hit the curb and mounted it, rear-ending the van in front. Sam pinned the gas; tyres spun and sparks flew from both flanks as we forced our way through, pushing the BMW further onto the pavement. Once in the inside lane, we left the crescendo of noise behind and raced to the junction ahead. Electing to ignore the red light, Sam bullied his way through the intersection. Our only thought: to get away *fast*.

The I-10 was approaching. The Hyundai roared and we joined the five-lane highway, forcing disgruntled drivers out of our way.

My eyes were out on stalks as Sam manoeuvred in and out of traffic. Looking sideways at his familiar face, I was glad to have him with me.

The BMW emerged behind, switching lanes and gaining ground. Determined to lose our tail, Sam pulled onto the hard shoulder and floored the Hyundai. It responded well and we hit a frightening speed. We seemed to be losing them, but our tail had lengthened. Sirens rose up; LAPD had entered the chase.

Re-joining the traffic, I scanned the road and rear window. Sam seemed to welcome the police presence, expecting they'd scared off the BMW or pulled it over. In what seemed like no time our rear window was full of cruisers.

Helicopters appeared overhead. With the cops now in heavy pursuit it was time to end the chase. Despite Lisa's "trust nobody" plea I was ready to take Sam's advice and involve the cops.

Yelping sirens followed us down an exit road as we looped round below the Interstate. Cars scuttled sideways letting us pass and merge with the CA-90. As the road straightened, Sam pulled over, stopping at the roadside. Red and blue lights flashed like fireworks as police cars swamped us. We were glad it was over.

* * *

Kester's last words to Skid before he joined Tino and they headed for Koreatown: *You lost him, you find him!*

Skid feared Edson Taylor was slipping away from him a second time but he wasn't about to give up.

'The boss is gonna fry us,' bemoaned Tino. 'If the cops get 'em we're toast.'

On hearing the familiar sirens of LA's finest, Skid had ordered Tino not to follow the Hyundai onto the hard shoulder. Instead, Tino was instructed to wait, follow the speed limit and allow the cops to pass. Once they had, Skid knew all police eyes and cameras would face forward. Providing the BMW kept back they could easily keep pace with the chasing cruisers.

By following the Hyundai's lengthening tail, Skid saw that they must have taken exit 3A. The BMW had followed them off the Interstate, taking the exit road until a roadblock stopped them. Kester's orders were clear, twofold: *to find, and then kill.* It had seemed routine but failure was looming. The roadblock was forcing cars back onto the Interstate. Reluctantly, the BMW stayed on the loop.

Then Skid's luck changed.

Cars in front had slowed: twenty feet below them, something was happening. A megaphone barked orders beneath them.

Step out of the vehicle!

The traffic on Skid's slip road had slowed to take a look.

Leaning out of his window, Tino looked down and saw police surrounding the silver Hyundai.

Show me your hands. Walk slowly, blared the tinny voice.

'Quick, now's our chance,' said Skid.

Tino released an indecisive groan, 'You want me to pop him with cops everywhere?'

'You've gotta perfect view,' snarled Skid. 'A free shot. What you waitin' for?'

With the police focused on the road below, Tino twisted his huge body into position, taking careful aim. *Find, and then kill.*

The megaphone sounded again: *Now, slowly, get down on the ground!*

Tino held fire. He sensed that he was about to get an even better shot. The men stopped walking, lowered their hands, bent down. Tino watched as they sank slowly to the ground.

At the ideal moment, he squeezed the trigger, recoiled back into Skid.

Without missing a beat, Tino rocked back into his seat and hit the gas. Like every other car up on the loop, they fled the danger, leaving pandemonium below.

'Tell me you hit him?' said Skid.

Tino smiled proudly. 'Took his fuckin' head off.'

Chapter Forty-Two

10.19am
Santa Clarita, CA.

For the senior guard of *Special Prisoner Transportation Services*, this was no ordinary run.

He turned the Ford E-350 cargo van onto Carson Way, a quiet stretch halfway between the County Jail and Federal building. The route was familiar: the usual direct line. The prisoner: just another Ali Baba off to the FBI. And yet, this was no ordinary run. It was the senior guard's first chance to work with the only single white female on the payroll, a woman reputed to flirt with the subtlety of a hooker.

But the senior guard was confused. For a reason unbeknown to him, his younger, thinner, better looking, cleaner smelling workmate was knocking back his advances.

'We're in different leagues,' explained the impervious SWF.

'Maybe, but I'm prepared to drop my standards,' kidded the pot-bellied lothario.

Up ahead he saw a LANE CLOSED sign and police presence. *That's strange.* He glanced at his planner: *Road closed for electrical wire installation, permission to proceed as planned.* A lone worker was moving a traffic cone, allowing access through the road block.

He dismissed the problem, tried again to win her favour. 'Okay, so you find me physically repulsive,' he acknowledged, 'but my personality rocks. You can ask my wife.'

She tut-tutted. 'Does your wife know what you're like?'

'Sure,' he gave the SWF a look, 'I don't cross the line.'

'*Really?*' she raised an eyebrow.

'Well, I don't cross the panty line,' he winked, 'anything above is allowed.'

Finally, the SWF smirked, rolling her green mascara-applied eyes. It only encouraged the senior guard. 'My wife is so self-obsessed,' he complained. 'She moans that I won't pay for her to have a breast reduction. It's a little cruel on my part because she would look better with just the two.'

Drawing no laughs, the guard noted *this gal has no humour*.

* * *

The SWF felt uneasy, but not at the sweaty guard's feeble advances. The police car was now in front of them, signalling a stop. Cutting through the chat, she alerted the senior guard and following procedure, he pulled up behind the black and white.

Speaking on his radio, a cop climbed out and headed back, strutting towards the cargo van. Attached to his belt was what looked like a flashlight. Neither guard recognised the elderly officer and they should have done. Prison runs were normally undertaken by rookies and this man was way too old.

Finishing on his radio the cop tapped on the window. 'Open up,' he ordered sharply.

Procedure rarely involved *opening up*. The senior guard's suspicions intensified. 'What's up?' he spoke anxiously into the talk box.

'There's a change of plan I need to run by you,' the cop said, matter-of-fact. The blacked-out windows offered the guards freedom to stare at him. Protruding out of the cop's heavily age-spotted face was a narrow nose on which sat shades. Uncombed hair, thin and white, dropped from police cap to narrow shoulders, he was probably only in his sixties, but could pass as older.

The senior guard clicked on his radio. 'Goddamn it, there's no signal.'

'10-10,' called the SWF, her radio was also dead. Her fearful eyes looked across. 'Don't open the door.'

The senior guard had no intention of doing so. They were in an armoured vehicle behind antispall laminated glass, resistant to high-powered gunfire. Unless the frail man quickly convinced them otherwise, they were about to drive off.

The cop banged on the door. 'What's the problem?' The regulation sunglasses failed to hide his small skittish eyes.

'You'll have to wait while I call in.' The senior guard noticed the SWF reach for her handgun. With the radios down, he reverted to procedure, pulling out his cell-phone.

The phone was missing. And when he looked up, the cop was gone.

* * *

Victor Lapenza dropped into a crouch. He knew he'd aroused suspicion, his appearance had seen to that. He also knew of the guards' reliance on due process.

And that made them predictable.

They would resist opening the door. Instead, they would discover the useless radios and correctly assume this was an attempt to get at the cargo: a Mr Sadiq al-Barabi. What Victor Lapenza also knew was that in a few moments the guards would be dead. But he had to be quick, before their procedure dictated they drive away.

Reaching for his back holster, he whipped out his gun – safety off, silencer on – and blew out the front tyres. From his belt he ripped out the small metal canister and in an instant had put it in place. Just as he'd practised, it was attached beneath the van, pointing up into the semi-sealed driving bay. All that remained to do was to push the valve, releasing a pressurised dose of highly lethal nerve gas.

* * *

The van dropped forward. 'What the…Where is he?' panicked the senior guard. Then, turning the ignition, 'We're out of here.'

As they swung clear the SWF yelled, 'You hear that? He's shot the engine, listen!'

They could hear what sounded like a gas leak spraying out, but it wasn't the engine.

Suddenly their throats were closing up.

Don't breathe in, the SWF told herself. Recalling her training she reached for the compartment above. It was empty, the gas masks were gone. Now the pain arrived, like a thousand razor blades cutting inside her forehead. Hiding her mouth under clothing she sucked in more gas as her desperate eyes pleaded for help.

The senior guard could do nothing to help her. He held his breath whilst pounding on the pedal, his head felt like a pressure cooker. The pain was unbearable, but he had to focus on keeping control of a van running on its front rims. The air conditioning couldn't cope, and the windows wouldn't open. Hoping speed would increase airflow inside the cabin he kept going, but it was too late. The damage was done. Vomit erupted from his mouth. He gasped for air, but his breath was gone. Next to him the SWF endured a violent convulsion, her muscles randomly twitching, throwing her green, deathly face up and down.

Fuck procedure! There was only one thing to do.

* * *

Victor Lapenza was growing concerned. There was only a mile left before his lane closure ended and other traffic may inhabit the road. Yet still the van motored. How? Why weren't the guards dead? The only gas mask was with the prisoner.

As his fake police car closed in on the van, Victor Lapenza saw the problem. *Air.* The driver's door was swinging open. He looked at his gun on the seat beside him, silencer still attached. Then he picked up the radio.

* * *

The influx of air had allowed the senior guard to breathe but his health was deteriorating fast. To his right the woman had stopped shaking, but the oxygen had come too late for the SWF. Her staring eyes told him she was dead. Held up by a seat belt, her lifeless body flopped to the van's unsteady movement.

The police car appeared in his left mirror, growing larger as it neared. Failing muscles made driving impossible and survival a priority. It took a massive effort to ease up the parking brake, but he managed it. With the van slowing to a stop he scooped up his gun and fell out, collapsing onto the road below. Trying hard to recover his breath, he turned onto his side, fighting to control the fire raging through his lungs. He squinted at the police car heading right at him.

It stopped a metre from the guard. The old cop got out.

Unable to move, the senior guard played dead, sensed the cop's piggy eyes on him.

A second vehicle arrived. The guard heard two men talking. They were after the prisoner.

Who the hell is he? The guard wondered as a high-pitched drilling screeched out. They were cutting into the doors at the back of the van. The prisoner was in the single compartment, he would take some getting at.

Man, they're good, thought the guard listening to the familiar pop of the rotary latch being released.

He felt some strength returning. Placing his palms down, he pushed himself up into the press up position just as the slam-latch handle opened. They were nearly in. *If I can just get to the gun...*

Crawling, the guard heard a voice.

'I don't think so,' said the old cop, raising his firearm. His piggy eyes were the last image the guard saw. The last thing he heard was the first of the four bullets that ripped through his body.

CHAPTER FORTY-THREE

12 noon
Westwood, Los Angeles.

My eyes scanned the meagre surroundings of the FBI reception room, but my thoughts were with Sam. I was in shock, unaware if he had even survived. When I had been taken away his legs were moving, but there was so much blood.

How the hell had it come to this?

Two men entered, looking me up and down before sharing an inquisitive glare. They sat down opposite me, and the older man placed a manila carded file on the table. 'I'm Special Agent Donnie Guzan and this is Special Agent Tyler Derego.'

'Is he dead?' I asked.

They looked puzzled. 'Who?'

'Sam.' My hands reached for my gut. 'Is that why the FBI are involved?'

Agent Guzan spoke again, 'Mr Chapman's shooting is not the reason you're here.' His voice carried impatience. 'It's because of what you told the police.'

What did I tell them? All I could recall was the horrific image of Sam rolling towards me, his head a mass of red widening into a pool of blood. My stomach cramped again. I gagged, coughing away the contraction.

It was explained to me that I was entitled to legal representation. Then the date and names of those present was repeated for the benefit of a tape.

'So Mr Taylor,' said Guzan, his copper hair turning dark with sweat, 'about what you told the police?'

'How is he?' I demanded. 'How's Sam?'

The muscular agent, Derego, answered me, 'No change. His condition is still critical. Tell you what, as soon as you finish answering our questions I'll provide a ride to the hospital.'

'He's got a wife and kids,' I thought aloud. *How can I tell them?*

Guzan kicked a table leg, breaking into my thoughts of sadness and guilt. 'You are here because you told an officer that Kester Hardwick is involved. Can you elaborate?'

Damn. In the aftermath of the shooting I'd broken Lisa Connelly's rule again. *Trust nobody. Not the police. No one.*

It was too late now. The rules changed the instant that bullet hit my friend. Shock was turning to anger. There were bad men behind this and I could name them. My talking could be putting Elaine in danger, but I had no choice. What else could I do?

Guzan pressed. 'Why would Kester Hardwick be involved?'

'Because he employs the men who shot Sam,' I said. 'The driver's name is Faustino Ricard, he's the one with the rifle; a man called Fernando Sanchez was with him.'

Guzan pulled on a puffy face. He seemed to be getting grumpier by the second; his craggy edges extending to his personality. 'Is this the driver?' He slid over a photograph from the file.

I looked at the black and white image. Nodded. 'That's him.' It was Tino; the same mug-shot Sam had shown me.

Derego spoke, 'For the record, Mr Taylor just identified Faustino Ricard.'

Guzan read my statement. 'Apparently he was chasing you in a BMW. You said, "Tino had the rifle. He was going to shoot me".'

'That's right. You should be talking to him. I gave the police the number plate.'

'Why would Faustino Ricard shoot Sam,' Derego glanced down, 'Chapman?'

'He was probably aiming for me.'

Derego shook his head dismissively. 'The accuracy of the shot is hard to question. And it would be difficult mixing you two up.'

Why would anybody want Sam dead?

The agents seemed to be eyeing me disbelievingly. I was suddenly aware of my appearance: my bandaged hand, the stains of blood under my armpit that hadn't come out.

A second image was pulled from the file and placed face down. Slowly, Guzan pushed it towards me, keeping a hand on it. 'We know that Sam Chapman is a policeman and we also know that he's inquired about both Sanchez and Ricard in relation to the disappearance of an Elaine McAdler.'

'So you'll get these men. You're taking this seriously.'

'Any shooting is taken seriously,' said Guzan. Staring knowingly, he turned over the paper. 'Is this Elaine McAdler?'

I was surprised to see an old photograph of Elaine, taken when her name was Claire Needlam; her young, delicate features were partly hidden behind dark curls. I couldn't think straight, my clouded mind flickered between Sam and Elaine; my pain was too raw to linger on either.

'We know you're looking for her,' said Guzan. 'That's why you and Mr Chapman came here?'

'What has this—'

Derego jumped in, 'Did either of you make contact with Kester Hardwick regarding her disappearance?'

Trust nobody. Too late. 'He said he could help, but I think he wanted to use *me* to help *him* find her. I know why she escaped fifteen years ago and that the FBI helped her. So you tell me, why would she come back here?'

'We don't know that she has.' It was Guzan's turn to look puzzled. 'And as far as the FBI helping her escape, we've no knowledge of that.' He raised his palms. 'All right, given the timing of her return I accept that she might be in LA, but I'm curious to know what you think happened fifteen years ago?'

'Elaine was witness to a murder committed by Kester Hardwick. She had to change her name for her own safety, but you know all this.'

'Indeed we do,' acknowledged Guzan, and his freckled jowls tightened, giving birth to a smile. 'I remember her as a juvenile, quite a strong character. She needed to be,' he added, putting his palms back on the table and leaning in. 'Elaine. She took her mother's name. That's nice.'

Her mother? *The name badge read Elaine. Like an older version.* I suspected as much, but felt the need for confirmation. 'The woman she witnessed Kester murder, that was her mother?'

Guzan nodded.

It explained her willingness to testify, but why didn't Lisa tell me? *If there are things Elaine didn't want you to know it was for your own safety.*

Elaine had seen her mother shot dead! My poor Angel. Previously I had let the meaning of this wash over me, but of course that also meant that Elaine's mother was Kester's partner.

It took Guzan to spell it out for me. 'Kester Hardwick is Elaine's father.'

I was stunned, frozen speechless. I just couldn't believe it. What did this mean?

My trance was broken by what looked like a third agent entering the room; a powerful looking woman, black, mid-thirties. She bent down next to an annoyed Agent Guzan. 'Ethan Knight for you; says it's urgent.'

Guzan looked like he was drowning in frustration. He pushed himself up and left the room. The woman then turned to me. 'And your lawyer's on hold.'

Lawyer? I suddenly remembered that I was in trouble for aiding and abetting the theft of a car. Actually I no longer cared.

'Lawyer, huh?' shrugged Derego. 'Knock yourself out. We've not charged you, LAPD will do that. If that Tiburon was stolen they'll be talking jail time.' He nodded to the door. 'Go on then.'

I got up.

Derego called, 'When you get back you can tell me what you've done to your hand.'

I nodded. With Sam in hospital I decided to offload everything, without mentioning Lisa. All about Surgeon and Bruno, about the furnace house that Gina had been taken to. I was ready to spill, just after I'd spoken with the lawyer.

The woman led me into a four by four closet, just room for me and a phone. She shut the door behind me.

I dialled 0 as instructed.

It rang once.

'Ed?'

My heart somersaulted on a wave of emotion. The voice I longed to hear spoke my name. For a moment I thought I was hallucinating.

'Elaine?' I croaked.

'It's me, Ed. Listen carefully.'

CHAPTER FORTY-FOUR

She was alive! I was aware that I was weeping. I didn't care.

It was Elaine's voice, only different. She was curt, devoid of emotion. For weeks I had thought of what I'd say to her, longed for the chance to talk, but the chance didn't come. It was a one-way conversation. Quick instructions, then she hung up. Was it really her? Were my prayers really about to be answered? Something was wrong. Different. Maybe she knew about Sam.

Her instructions were clear. *I'm listening carefully, my love. I know what to do.* I had to get out of there. I stepped into an empty corridor as Derego burst out of the reception room, a phone to his ear. With him out of sight I headed for the lift. Up ahead, voices grew louder, footsteps quickened and doors closed. I pressed for the lift. *I'm coming, my Angel.*

My emotions were everywhere, so much rattling around in my mind. I had only just discovered that Elaine had witnessed her father killing her mother. I thought about this. How she'd never talk about her parents, but would often say, 'Good parents say two things: no, and I love you'. How did this apply to Kester Hardwick?

The lift couldn't arrive quickly enough.

3…4…5 *Come on!*

Sounds of commotion came from the offices. Something was up. Have they caught Skid and Tino? Kester Hardwick? Whatever it was, it was keeping the agents busy.

Someone was coming, their shoes clicking ever closer.

10…11…12.

A ding alerted everyone that the lift had arrived; the door was opening. Then a voice called out, 'Hold the elevator.' It was the female agent. Before the door could close she had joined me inside.

She was tall, broad-shouldered, and together we filled the lift. She broke into a smile. 'Everything all right?'

'Sure,' I smiled back, wiped my eyes, nodded a change of subject. 'Some problem up there?'

'You could say that.' She didn't divulge. 'Put it this way. If the agents want to talk to you again it's unlikely to be today.'

The lift opened into the large oval lobby that boasted marble columns and a high panelled ceiling. The agent wished me a safe day and I strode across the shiny wooden floor, my feet and heart quickening with every step.

Warning signals were going off in my head. Could Elaine really be waiting outside for me? After yesterday I didn't know what to believe. Lisa had said that Kester wanted Elaine dead. Then an agent tells me Kester is Elaine's father.

As I left the federal building, all caution left with me. I was desperate to end the agony, to collect Elaine, to get to the hospital and get Sam home. If Elaine was there anything was possible.

I walked down concrete steps, into the brightness of the sky and roaring of the traffic. The sudden stimuli made me feel claustrophobic. It was like I was on a stage, under a spotlight and unable to see the audience. I hid my eyes from the sun and frantically scanned for faces. Six lanes of vehicles sped past, but not a face to focus on. No Elaine.

Through the mass of motors I spotted a car parked opposite with a woman waving out of a window. I jumped with excitement. Elaine.

The wide road separated us. I could only guess at her expression but despite tears blurring my vision, I knew it was her. The face I'd longed to see. I was waving back and shouting over to her when all the breath was knocked out of me.

I was struck from behind. Hit so hard, the back of my head slapped my spine as I flew forward, skidding into the road. I was jerked back, dragged onto my knees. I looked up to see Tino strike me again, harder. Next thing I knew I was being pulled into the back of a car. Right there in front of the federal building. My head was spinning, my eyesight a kaleidoscope of red and black. I was being held face down, but could hear Skid giving orders as my arms were tied behind me.

We sped away leaving the image of Elaine fading from my mind.

CHAPTER FORTY-FIVE

12.21pm
Westwood, Los Angeles.

News of the escape swept through FBI headquarters like a Californian forest fire. Agents learned of the attack on the secure cargo-van and its dire result: one guard killed with nerve gas, the other shot dead as the convict escaped custody. The man's identity had yet to be released, but soon everyone would know that it was Sadiq al-Barabi – a dangerous terrorist.

Isolated inside his glass office, Guzan placed Ethan Knight on speaker-phone.

'This is fucked up, Don,' spoke the CIA official, 'his route was never divulged. Christ! Nobody even knew his destination. We're talking inside information here; and a professional hit.'

On knocking and entering the office, Agent Beasley was met with a raised finger. The wiry agent held his breath in frustration as he waited for Guzan to finish speaking on the phone.

Guzan ignored him. 'We don't know who attacked the van, Ethan, but can we at least rule out Ali Afshari and Syrus Meybodi?'

'You'd like that, wouldn't you?' said Knight. 'Feared losing them would bite you in the ass, huh? Well they may have been smart enough to give you the slip, but I don't believe they sprung Sadiq al-Barabi. For me, it comes back to Kester Hardwick. He would still have the means to pull this off. I want you to step up your efforts, find out what the hell's going on. It's no coincidence they shared a prison cell, now this happens.'

'Any suggestions?' Guzan rubbed his neck.

'Check out a guy named "Feely Grub". He roomed with Hardwick before Sadiq al-Barabi. He's a deadbeat, a small-time crook, but he might have caught something.'

Inching closer, Beasley waved impatiently, he looked fit to burst.

'Listen Ethan, I gotta go.'

'Keep me informed.'

Before the line went dead, Beasley spilled, 'According to Mal on floor two, a man matching Edson Taylor's description has just been forced into a car in front of the building. A black BMW.'

'Shit.' Guzan balled his fists, struck the desktop, rattling stationery. With all the furore surrounding Sadiq al-Barabi's escape, Guzan had overlooked the threat to Edson Taylor. 'He should have been given protection,' he said, angry with himself.

'We pulled the license plate off surveillance,' said Beasley. 'The EVL had already been checked by LAPD an hour ago. It belongs to Faustino Ricard.'

'Get it out on the wire. I want that car found immediately. And put an APB out on both Faustino Ricard and Fernando Sanchez.'

Beasley hurried off. Guzan frantically loosened his tie. *Kester wants Edson Taylor, but for what?* He thought. *To kill him? To help find his daughter?*

Derego returned, looking fraught. Guzan was aware that his partner, like most of the bureau, had never heard of Sadiq al-Barabi until now.

'Relax Tyler. It's unlikely the Iranians are directly involved,' Guzan assured him. 'We won't be blamed.'

'What? No, it's not that,' dismissed Derego. 'I've just had to hold off a detective wanting to speak with Edson Taylor. LAPD have just had word from the hospital about his friend, the cop.'

Derego turned down his mouth, shook his head. 'He didn't make it. Died in the ambulance.'

CHAPTER FORTY-SIX

When his sentence was up, it wasn't just Kester Hardwick who was released, thought Donnie Guzan. There was something else, something inside himself. The demons he had drunk away before arose once more to haunt him. The false hope that once had held them down was fast disappearing. Just when his best was needed, he was found wanting. He had nothing to hide behind. No Cliff Donachie. No Jack Daniels. No control over a situation he didn't understand.

This is no time for a breakdown, Don, nor is there time for one.

Struggling with conjecture, Guzan abandoned all hypotheses and focused on the facts. He drew a sheet of paper towards him and listed what he knew:

Sadiq al-Barabi (recently escaped terrorist) – location
unknown.
Shared cell with:
Kester Hardwick – current location unknown.
Employs:
Fernando 'Skid' Sanchez and Faustino 'Tino' Ricard
- BMW?
Linked to both:
Sam Chapman – deceased.
And Edson Taylor – abducted.
Who were both looking for:
Elaine McAdler (Claire Needlam) – missing.
Daughter of Kester Hardwick.

As he stared at the list, Guzan couldn't help thinking
that he was missing something. He sat perfectly still
and focused his mind. The buzzing phone acted
as a defibrillator. He shot up and straightened his
spine as Derego took the call.

A briefing was taking place in five minutes. There
would be some explaining to do. It was bound
to concern Sadiq al-Barabi; a terrorist Guzan had
known about only because he had conspired with
the CIA to keep it from the bureau. His justification
for this secrecy was that his own colleagues could
not be trusted. It wouldn't play well.

Subsiding back into his chair, hands to his knees,
Guzan planned his response. He would accept
that he'd made a wrong call. His defence was
that Sadiq al-Barabi was in custody and therefore
not an immediate threat. Now he had to prepare
Derego. He swivelled his chair in the direction of
his partner. 'Tyler, before we head for that briefing

there's something I need to tell you about the escaped terrorist.'

Derego stopped typing, leant back.

'Recently the CIA became aware of Sadiq al-Barabi. With the permission of the director of counter terrorism they elected to keep this information to themselves and just a handful of agents; a secure ring. Once the CIA had him in custody, FBI was to become involved, but until then he needed to be treated as a normal prisoner, at least until his plans were uncovered.'

'You're saying you knew about this man?'

Screwing up his face, Guzan rubbed his mouth. 'Someone within the agency had been talking. The director was trying to shut off the leak while keeping us operational.' Guzan saw disappointment strike his partner's face. 'I'm sorry I couldn't bring you in on this. The CIA only involved me because of my history with Kester Hardwick. The leaks concerned Sadiq al-Barabi and a chemical formula. For over a year he shared a cell with Kester.'

Derego's eyebrows lifted as Guzan continued, 'Ethan Knight asked me to look into their relationship. Any reference to Kester was to be referred to me. That's why *we* just questioned Edson Taylor. I'm sorry,' he repeated, 'my hands were tied.'

'But now the whole agency is about to be briefed you thought you'd better let me in?'

Guzan diverted his eyes. 'Not exactly. Now this information is out I need your help. I have to miss this briefing. There will be an internal inquiry that will only delay the operation. I have to pay someone a visit, see if I can shed some light on the relationship between Kester and Sadiq al-Barabi. Fancy tagging along?'

'And miss a briefing? Consider my arm twisted.'

'Thanks,' Guzan hid his relief. 'I might have to go dark, but with your help I can get to Kester. I'm sure he's behind this.'

The men headed down the corridor, overtaking agents on their way to the briefing. As they walked past the briefing room they saw agents looking their way, nudging one another. Then Guzan and Derego caught sight of the whiteboard. It was the first time they had seen a picture of the escaped terrorist and it left them dumbfounded.

Going dark was no longer an option. Guzan didn't know it yet but given his unique position he was about to lead the Federal response.

CHAPTER FORTY-SEVEN

12.50pm
Griffith Park, Los Angeles.

My body was besieged by pain; my head reeling
with shock.

Tino had tied my wrists together; my wounded
hand throbbed out of sync with my racing
heartbeat, but it didn't stop him warning me not to
try anything, threatening to shoot me like he'd shot
my buddy. Anger squeezed hold of my stomach.
I wanted to throw myself at his smug grin. 'Don't
like cops,' he shrugged, his huge body wedged in
behind the driver's seat.

I looked down at the gun almost swallowed
by his hand, noticed the rifle by his feet, the one
that I guessed had shot Sam. My hatred for Tino

was unbounded, as was the dread I felt for Sam's condition. In the meantime, my only salvation was that I had seen Elaine. The knowledge that she was alive gave me strength. Purpose. In the corners of my mind I was horribly aware that her waving might have led me into a trap, but I couldn't focus on that; refused to entertain the possibility that it had been deliberate. I had to get through whatever Tino and Skid had planned for me.

This time Skid was driving, leading us up a winding dirt road. It was quiet, in shade. Every few seconds a gap in the trees allowed a flash of sunlight onto the dark, uneven track. The car rolled over every bump lifting my tired and battered body off the back seat before dropping me like a stringless puppet. Eventually we reached a clearing and the car stopped its ascent. My body welcomed the respite but it was short-lived. Tino ordered me out, saw that I was incapable of movement and hauled me roughly from the car, whereupon he slipped the rope off my wrists. I stood, swaying; the burning sun sapping my remaining energy and forcing my hands to my skinned, shredded knees. We were standing on a level opening at the end of the dirt road; about the length of a bus. Arching trees surrounded the space, springing like whiskers from the steep terrain. I sucked in the warm, thin air and looked up. Tino's gun was still on me.

I heard car tyres approaching on the gravel road. Who was it? Could it be the FBI? The feds must have seen me, snatched from under their noses.

Tino gestured for Skid. They were both edgy.

I dared to hope.

After waiting an age, the car finally emerged from the trees. A black Range Rover parked up behind the BMW. A man got out. Dark grey suit, light grey hair, blue challenging eyes.

Kester Hardwick.

He patting Skid on the back as he strode by. 'Good work men.'

Tino looked like the know-it-all kid who'd topped his class. Kester met him. 'Your Glock,' he said.

Confused, Tino handed over his gun.

Kester clicked his fingers. 'Now take off your jacket.'

As Tino followed orders, Kester's eyes locked on mine. 'Now throw it on the floor.'

The jacket landed behind us. I looked at Tino. His shirt was sticking with sweat to his massive physique. He rolled up his sleeves displaying his trunk-like forearms and smiled, clearly believing he was about to hand me another pounding.

Kester spoke again. 'Now Tino, I need you to hold Mr Taylor, keep him still.'

Tino came at me, feigned a punch. Succumbing to his decoy I flinched, raised my hands to block. Tino caught them, and my left hand nearly exploded with pain. He stepped behind me. I kicked back but it was like hitting a wall. Tino had my arms locked together and my hands twisted excruciatingly sideways. I couldn't move without breaking my wrists.

Kester looked disappointed. 'You should have stayed at my place, Edson. My hospitality not good enough for you, is that it?'

I stared at Kester, every muscle straining against Tino's grip. 'What if I had stayed?'

'Then this would not have to happen.' Kester pulled something from his pocket. It was an attachment for the Glock. Realisation brought panic. *I'm not being held to be punched.* As Kester screwed the attachment onto the gun my heart thumped against my ribs. I screamed out as Kester lifted the weapon, twisted in vain as Tino tightened his grip. I couldn't move. I was pleading for mercy. Sweat streamed into my eyes to mingle with my tears. Involuntarily I voided the contents of my bladder, felt the stream of hot liquid gush down my legs as I saw Kester take aim.

The gun fired.

I flew back, landing on Tino. He let go of me. Blood was all over my face and neck. I rolled away in pain to the sound of a deep moaning. But the moaning wasn't mine. Tino had been shot. He gasped like a fish, gurgled blood. His eyes wide with shock. Kester dispatched several more bullets into him. What remained of his head jerked violently with every hit before flopping onto one side, his face a mass of dark flesh, his eyes suddenly unseeing.

I could hear Kester, doling out orders to Skid. He obeyed without question, picked up Tino's jacket, removed his wallet and handed both to his boss.

Wrapping the jacket around his foot, Kester eased it under Tino's lifeless body. Puffing with effort, he and Skid rolled the heavy carcass to the edge of the clearing and kicked it over.

I was on my forearms and knees, shaking and wiping Tino's blood from my face. Kester crouched down at the edge where Tino had disappeared. He sat, called me over, pointing the gun to where he wanted me to sit.

I slowly got to my feet, circled around Tino's blood, which seemed to ebb south in search of its body. A combination of shock and the stench made me gag. It all reminded me of Sam. I couldn't feel sorry for Tino. *I'll shoot you like I shot your buddy.*

The smell of death and piss travelled with me as I approached Kester. He was sat down, looking out into the distance. The gun lay idle by his side.

'Let's talk,' he spoke calmly, like the past minute had never happened.

Still nauseous and shaking, I crept to the edge and looked down where the land dropped sharply away. Dark blood stained the grass where Tino had slid; his weight had kept him falling from sight.

I sat down, about six feet from Kester. From the murderer. From Elaine's father.

I was never more alone.

CHAPTER FORTY-EIGHT

We were perched high above the city, Tino's corpse lying somewhere beneath us.

Skid positioned the BMW at the top of the dirt road, under strict orders that we were not to be disturbed.

'This area was designated for sightseers,' said Kester in his laboured voice. 'But nobody comes up here. In the old days they did, not for the view, but to cut across the hills and climb the HOLLYWOOD sign' – he rolled his eyes – 'some kind of metaphor.'

Still trembling, I studied him. Looked into the eyes of a murderer. Now I knew to look for it, I could see Elaine in him. It made me uncomfortable, jittery. Their eyes were the same shade of blue. Only his were cold, inhuman.

I turned away, struggling to focus on anything. My breathing quickened, I was swamped with anxiety; visual distractions in every direction: the unnerving height, the scorching sun, Kester's blue eyes, Skid's repulsive face, Tino's smoking Glock, and his creeping blood.

Steadying my head, I gazed into the panorama of Los Angeles. The sun had burned away most of the smog revealing a surprisingly flat landscape, all areas appeared the same; they were anything but.

'Relax, Edson, we are on the same side.'

'I don't think so,' I spat out, my voice unstable. How could I be on the same side as this killer?

'I guess you know by now that I have a daughter?'

I said nothing.

'Are you perturbed by Tino's death? I am surprised. Don't you believe in the death penalty?'

Again I said nothing. I wasn't going to admit I had wanted Tino dead. It was the manner of it I objected to.

Kester pulled sunglasses from a pocket and slipped them on, almost as if he understood my difficulty in looking at him. 'Tino died because I have trust issues with black men.' Stretching out his legs, he turned to face me, his lips lifted in a slight smile. 'No offence.' He was calmness personified, practically sunbathing. 'You should have stayed the night as I had asked. Then nobody would have been shot today.'

'Does that include Sam Chapman?'

Kester shifted uncomfortably. 'Messrs Sanchez and Ricard were given instruction to find you and then...well, let's just say that after your friend led them to you he was a problem waiting to happen. His presence here was always going to be ephemeral. Much like our Elaine's.'

I hated to hear her name on his lips. All the rage I had bottled up inside surged out and focused on this cold, hard, executioner. I tried to sound tough, but it came out like a whine: 'What do you mean to do to her?'

Kester locked his hands, put them behind his head, and tilted towards the sun. 'Back in '93, she needed to leave town. I helped her. She had made dangerous enemies – me for one – but I called on a favour. Set her up in Europe. Madrid. When she disappeared, rumours circulated that she had run away and that I had assisted her. I couldn't let that happen. Daughter or not, she had to be seen to be punished. As I told you yesterday, I have a reputation to protect. It's very important to me. Revenge was expected.'

'So you brought her back here to punish her.' I gasped as the implication hit me. 'To kill her?'

'Let me finish,' he freed a hand, used it to block off the sun. 'I have had a lot of free time lately,' he shot me a wry smile. 'Time to plan. I decided that by faking my daughter's death I could restore my reputation. So we staged an elaborate murder right in front of Bruno's eyes – one that would ensure the word got around. She was quite the actress...' Kester paused, momentarily lost in his thoughts. 'But then again, maybe her fear was real. Either way, it was very convincing.'

All are dead. I tried to imagine what it must have taken to convince Bruno. And what Elaine must have gone through.

'We didn't part on the best of terms,' said Kester. 'My killing her mother and her willingness to testify saw to that. Maybe she never totally trusted me,' he mused, half to himself. 'I did fear she might negate on our deal.'

'What deal?'

'I helped her leave town on the condition that one day she repaid my favour. I asked Elaine to help undo the damage she'd caused my reputation. I knew she'd agree; the chance to get Bruno off her back was too good to refuse. So I arranged to have her roasted alive in a furnace. Bruno was ecstatic! But before the heat became dangerous she was away as planned. Furnace 17 has a back hatch for external access. She used it to slip out.'

I recalled Bruno boasting that he took Gina to the furnace house. *Set to fry at three.* He had killed Gina the same way he believed they had killed Elaine? A horrific thought. But would Bruno still believe it? After all, Skid now knew she was alive; he had seen her waving out of a taxi. I raised my concern with Kester.

His reply was to glance back at the BMW; 'I don't worry about Skid; the little stoat owes me his life, but I couldn't trust Tino not to talk.' Stretching, he looked down to where Tino's body would by now be attracting flies.

The situation was surreal. All that was missing was the picnic hamper. Here I was, sharing a postcard view with a vicious murderer, while in some hospital my best buddy was fighting for his life. Nothing Kester said gave me any comfort, aside from my belief that Elaine was unharmed.

He went on to explain that when she'd called me – pretending to be my lawyer – it was at his instigation. He had been with her in the car and had forced her to attract my attention. I was dumbfounded: it seemed Elaine had been in Kester's custody all the time. At least it explained the phone call; why her voice had seemed so sullen. And yet I had thought that he was using me to find her. The cogs in my brain slowly revolved as I tried to assimilate this information. It left a question: 'Why did you want me at your house so badly?'

'Ah,' he sat up straight. 'The main reason I brought my daughter back to LA was to get *you* here. Elaine thought that her favour was all about restoring my reputation, but in fact that was merely a bi-product; she was my pawn. You are the most important part of my plans. The red envelopes, Gina's e-mail. All my work. Designed to coax you here of your own accord.'

I didn't understand. All this to get me here! Anger edged out confusion and I grasped at one salient fact: 'Gina died because Bruno thought that e-mail was from her.'

'Yes,' Kester sighed. 'That was unfortunate. I didn't anticipate you going to the club, at least not straight away. But from the moment I relieved you of Bruno's company you were never in any danger from me. Once you were at my house I told Skid to make sure you didn't leave. He was to keep you safe, at gunpoint if necessary, but he knew not to harm you.'

I recalled the moment I jumped into Lisa's car; Skid had already put away his gun; he was speaking on the phone.

'When you evaded Skid's protection I made it clear to him and Tino that their priority was your safe and speedy return.'

I flashed back to the moment in Koreatown when Tino delayed his shot. He never intended to shoot me.

My mouth dropped open. One word fell out. 'Why?'

'I have a job for you,' revealed Kester. 'One that only you are qualified to do.'

'A job? What sort of a job? And why would I agree to do anything for you?'

Kester raised a sardonic eyebrow. 'Why wouldn't you? You could be back with my daughter in no time.'

I shook my head, bemused. 'And if I refuse?'

'You two are only alive because I need you. Refusal would be very foolish. Daughter or not, after Elaine's betrayal I could kill her in an instant. As for you – I might just let you live long enough to watch her die.'

I believed him. He spoke quietly, almost conversationally. It made his words all the more menacing.

I succumbed. 'But what can *I* do?'

Kester stuck out his chin and released a smile. 'You'll see.'

Chapter Forty-Nine

1.26pm
Huntington Park, Los Angeles.

There had been opposition to Guzan's appointment. The main objection was that it had been on his watch that the Iranians – Ali Afshari and Syrus Meybodi – had ducked surveillance. Defending his decision, the director cited Guzan's unique insight and explained that he was best equipped to lead LA's fugitive unit in the search for Sadiq al-Barabi.

Agents were soon critical of Guzan's leadership, noting that his obsession with Kester Hardwick was clouding his judgment. Unperturbed, Guzan dispatched a team to apprehend the black BMW licensed to 'Tino' Ricard. It had been picked up on satellite heading for the Hollywood Hills.

Regarding Sadiq al-Barabi, Guzan's only direct action was to set up a press conference for five o'clock. This gave the agents under four hours to find him before news stations alerted the public that the man escaping custody was a terrorist. This window of delay provided the bureau with the opportunity to avoid the widespread condemnation that would be heading their way. In return for the media's cooperation Guzan had released a picture of Sadiq al-Barabi, together with a statement that he was not to be approached. Despite the urgency, Guzan referred to the search as chasing shadows, insisting that Kester Hardwick was the key to the terrorist's whereabouts.

* * *

Opting to flee the politics of FBI headquarters, Guzan had headed to Huntington Park. Joining him in the field was Tyler Derego.

'It won't take long,' assured Guzan, anticipating his partner's concerns. Questioning an ex-con was not proactive enough for Derego and as he slipped his silver Saleen Mustang into park, Guzan detected hostility.

Derego anxiously locked the car. 'He'd better be in. Not sure my insurance covers Huntington.'

The two agents paced Seville Avenue, a mix of low and no-income families. The letters FBI emblazed across the back of their navy jackets was enough to cause a stir that so far had confined itself behind the doors and windows.

'Instead of lurking around Shitsville shouldn't we be focusing elsewhere?' complained Derego as he negotiated the litter-sprayed sidewalk. 'We might've captured the terrorist by now; before a Marshal is brought in and gets all the fun.'

'Whoever sprung Sadiq al-Barabi had inside information,' Guzan replied stepping over a wheel-less shopping cart. 'That points to Kester Hardwick. It all does. You saw Sadiq al-Barabi's picture.'

'Still doesn't explain why Edson Taylor was hauled off in a BMW, or why his cop friend was murdered.'

'But it links them to the case. Okay, so we could be wasting our time here, but I have to follow my instincts.'

Derego looked back to his Mustang, shook his head. 'Man, this place is landfill. My wheels get touched I'm holding you responsible.'

Stopping, Guzan noticed 45 etched into a front door. 'This is it,' he said, eyeing the Grub residence. One window was boarded, the other duct-taped. Burnt yellow grass battled with concrete and dog shit for the right to cover the front yard.

The sight of the house was enough to make Derego scratch himself. 'So what's Feely Grub's story?'

'Hangs around with DPW members. They're a street punk gang from Oakland. Small fry, not turf claimers. Apparently he sells them hooch.'

'How're we playing this?'

'Haven't decided yet. Getting him to inform on Kester mightn't be easy. Just secure the rear and be ready to come in if I need you.'

'You're kiddin', what about bringing me in on this?'

'Let me try softly-softly first,' said Guzan.

'As if coming here wasn't a big enough waste of my time,' grumbled Derego.

'Do us a favour,' – Guzan's patience was shredding – 'just cover the rear.'

'I get it,' moaned Derego, 'you only need me for my brawn. I'll be out back working on my guns.'

Once Derego was out of sight, Guzan stepped up to the screen door, opened it. A scrawny cat darted out, followed by a waft of marijuana. Before he could knock, a man appeared at the door. His eyes were red and aggressive; his grey Mohican brought him up to Guzan's five foot ten. Hanging over his tight, black denim jeans was a saggy belly, but muffin-top apart, he was unusually thin: it was like all his fat cells were on a pilgrimage to his gut. The man folded his arms, spoke in Southern drawl, 'Who the f—'

'Feely Grub?'

'Uh-huh.' Grub had spotted the FBI insignia.

'I'm Special Agent Donnie Guzan of the FBI. May I come inside?'

'We can talk here,' Feely Grub snorted through gapped teeth.

'Fine, it's about an old cellmate of yours.' Guzan waited knowingly.

Slack-mouthed, Feely Grub elbowed open the door. Gave a bloodshot squint as he looked past Guzan, nervously surveyed the street. 'Better we talk inside.' Grub waved the agent into his dank and dingy digs.

A dark carpet, patterned with trodden-in food ran into a cluttered living area in which hid a brown sofa and box-style coffee table. On the table was a porno mag, a cardboard bucket of chicken bones and several mugs stained the same brown as Feely's remaining molars.

Guzan wrinkled his nose. 'I'd take a seat, but I'm not up to date with my immunisations.'

'Wise,' Feely eyed the mess as he sat down. 'Must remember to sack my cleaner.'

Guzan puffed out a laugh, enquired, 'The DPW gang still going, huh?'

'I ain't no Dog Patch Wino,' Feely frowned defensively.

Hit a nerve thought Guzan, *ease off.*

'You wanna know about Mr Hardwick or not?'

'Congratulations,' said Guzan. 'You guessed the right cellmate.' Sharing a cell with Kester Hardwick had probably turned Feely into a local celebrity. Guzan was hoping his desire to talk held out to FBI agents. 'So, Mr Grub. What can you tell me about him?'

'We wound up in the same cell's all,' Feely Grub sunk back into the sofa.

Acting dutifully impressed, Guzan remained hopeful of Feely's cooperation. 'But then you moved cells. Why was that?'

'One day I was Mr Hardwick's roomy, the next I was gone.' Feely shrugged. 'You never get to hear the reason.'

'The man that got your bed, Sadiq al-Barabi, what did you make of him bunking up with Mr Hardwick?'

'Surprised man, Sadiq ain't white. Mr Hardwick only talked with whites. You know his father was killed during Watts, burned alive by a pack of rampaging niggers.'

Guzan winced at the abhorrent expression, but not wanting to stop Feely's flow, reluctantly ignored the racism. He was aware the Hardwick residence had been burned down during the Watts race riots of 1965. Kester was a small boy at the time and he got out unscathed, but only after watching his father perish. The incident led to Kester using fire as a preferred method of punishment in later life; his link to the death of Cliff Donachie's family being a case in point.

Reigning in his thoughts, Guzan focused on the case in hand. 'So given that he only talked to whites, how come he ended up in a cell with Sadiq? He must have had some say in who he roomed with.'

'Money,' boasted Feely. 'Sadiq was stacked, he paid Mr Hardwick.'

'Paid him?'

'Inside there are some people you just don't fuck with, not without losing a digit or a family member. Mr Hardwick was top of that list, not because of what happened in prison, but what he could do outside. Sadiq was a scary fucker in his own right, but in the end he needed Mr Hardwick's protection – at least, that's how I saw it. You see, inside you're either black, white or Mexican. Not sure which, you'd better pick one. Real quick. Sadiq didn't. But fighting gangs just got him sent to the hole. He was pushing his luck. You know what I'm sayin'? Without the protection he'd have wound up dead.'

'Did you ever talk with Sadiq?'

'Not really, he was quiet, apart from when he was with Mr Hardwick. Suddenly he'd find his mouth. If half of what he said was true he'd have a list of war crimes longer than a magician's hanky.'

'Did he ever mention a formula?'

'Formula?' Feely shook his head. 'Not that I remember.'

'Do you think Sadiq could have paid Mr Hardwick for anything other than protection?'

'What you sayin'?' Feely pulled a face, like he'd just smelt his room for the first time. 'The only thing Mr Hardwick liked about "Sadiq the psycho" was his green paper.'

'And there were no other theories as to why he might be paying him?'

Feely scratched his crotch. 'I heard that Sadiq wanted revenge on someone or something. But he never said revenge, he said—' Feely's eyes fished around before catching a thought. 'Retribution. I heard that Sadiq was payin' Mr Hardwick to exact retribution, or some shit like that, but if you ask me he was paying to be kept alive.'

'Retribution for what?'

Shrugging his bony shoulders, Feely Grub sculpted his Mohican and closed his mouth.

Sensing that he'd nothing more to say, Guzan informed Feely that he'd be in touch and left the Grub residence the same way he'd come in, sucking in a lungful of clean air and resisting the temptation to head for the nearest washroom.

Having listened in to the conversation, Derego had made his way to the front yard. Guzan joined him and they headed back to the Mustang. Not sure they were any closer to finding Sadiq al-Barabi.

Derego said, 'You should have asked Feely the question.'

'Question?'

Standing still and stony-faced, Derego struck the pose. 'You feeling lucky, punk?'

'Sorry, I missed that,' said Guzan. His cell buzzed. He removed it. Seeing it was Ethan Knight, he hit green.

Ethan sounded anxious: 'Just got wind of a meet that Hardwick will be attending, you need to drop what you're doing and haul your ass over there. I heard about your appointment, Primary Lead Supervisor, huh? Well that should make things easier, but you still answer to me on this and I need you over there pronto.'

'What sort of a meet?'

'I don't know, but we picked it up off frequency, sounds like he's got company, could be Sadiq al-Barabi. I have just dispatched a SWAT team but you are closer. This time bring the bastard in, Don.'

'Where are they?'

'Lincoln Heights.'

Chapter Fifty

Having ditched the BMW, Skid replaced Kester as driver of the Range Rover. They both seemed relaxed, unmoved, like they hadn't given Tino's murder a second thought.

I was in the back. My wrists had been bound together with tape; causing pain that was becoming familiar. My ankles were also tied. Cuts and gashes covered my body. Dirt and blood mingled into my shredded clothing and onto the leather upholstery. We were on our way to a big meeting. That's all I knew.

The journey gave me time to think and boy did I need it. It was like Kester had tipped a jigsaw puzzle in my lap and I had to describe the image. I didn't know where to start. I recalled what Lisa had said, *you don't know what you're dealing with*. I didn't.

According to Kester, Elaine had required his help when she needed to leave Spain. He obliged, using his contacts to relocate her to Northampton. It was evidently no coincidence that she had arrived in my life. She was deliberately dropped into my inner circle, given a job working with my best friend's wife. As far as Kester was concerned, it was the logical location. Apparently he already had somebody keeping tabs on me. Elaine had become just another person to watch.

I could not even begin to imagine a reason why Kester would go to such trouble for me. I scoured my brain for something I might have heard, seen, or done that would qualify me to do a job for him. All I kept coming back to was that it was somehow to do with my attack in the park and the vicious murder of my father. I felt like a fly; trapped in a web of questions for which there were no answers.

I thought of Janet, another innocent victim in Kester's plans. It troubled me that I hadn't called her about Sam or even located his hospital. What could I tell her? I didn't even know if her husband was alive – and that troubled me even more.

Kester had deigned to inform me that my relationship with Elaine was not part of the plan. It had been a shock to him when she fell for me, but he had used it to his advantage, making Elaine the bait when the time came to get me to LA.

In addition to looking for Elaine maybe I was escaping my nightmares and all the furore surrounding my father's death, but whatever the reason, it had been my decision to come here. Or so I had thought. Now Kester had told me it was all part of a plan: the letters were from him; postmarked Los Angeles because he needed me here.

I questioned him about the message: *Gary Jasper. Edson Taylor. Third time lucky? Start counting.* He denied that Gary Jasper's murder or my attack were part of the plan. Once again, as far as Kester was concerned these incidents had been fortuitous. Knowing of them, he had used them to add weight to his letters. I now realised the messages were designed not simply to lead me to the destination of his choice, but to make me believe I was in control. *Third time lucky? Want your Angel back? Go Seek.* Everything had pulled me to Los Angeles, but I still didn't know why.

In case I had doubted the authenticity of the notes, the e-mail was added, complete with picture attachment. He spoke with regret that he had used Gina's name. His pain seemed genuine, his anger real.

I recalled Surgeon's words: *In your photo all are dead.*

Surgeon may have been right about Gina Sipple and Elaine Needlam, but as for my Elaine, it seemed that the plan to fake her death had worked.

But why me?

'You'll see,' Kester had repeated. It was the last thing he had said.

* * *

A graffiti-splattered road sign told us that we were on the High Street, and that *Maggot is a Faggot*. I recognised the six-lane highway. I was back in Lincoln Heights. I had heard that people don't walk in LA. Well, they did here, nearly all of them eyeing up the Range Rover through palm trees and fence posts.

'Are we there yet?' I asked like a child.

No answer.

After a couple of left turns the pedestrians were gone. The last ones we saw were a handful of shirtless Mexicans standing under a sign that read: THE SAN ANTONIO WINERY. They stopped talking and scowled as we passed. A hundred yards further, we turned into an empty parking lot behind a lone, brick building. Skid reversed and parked.

Kester lowered his window, breathing in the warm, close air. 'We are here to meet an old friend of mine.'

The place was too quiet; as if someone had blown the city power supply. Behind us was a heavily tagged concrete wall, which tilted at the weight of the grassy bank behind. On either side were the obligatory metal fences so prevalent in the area. The Range Rover faced the only way in or out of the car park.

After a couple of minutes' silence, a black Lexus joined us. The driver's window lowered.

Skid was first out. Then Kester, a wide smile on his face. 'Victor, impeccable timing. Hope the destination is quiet enough for you.'

I couldn't see who he was talking to. This *Victor*. As for his timing, a clock on the dashboard showed 2.30pm.

As Kester moved around the car, I heard snatches of conversation: something about *good work* and the *prisoner*. Victor's reply was hard to make out, but I caught the words *trouble* and *guard*.

I looked again at the brick building. The windows were barred and boarded up. I had the feeling they were not just to stop people getting in.

I remained in the car as Kester's colleague climbed out of the Lexus. From the side he looked familiar. He was short and thin. His white, pony-tailed hair suggested he was a rocker in the seventies – or maybe a hippy in the sixties. Given that he had age spots as large as his eyes, I plumped for the latter, but he didn't look the sort to wear flowers in his hair.

'Let's get him inside,' he said in a high-pitched voice that pierced my mind, breaking me into a cold sweat.

The more I struggled, the tighter the bond dug into my swollen hand.

I tried to fight back panic as a horrible realisation materialised. Victor was the old man from my nightmares.

CHAPTER FIFTY-ONE

2.45pm
Lincoln Heights, Los Angeles.

Putting binoculars to his eyes, Derego surveyed the scene, catching sight of movement near the boarded-up building. A parked Corvette limited his view.

Deputy Platt of the County Sheriff's Department spoke in a nasal whine: 'The Corvette arrived one minute and fifty-three seconds before you guys.' Platt was first on the scene; neatly turned out as if he had just arrived from a uniform inspection. He had welcomed agents Guzan and Derego as they arrived. They had joined him by his department car, observed the building; waited for signs of Kester Hardwick and the men he was meeting.

Derego turned to the meek looking Platt. 'Have you run a check on the Corvette?'

'Don't need to,' bragged the deputy, 'that's Bruno Meyer's car.'

'Who the hell's he?'

'Bruno Meyer runs Kester's strip club not far from here,' said Guzan. 'He acts as an enforcer for local pimps and dealers.'

'A right nasty piece of work,' added Platt. 'He went in there with another man – five-seven, Caucasian. I got a picture of them on my i-phone.' Platt displayed the image, like a proud parent showing off baby photos. 'I zoomed in from here.'

Looking at the fuzzy image, Guzan recognised Bruno Meyer, but not the other man. Dressed entirely in black and looking barely 100lbs; standing next to Bruno he looked like a bit broken off. Ethan Knight's tip-off suggested that other men could be with Kester, but who else? All heat sources could confirm was that multiple bodies were inside.

This time bring the bastards in.

Still watching through binoculars, Derego looked for any movement. There was none, the place appeared desolate. Like many of the so-called business plots in the area there were no takers. Every window was covered, every wall a canvas for graffiti. 'What is this place used for?' he asked the know-it-all cop.

'Before it shut down it was a clothes factory,' he explained. *Shirts 'n' Suits.* They ceased trading on the—'

Guzan cut him short, his cell was buzzing. It was Ethan Knight wanting an update. Guzan obliged, 'Bruno Meyer is in there, and he entered with another man before we could confine the situation. LAPD are setting up an outer perimeter so the building will shortly be isolated. All traffic's now been diverted; we're a civilian-free zone. I'm putting through an image for identification of the second man.'

Knight responded, 'SWAT are employed, but I don't have an arrival time. Wait on their instruction, and Don, don't let personal feelings get in the way, we need cool heads. This could be a trap. Anything.'

Guzan was concerned. 'If Kester sees SWAT we could have a problem, he won't go quietly. Isn't it better to wait until he emerges?'

'SWAT are aware of the situation, they are just a precaution. Intel suggests that Hardwick is in there with two other men. My hunch is that Bruno Meyer and his buddy make five. Hardwick owns the building, who knows what security he has. The Unit is backing our theory that he is planning to sell a chemical formula to Sadiq al-Barabi. This could be the meet. Remember; our number one priority is recapturing the terrorist. You are only there because you know Hardwick. That must remain *our* advantage not his. No playing heroes. We want everyone alive, including you.'

The call ended with Guzan deep in thought. *Intel suggests Kester's in there with two other men.* Who? 'Skid' Sanchez, 'Tino' Ricard, Edson Taylor, Sadiq al-Barabi?

'We stay back, wait for SWAT,' instructed Guzan, his eyes scanning for their presence. 'Not you.' He turned to Platt. 'I need that photo of yours put on the system.'

The deputy perked up. 'Wait for SWAT, hey? I could tell you a thing or two about them.'

'Why doesn't that surprise me?' said Derego.

Platt continued regardless, 'Did you know the first deployment of a SWAT unit was on December the 9th 1969, in a four-hour confrontation with the Black Panthers?'

Derego rolled his eyes, glanced at Guzan, 'Can you believe this guy?'

Guzan's patience had already deserted him. 'The *photo?*'

As Platt retired, a SWAT team arrived, piling out of a van. A tall man whom the agents assumed was the team leader headed for them. He was pulling fire-resistant Nomex coveralls over his armour vest and strapping on an outer, load-bearing vest. In short, he was preparing for possible combat. Up close, Guzan recognised him from previous missions, though this was the first time he had seen him lead.

The man's name was Kromkamp. He cut a formidable figure: the look of Van-Damme; the voice of Earl-Jones. 'Follow me as I brief you,' he said.

Neither Guzan nor Derego responded well to orders, but they followed Kromkamp. 'We are a ten-man team,' he bellowed. 'Two five-man squads. Mine will secure the building while squad B prepares to enter. We will have marksmen on the East and West corners and an observer on top of the bank. A scout and rear guard will secure the south, roadside. As soon as we have presence on the roof, we will be ready to move in and secure the building.'

In the distance Derego spied the teams move quickly into position. They were already in full gear; tactical gloves, Kevlar helmet, gas masks, and combat boots.

Kromkamp's determined stare found Guzan. 'Once we are in, wait for confirmation that we are secure. At that time you may enter the building. Until then, stay here and cover the exit route. We are prepared for the risk of chemical involvement, so leave the action to us. I repeat, don't leave your post until we are on the roof.'

Guzan nodded. Making haste, Kromkamp went to work.

'Look at them,' said Derego.

Detecting concern Guzan snatched the binoculars. 'What?'

'The weaponry,' said Derego. 'They're starting a Goddamn war!'

Twisting the building into focus, Guzan zeroed in on the SWAT members primed on the East corner. He saw a 9 mm Heckler & Koch MP5, and what he thought was a high-power anti-sniper rifle. Scanning frantically across to the West corner he saw two .223-calibre semi-automatics. Letting the binoculars drop to his chest he put his hands to his face. 'Shit!' There were no Pepperball guns. No Tasers. No OC canisters. The rounds were ammunition, not bean bag. Wide eyed with concern Guzan panicked, 'They are going in there for the kill.'

'What should we do?'

We want everyone alive.

Thinking fast, Guzan, fixed his gaze on the building. 'We have to stop SWAT.'

'Call Knight,' urged Derego.

Red drained from Guzan's cheeks. 'There's no time,' he called back, already on the move, 'They're on the roof.'

CHAPTER FIFTY-TWO

Running like hell towards the inevitable blood bath, Guzan's neck was a vein-fest. He didn't know how he could stop the carnage, but he had to try. His harboured dreams of killing Kester Hardwick didn't end like this. Not when Kester was the best link to Sadiq al-Barabi and the rumoured formula. Killing him now would be surrendering the last laugh. And was Sadiq with him? A terrorist in custody beat one in the morgue. And what of Edson Taylor, an innocent man Guzan had already let down once today.

A college sprinter, Derego passed Guzan and had Kromkamp in his sight. 'Abort,' he yelled now close enough to see the whites of the team leader's eyes. Kromkamp stared back momentarily before signalling to the roof.

Then all hell broke loose.

With no warning, SWAT stormed the building, battering through doors and boarded windows. All guns blazing.

Listening to the barrage of bullets, Guzan dropped to his knees.

What have they done?

He felt a hand on his shoulder; Derego pulling him up. Things were quiet. The operation had ended as quickly as it had begun. Catching his breath, Guzan continued wearily towards the building. The familiar blare of sirens erupted as LAPD moved closer. A chopper appeared, hovering above with the effects of a giant hairdryer. Widening their stance to remain upright, the two agents staggered toward the carnage of the disused factory.

The main door burst open. Two men swung out, both SWAT. One of them had taken a hit but his armour looked intact, the other man was propping him up. Kromkamp was next out. He looked pissed, even before he noticed Derego in his face.

'We said abort,' raged the agent squaring up to the SWAT leader.

'I had orders,' defended Kromkamp shouting over the chopper. 'We were dealing with a potential chemical response. You don't fuck with that.'

'Potential?' yelled Guzan. 'What happened in there?'

'I don't have time for this. Go see for yourself. But know this, they were armed.'

A paramedic car arrived in the parking lot, FBI assistance close behind. Guzan and Derego carefully entered the clothes factory. A smell met them, empty shells, the remnants of which lay under their feet. Dead bodies were sprayed across the floor. A paramedic followed them in, her check for life just a formality. She was careful not to disturb anything. She knew the drill.

Standing over the first body, Guzan knew contamination of a crime scene wouldn't be an issue here. He looked at dead bodies professionally, as empty vessels, the ultimate piece of evidence, but the eyes of the dead never failed to spook him. It was the emotions they carried. Bruno Meyer was on his back, almost looking up at Guzan. His eyes were bloody - the line of red in his hair seemed to flow into his wide, frightened gaze.

Like Meyer, the next corpse was on his back, but his head had fallen sideways. The man's face was ghostly white; the body could have been there for days if it were not still warm.

'Is he wearing eye liner?' Derego asked. 'Looks like a Goth.'

They kneeled, twisting for a closer look.

Strangely devoid of emotion, the Goth's eyes sank slowly back into his skull. Probably one of the insalubrious characters Bruno Meyer associated with, thought Guzan.

The paramedic headed down the stairs. 'Two bodies, that's your death toll.'

'Nobody up there?' queried Derego.

The paramedic shook her head, confirming Guzan's surprise. *No Kester. But the CIA thought he was here;* and whatever their source, they had believed it strongly enough to employ SWAT.

A familiar voice came from behind Guzan. 'We found something.'

It was Agent Beasley. He glanced down at the two dead bodies. 'We've found another one,' he said. 'In the Corvette. You'd better take a look.'

CHAPTER FIFTY-THREE

As they rode along in Victor Lapenza's Lexus, Kester felt strangely alive. Prison had denied him what he craved the most; the feeling of accomplishment; he had almost forgotten how good it felt.

With its windows blacked out, Kester was worried the Lexus might attract unwanted attention. As they turned past the old winery he ordered Skid to keep to the speed limits; took a look down Lamar Street. He could see a road block in the distance and noted the time. 2.53pm. 'Excellent,' he said, giving a brilliant – if accidental – *Mr Burns* impression.

By now, Bruno and his psychotic confrère would be dead. Kester had arranged for them to perish inside the old clothes factory, one of the many buildings he owned in Lincoln Heights. He had arranged the meet, telling Bruno to wait there for a VIP who wished to do business with him. All Bruno knew about the man was that he was extremely wealthy and inclined to get heavy. Kester had known this would secure Surgeon's presence.

Two birds with one stone.

Were it not for Kester's incarceration, he would have disposed of Bruno years ago, but he recognised the need for a vehement presence on the outside and Bruno had fulfilled that role. His fate was sealed the moment he boasted about killing Gina Sipple. Aside from the fact that she had been the only girl remaining from Kester's *Flesh Dance* days, by using the furnace to kill her, Bruno had challenged Kester's authority. He simply had to die. Surgeon's demise was an added pleasure. Whilst in prison, Kester had heard reports of the man's extreme violence and ability to avoid capture. He was of no use to Kester: unpredictable; controlled only by his need for sadistic gratification, he had needed to be removed.

The opportunity to use SWAT to murder them both was too good to refuse. With Kester's contacts, it was easy to ensure news of the meet would be taken seriously. Given his known association with Sadiq al-Barabi, SWAT's involvement would be routine. It had amused Kester to pull the strings and watch the puppets dance to his tune. And he had done society a favour: there would be no mourning or public outcry where Bruno was concerned. Kester gave a satisfied smile, enjoying once again the pleasure of accomplishment. He was back – with avengeance!

As soon as Bruno had bragged about taking Gina to the furnace house, Kester had arranged for the power to be axed. It was too late to save Gina, but in time to preserve her remains. She was shrink-wrapped and placed in the trunk of Bruno's Corvette; a present for the FBI. Pathology would be consistent with Bruno's boast, and his DNA should be all over her. *Revenge was expected.* People would know that Bruno had been punished for what he did to Gina. To Kester's employee.

Kester sighed: all things considered, a job well done. He turned his attention to the rear of the Lexus. Now for the big one, he thought, glancing back at the unconscious passenger. Victor was sat with him, monitoring his condition. It was important the drugs wore off soon. Edson Taylor had a job to do.

CHAPTER FIFTY-FOUR

4.14pm
Lincoln Park, Los Angeles.

My eyes slowly opened. I was awake inside my
nightmare, consumed with fear. The white hair
touching my face, the piggy eyes staring down
through John Lennon specs, the sharp nose pointing
right at me; they all belonged to Victor.

I shut my eyes, hoping to erase his image, hoping
to change the nightmare.

Fear was joined by regret. *I should never have come
to Los Angeles*. Despite Kester's coercion, it had been
my own decision. I had ignored Sam's sound advice
not to come and my actions had accomplished
nothing but get my best friend shot in the head.
A good man, a family man in God knows what

state. At best he was all alone, fighting for his life, needing me. But then, maybe I needed him more. As for Elaine; what had Kester done with her? *Just how much is she involved?*

A voice like a badly played viola brought me sharply back into full consciousness. *Victor.* It wasn't until I forced open my eyes that I could understand him.

'Ah, good, Mr Taylor is back with us,' he hissed, holding a small light that flashed across my eyes.

I gingerly pushed myself up. We weren't in the brick warehouse. This ceiling was low and mirrored, a hard floor shone back at me.

Where am I? My throat felt like I'd swallowed hot coals.

Kester's voice came from the side. 'You are at a place I call my *refugio seguro*. Don't worry you haven't been away for long. Victor is very pleased with you.'

'Impressive,' Victor agreed as he moved away, taking the light with him. Suddenly my feet raced to the floor and my head flipped forward as the bed transformed into a seat. My blood failed to keep up and I nearly passed out.

As their eyes bore into me, Victor and Kester shared a laugh. I held myself still as the room spun. It was small and windowless, maybe ten by ten, like a bedroom. They were stood next to the door, arms folded, seemingly admiring their view of me. Standing against the back wall was another man; suited, booted and bald. He sported a tidy beard not uncommon with men who can't grow hair on their heads. He was a little taller and younger than Kester – I'd say six foot, late forties. His eyeballs were hyperactive. His hands were shaky. His right knee bounced uncontrollably.

I dry swallowed, turned to face them. 'Who's the cue-ball?'

'You can call me Al,' he said.

I frowned. 'Like the Paul Simon song or is it short for alopecia?'

Al scoffed. 'Wise guy, huh?'

Kester spoke next, 'Enough with the intros, let's get down to business.' He glued his stony gaze my way. 'You were targeted two years ago. Because of your face. A face that wasn't quite perfect. A couple of months back Victor put that right.'

I found myself slipping back into my nightmare, where nothing made sense. I stared at Kester; tried reassembling his words. In the end I was forced to ask, 'What are you talking about?'

Victor piped up. 'Don't tell me you've forgotten our romantic summer's evening in the park? You, me, Tino, my medical bag?'

The park. My blood boiled. Kester had lied. Why did that surprise me? More importantly, what did they do to me? I struggled to stand, fists bunched. It was a pointless gesture.

'Calm down,' Victor chuckled. 'It was Tino who got a little heavy. I told him not to be too rough, to let the chloroform do its work.' *Like a hand gripped my face.* 'Once you were down, I anaesthetised you. I then took a mould of your face. Your measurements were perfect. Unfortunately so too was your nose.

But that was successfully rectified, with a little cosmetic surgery. Your bruising has cleared up nicely.' He turned to Kester, 'The bump on Edson's nose is perfect wouldn't you agree?'

'Perfect,' nodded Kester.

What the hell? I put a hand up to my nose, felt the bump.

'Let me explain, Edson.'

About bloody time.

Kester tented his fingers. 'The time has come for that job I mentioned. Your task is a simple one. In an hour or so you will be driven to a downtown location. Once there you will remain in the car until a white Nissan joins you. At that point you will get out and walk over to the car where you will be handed a briefcase. All we need is a good shot of your face' – he glanced at Victor – 'perfect bump and all. The security camera will do the rest. You won't have to speak, or do anything illegal. And once this task is complete you will be free to be with Elaine.'

Kester's explanation was another riddle; I was not wholly convinced I wasn't still dreaming, but the last few words registered; *be with Elaine*. I clutched at the straw. 'Let me see her now,' I insisted. 'How do I know she's even alive?'

Kester exhaled, like he was expecting my question. 'Pass him the phone.'

CHAPTER FIFTY-FIVE

Al handed the phone to me, told me to press the green key. It was a video phone. The screen read *internet connected*. I hit the key and Elaine appeared on the two-inch LCD. I gasped. She was tied to a chair, gagged. I struggled to hold it together. My heart pounded in my throat. Even on the tiny screen I could see fear in her bloodshot eyes.

'How do I know when this was taken?'

'Press green again,' instructed Al, 'and speak into it.'

I did. '*Elaine*. Can you hear me?'

Her eyes sharpened. She looked into the camera. Nodded. Tears flowed onto her chest; her eyes said *I'm sorry*. Then her face reddened, her neck bulged. She was straining for something.

What is she doing?

As I watched, Elaine shook. So did the image, as if her feet gripped whatever the camera was resting on. She disappeared for a moment as the image rocked. When it returned Elaine was to the right, trying to show me something to her side? *What?* Her eyes gestured over her shoulder. Mine followed. There was a shelf with a candle, above it a picture on the wall, a print. *Picasso.*

What Elaine? My mind screamed.

'He's seen enough,' said Kester and Al swiped the phone from me.

But Kester was right, I *had* seen enough.

Not the Picasso, but the glass protecting it. Light from a window had reflected back an image of what looked like a Mayan pyramid rising above trees.

She had been trying to tell me where she was being held. Find that pyramid, I find Elaine.

I hid my discovery and faced Kester. 'I'll do it, but I want to know why? Why is my face so important?'

Kester put a hand on my shoulder, and slowly released a smile. 'We need you to impersonate someone. Had you been able to watch TV you would have noticed your face plastered across every news station. But it is not your mug, it belongs to a recently escaped prisoner, some might say, terrorist.' He gestured to Victor who passed me a glossy picture. 'We need you to look exactly like him.'

I sat forward and looked at the 8 by 10. It was of me, nose bump and all. But the image had been doctored somehow. I had a full beard and was wearing what looked like a cape of cotton cloth that hooded my head.

Kester spoke, 'That man is Sadiq al-Barabi. Your task is to impersonate him.'

'But that's me. How is that me?'

'Uncanny isn't it?' said Al.

I rubbed my eyes, prodded the photo. '*That's* supposed to be a terrorist?' I sank into the chair. My head still dizzy. 'Is that what this is about? You want me to help a terrorist?'

'No, it's about helping ourselves,' said Kester.

Victor agreed. 'Sadiq al-Barabi paid us well for springing him, but that was only part of the deal.'

I dropped the picture, fought off the panic caused by his voice and tried to listen.

'He is a rich man and his money gets him you. It's not his mother he wants us to fool, it's the FBI. They will use digital image processing algorithms on the footage. Noise will be removed and contrast increased. No face is unique but, thanks to the mold, my measurements are precise. As a result they should determine without doubt that the man in the image is Sadiq al-Barabi. You are the chosen decoy, part of a meticulous plan hatched by both him and Mr Hardwick.'

'A decoy? What is this plan? And why do I look like him?'

Kester folded his arms. 'We just need you to appear on camera being handed a case. Think of it as an acting job; playing a body double. Sadiq needs the FBI to think he was in a particular place at a particular time. Why is not your concern.'

'But too many agents have seen me,' I protested. 'The FBI won't fall for it now.'

Kester retorted, 'It was never expected that you would come into contact with the FBI, but it seems that by whisking you away when we did we have got away with it. You see, Sadiq doesn't know that members of the FBI have seen you. And we're not going to tell him. He will still pay us, and you will still get back with Elaine.'

Victor pursed his lips. More doom-laden words strained from his voicebox, 'There were probably a hundred men I could have worked on, but Sadiq specifically requested you.'

'How the hell does he know about me?'

'I must admit it did make life easier,' Victor ignored the question, 'but sometimes the simplest work can have hidden problems. You wouldn't be the first identical twins to fail the FBI's tests.'

'That's bullshit,' I fired back.

'Twinned with a terrorist: officially identical, but in reality not quite.'

Shuddering, I tried to stand but my legs were numb. 'I don't have a brother – never mind a twin.'

'Sure about that are you?' smirked Victor.

I gazed at him. No. I wasn't sure. I knew very little about my origins. 'How can that be?' I croaked, dumbfounded.

Victor let out a yelp of laughter, 'I would imagine like any other baby is produced, only there's two of you.'

My life had spun upside down and was now unravelling. I was stunned. All along I had thought that Elaine's past had caught up with us, but it wasn't hers at all, it was mine. I looked at each of the men. Their faces were deadly serious. They wanted me to become a decoy for someone they thought was my twin. *We need you to impersonate someone.* If this was the only way to end this nightmare, what choice did I have?

I sighed. 'I'll do it.'

CHAPTER FIFTY-SIX

4.41pm
Piru Creek, Los Angeles.

The climate reminded Sadiq al-Barabi of his childhood, being forced to stand in hot sun for hours on end. That was his life in the orphanage. His upbringing. His suffering. They'd said he was put there because of poverty, but Sadiq knew different: he'd been put in that orphanage to experience pain, and for him the abuse was always the worst. Born to a single mother – a black Christian no less – his regular punishment had been vicious beatings with leather whips. Before his mother died, he was taken from her. It was in the orphanage that he became Sadiq al-Barabi and endured heinous suffering. Islam was beaten into him. Prayer-time became his only release. But Sadiq was not with Allah, his thoughts were elsewhere. He wasn't prepared to suffer in this life on the promise of reward in paradise. He knew at a young age that he was suffering in order to gain knowledge of pain; learning to live with it, embrace it, and one day to inflict it on others. If he was fanatical about anything beyond that it was money, power, legacy. Ordinary things. Western things.

When old enough to work, Sadiq was sent onto the streets of Khartoum, the capital of Africa's largest country, Sudan. He found a city in turmoil: its residents in the process of Arabisation, forced to live under Islamic Sharia law. Sadiq may have rejected Islam, but in public, any rebellion was confined to his mind. Being seen as Muslim provided him with acceptance and a job. The state employed him to promote and enforce Islam within the Christian and English-speaking community. His non-Arab looks and effort to learn English had endeared him to a group who were desperate to appear comfortable with Sharia law. Sadiq knew the non-Muslim population was – as he saw it – *looking for loopholes*. For a price, he offered ways of living within Sharia law without the inconvenience. Sadiq extorted what money he could, sometimes for simply turning a blind eye. This money enabled him to break from the control of his elders and live for himself.

He was in his mid-teens when he discovered his father's nationality. By then Sharia law was no longer mandatory and there was greater freedom of information. Hospital records showed his father to be British; Britain's influence was everywhere in Khartoum. The city had started as a military town – its streets were designed in the shape of the Union Jack - but only when the slave trade was introduced did it prosper. That time was now seen as the beginning of the end for Khartoum. Those who didn't blame the British for the slave trade blamed them for abandoning the city. Having a British father was nothing to brag about and Sadiq kept it to himself, but when he was sixteen he came across a friend of his mother's and uncovered the circumstances of his birth.

His father – Gary Jasper – had visited Khartoum in 1969. The city was hosting the African Nations Cup the following year and he was there to help Sudan prepare for the tournament. Whilst in the city he met Amna, an English-speaking aide, and they conducted a brief affair. When Jasper returned in 1970 he found Amna to be pregnant. She begged him to take her to England, but he refused and after watching Sudan win the cup, returned to England without her. He paid for Amna to be hospitalised for the remainder of her pregnancy and insisted that he be informed of his child's birth. Jasper was keen for his offspring to be raised in England and in return for Amna's compliance in the matter, agreed to pay her handsomely. She was ill-prepared to lose her baby, but knew the financial impossibility of raising one alone. Her pregnancy had already made her an outcast; she had lost her job and had little chance of another.

When Amna went into labour, she was in despair, but her heavy heart was lightened by the birth of twin boys. Suddenly there was a way for her to keep one of her babies and have the money she desperately needed to raise him. Now she was faced with a different dilemma: how to choose? One son had to be handed over to his father; the other would stay in Khartoum.

After his help with the success of the African Nations Cup, Jasper was granted permission from the state for his son to live in England. Neither they nor Jasper were ever meant to find out about the twin; only Amna's friend knew the truth. But, as Sadiq learned, once his twin was safely in England, their father went back on his word. Amna received nothing from Jasper and as a result of desperate poverty was not allowed to keep her chosen son.

Enquiring further after his mother, Sadiq was told that the trauma of handing over her newborn son to Jasper had hit her hard. Then, when her other boy was taken – put in the orphanage – it all became too much. After being refused access to see Sadiq, she took her life.

On hearing this news, Sadiq was badly affected. Nurturing within him a well of hatred that focused on the man who had destroyed their lives, he became distant, unpredictable. As a result, the money dried up. Then in 1991, things changed. Sharia law was reintroduced to the Northern States. Regardless of religion, all of Khartoum was once again required to live a life of strict Islam. Sadiq was not physically strong, but armed with the blessings of his government he became the perfect enforcer. Stonings were carried out as punishment, often in front of family members. Sadiq revelled in their pain. Numbed to their pleas, he felt no remorse for his actions. He existed in the only world he knew: a world of fear.

By 1994 his name had reached Al Qaeda. He was taken to a large Sudanese training camp where he learned about explosives and discovered new methods of torture and murder. It became a science to him and he dedicated himself to finding new ways of using the simplest of chemicals and actions to provide the most effective weaponry. They even invited him to teach the art of detachment, paid him for it. There are *prophets* and there are *profits*, thought Sadiq. He knew how money equated to freedom.

Since that time, Sadiq had kept on the move, following any cause that funded his want for violence. War zones provided the biggest paydays, and it hardly mattered which side he was on. After his Iraqi base became demilitarised, Sadiq chased the dollar. Contacts in America provided an opportunity for him to enter the country via his US allies – the MEK – and in the USA, terrorism meant big business. His sights were set on developing a chemical weapon that could turn the US government's own weakness against them. In order to meet that objective a formula needed to be developed. But it wasn't Sadiq's plan to use the formula himself – he valued his freedom too much for that – no; once developed, Sadiq would sell his formula to the highest bidder.

Prison had delayed his plans. After a stretch for possession of illegal bullets, Sadiq was on the verge of securing the formula. It had needed to be perfected in his absence – and would cost more than he'd initially hoped – but finally it was ready. But he had a problem: whilst incarcerated his identity had come to light. Sadiq needed his freedom back, and his twin brother was going to get it for him.

CHAPTER FIFTY-SEVEN

Sadiq al-Barabi had to close the windows, at least until the wind changed. The dead farmer and his wife smelt worse than the animals picking at their remains.

He poured himself a glass of tap water. The kitchen was now baking hot. No air conditioning. Should have buried them, he thought, rummaging inside the deceased farmer's walk-in pantry. He located a jar of peanuts, wandered into a back room, put his feet up, popped the jar and stared at his cell-phone expectantly. The unforeseen delay in locating Edson Taylor had made Sadiq tetchy. They were cutting it fine, but at least by now his brother would know of his part in the plan. But would he come on board? If his twin's mistrustful disposition matched his own there could be trouble. Was it possible Edson would see through the promise Kester had made him? The wait was making Sadiq anxious, as was the heat – and that damned smell. He loosened shirt buttons, then his belt; *fucking Western clothing*, he thought irritably: designed for neither heat nor sweat.

Once again the smell of death alerted his nostrils like a gas leak at a fire-eating show. On reflection, he should have shot the farmer and his wife. It was just that they had a slaughter house. The temptation to inflict on them what they had intended for their livestock was simply too great. Which was why he'd slit their throats.

He picked up his phone, willed it to ring. Soon his brother would secure his freedom, and he, Sadiq al-Barabi, would have his formula. He would demand a fortune for it, promise unprecedented levels of paranoia. Skyscrapers, aeroplanes, undergrounds, could all be avoided. Water could not.

The call came at 4.59pm. Its chirpy ring preceded Kester Hardwick's staid voice. 'We're set; your brother's about to leave for the destination.'

'Is everything ready?'

'Affirmative. The moment Edson Taylor has the case, the bomb will be detonated, and you will be a free man. *Nobody* will question that you died in the explosion.' Kester coughed. 'I trust the second instalment will be duly wired. Then all that remains is our final exchange. My man has the formula ready for you; I trust you have the money ready?'

'Of course,' said Sadiq, thinking about the all-important formula. 'And it works?'

'It will. May I ask where you plan to go?'

'Maybe I will travel to England on my brother's passport.' The line went quiet. 'A joke of course,' smiled Sadiq. 'Speaking of my brother, I have one last request.' Sadiq knew what he was about to ask would not sit well with Kester, but it was his money. *His* plan. 'I want you to use the larger IED.'

'But we discussed this. It will be seen less as an assassination, more as terrorism. We decided one capsule would be sufficient.'

Sadiq slowed his voice, to Kester's level. 'If you want all the money, you will use the larger one.'

'It's your call,' conceded Kester. 'But it will probably take both cars out and everyone in them. My driver will be killed not to mention Ali Afshari and Syrus Meybodi.'

'Exactly,' said Sadiq. He didn't want to take any chances where his brother was concerned. As for the gullible Iranians, they would have served their purpose; the fewer people left alive who knew the truth, the better. 'I take it we are agreed?'

Silence. Then: 'Fine.'

CHAPTER FIFTY-EIGHT

We exited an internal garage and joined a narrow road that ran behind what I now saw was a three-storey townhouse.

A place I call my *refugio seguro*.

Doors had locked me inside the stuffy Dodge Charger; Plexiglas separated me from my chauffeur, a neck-less man whose silver hair matched the bodywork of his car.

Studying myself on the inside of a window I couldn't believe how quickly Victor had transformed me, and not just my clothes. *We need you to impersonate someone.* I could barely tell if they were my eyes staring back or those of the escaped terrorist; my twin brother. I looked older, a false beard framed my face and my hair was thicker. I wondered if I would ever get to meet the man looking back at me. I had heard about the bond twins shared, and how they finished each other's sentences. But mine was a terrorist; how could we have the same genes, share the same traits? How was that possible?

A crackly voice came through a speaker, 'Glad of the blacked out windows.' The driver turned. 'Your face is on the news.'

'That's not me,' I shouted, unsure if he could hear me. 'You understand I'm not the terrorist?'

'Yeah,' he laughed. 'You just have to play him. Collect a case, right?'

'Right.' Once this task was complete I would be free to be with Elaine. It was all that was keeping me together.

No-neck curved the car left, taking us back in front of the townhouse. On the opposite side, trees lined the road.

Something caught my eye.

In the park, poking out above the trees was the top of a pyramid – a children's slide – in the same Mayan design I had seen reflected in the Picasso. With my heart all but lifting me off my seat, I looked back at the townhouse: back at the window that was level with the top of the slide. Elaine was being held in *that* room. She was tied up in *there*, with Kester and Victor, only one floor above where I had just been. As we turned a corner her window was gone, but her image remained. I pictured her on that screen, fighting to show me where she was.

No-neck was checking his rear view mirror, probably wondering what was up with me. I banged on the Plexiglas. 'Do you know why we're doing this?'

He shrugged a no idea. 'I find it best not to ask questions.'

Once this task is complete you will be free to be with Elaine. Would I? Was it that easy? Just appear, collect a case, and return for Elaine? I thought through everything that had happened to us since that fateful night in the park. Fear clutched at my stomach; a feeling of dread that grew with every yard that took me away from the townhouse.

Come on, Ed, think. Things are different now.

You know where she is.

* * *

Elaine McAdler wanted to die. Even before she had heard Ed's voice, she was imagining how she might do it; how she might somehow slip off her restraints and kill herself. She could no longer live with what she'd done to him.

Coming back to LA had been about her freedom; about their future together. She had even hoped her father had changed; that he might be sorry. Since a young girl she'd clung onto the hope that one day he'd give her a glimpse of a hidden goodness. Who knows, maybe even show her his approval; God forbid, affection, or love? He'd never been a proper father. She'd even grown up without his surname, becoming Needlam, like her mother. Kester didn't want either of them advertising the fact that they were related to him. He feared that his enemies might come after him in the same way he punished them; by hurting his family. That was about as close as he had ever come to showing he cared.

She had been taught to wall up her feelings. Ed had broken the walls down, found the real her, the girl behind the act. And the more she was herself the more he loved her for it. She had heard the emotion in his voice: *Elaine, can you hear me?* His love was unconditional, but now it was going to get him killed.

Returning to LA, she had been highly suspicious of her father's motives. She had assumed he wasn't bringing her back simply to put an end to Bruno's vendetta, but she had genuinely believed in his need to protect his reputation. She had agreed – if reluctantly – to become Claire Needlam once more on the strength of that belief.

Any shred of affection she had felt for her father had disappeared on the night he had killed her mother. But even then she couldn't hate him. He was her father. The hatred had come when he told her of his plans for Ed. How she'd been used as bait, not only to get Ed to LA, but to kill him. 'It seems he will do anything for you, Elaine,' her father had said, the slight smile on his lips. 'Even get himself blown up.'

Time stopped still as she heard those words; unable to move, unable to scream, all she could do was listen to her father's voice engraving his cruelty on her brain. 'As we speak, Edson is being driven to his death: not because of revenge; not even because I cannot have a daughter of mine marrying a black – though God knows it is reason enough – but because it is going to make me wealthy. I am doing it for money. Pure and simple. Thanks to you, I've had fifteen years off and my cash flow has suffered.'

I am doing it for money. That was bullshit! How could killing Ed be about money? There were a hundred ways he could have made money. No. It was about vengeance. She had been prepared to testify against him and now he wanted his revenge; his ego demanded it. Just as it demanded that he prove himself all over again: to the cops who had locked him away; to the criminal world; to Lincoln Heights.

Gagged and bound, Elaine looked at her father through different eyes; saw a man who used low-life and their fears to get things done. The buildings he owned; the people he protected; his insistence on living in Lincoln Heights; it was all about control. He had not a shred of humanity; the hidden goodness she had hoped to find had been a child's whimsy. She finally saw her father for what he was; an evil monster. And in those few moments, Elaine grew up.

If it *was* revenge, she couldn't think of a worse punishment. Using her to get to Ed. It was the thought of this that she couldn't live with. Having lost her mother, Elaine knew what it was like to lose someone she loved. But this would be worse. Far worse. This time there would be no justice, only guilt.

The last image Ed would have of her was being tied up, gagged, desperate, bursting with tears of regret. Even if he knew where she was; what could he do? It was more important that he knew how much she loved him; that she'd die for him if she could; that she'd kill for him in an instant.

She was probably being kept alive only until they were sure he was dead. After that they'd have no more use for her. She prayed that they were going to kill her.

Without Ed in her life, all she could hope for was death.

CHAPTER FIFTY-NINE

5.20pm
Downtown, Los Angeles.

The security cabin was on level three of the Parking Centre; a giant 24-hour car park that made money out of the mainly disused space on the south side of the empty river. Bored, the guard swivelled his chair to look at the monitors. Nothing moved. Reaching for a pretzel, he noticed a flash of white hair brush across his oval window. He put down his pretzel, turned down his mp3 player, and called out, 'Hey! Are you the dude from *Vision360?*'

'Sure am,' answered a high pitched voice. It belonged to the ageing man pushing open the door. He slid inside. 'And you are?'

'Hank.'

'Hi Hank,' the dude squeaked. 'So, this is your nerve centre?' He spoke in a weird accent and had wispy hair over circular, rose tinted specs.

'My what?' said Hank, swivelling his chair towards the white-haired man.

'Your voyeur's paradise.'

Hank's thin face folded. 'Huh?'

'The room with all the cameras.'

Confused, Hank shook his gel-ridden mop, started again. 'So you're here to like, check for blind spots?'

Ignoring the question, Victor Lapenza reopened the door and gazed out over the concrete monstrosity that was the LA river, then down at the Southern Pacific Railroad. 'Nice view,' he muttered sarcastically.

Returning to scan the security monitors, Victor quickly confirmed the presence of the parked up Dodge Charger.

Hank had sat forward, knees wide apart. 'We had a spot check recently, every car space is covered, dude.'

'I'm sure,' noted Victor, closing the door, his voice now unpleasantly dark, sinister. 'And what about in here, is this office covered?' he mocked. 'Is this office *like*, a blind spot, *dude?*'

Hank slid back, a look of confusion and terror contorting his face as a silenced bullet made a hole in the centre of his forehead. He collapsed, his chair slipped away, dumping him onto the floor. An oozing halo of blood began to colour his hair.

Stepping away from Hank's dead body, Victor nonchalantly pulled up a chair, fixed his eyes on the monitors.

Whilst waiting for the white Nissan, he meticulously wiped clear all incriminating evidence – excluding Hank's body – which mainly consisted of deleting all recordings of his presence. As he did so a monitor vied for his attention. A metallic blue Mercedes was parking worryingly close to the security cabin. Frustrated, Victor reached for his smoking Glock, and watched the driver emerge. As he walked over to the cabin, Victor headed out to meet him, his ingenuous smile failing to hide his surprise. 'To what do I owe the pleasure?'

'Come to watch your little movie,' shot the reply, as Al brushed past Victor and went into the cabin. He took Victor's chair, flicked a glance at Hank's dead body, and immediately picked out the silver Dodge.

Victor stood behind, peering over Al's completely hairless scalp. 'Everything is under control here,' he said.

'So I see.' Al crossed his legs, turned to Victor. 'Kester just wanted me to cast an eye over things. So, when are we expecting the Iranians?'

'Anytime soon,' replied Victor, double-checking the position of the camera that was set to record the exploding Edson Taylor.

'So, Victor' – Al's chair pivoted – 'while we're kicking back here, you have any idea who has hold of this formula?'

'Formula?' said Victor defensively. 'I don't know what you're talking about.'

'And I thought you held all the cards.'

Silence followed. Victor was unwilling to discuss the formula or anything else, but he sensed Al wasn't about to let it lie. He had met him several times and didn't trust the man. His name for one thing; *you can call me Al?* What was that all about? Victor knew Al's game; he was prodding him for information. It was all about Victor's responses. His *visual accessing clues* they were called, Victor had read about it. As long as he kept his eyes still, he'd be giving little away.

'The formula makes water poisonous by using sodium fluoride,' said Al, looking carefully his way.

Victor flicked his eyes 90 degrees right. *Damn!* That suggested auditory remembering; meaning Al was telling him nothing new. He schooled his expression to deadpan and waited for the next probe.

'The whole nation could be living in fear,' said Al. 'Too scared to drink, even take a bath. *Living like the Third World* was how I heard it put.' Once again, Al was watching Victor like a hawk. Not wanting to be caught out again, he turned away to look at the monitor, relieved to see a vehicle approaching. 'The Nissan is here,' said Victor.

Both men edged closer to the screen as the target slowly emerged from the back of the silver Dodge. As instructed, Edson Taylor had used the door to his right, showing him perfectly to the camera. *Part one over with*, thought Victor, *now I just need to detonate the bomb*.

Syrus Meybodi climbed from the Nissan holding the shiny case of explosives; a case that he had been led to believe contained money, but he'd had no way of checking. There was only one way to open it, with the remote detonator; the one that Victor's finger was hovering over. *This would do nicely*, he thought, *Edson Taylor is nearly in range*.

* * *

I stepped away from the Dodge Charger. The hustle and commotion of downtown LA pounded my ears, but there was no sight of it. My immediate location was flanked by concrete. To my left, we were parked up against a wall separating us from a drop; to my right, a multi-storey car park. By now I would have appeared on camera as Sadiq al-Barabi. I had done my job.

A Middle-Eastern man had stepped out of the Nissan, carrying the case. Handcuffs were attached; one cuff to the case, the other waiting for my wrist. He gave me disbelieving, intermittent glances. There was another man in the Nissan, also Middle-Eastern, wearing a concerned expression. It was disconcerting, but all I had to do was collect the case and return to the car.

Soon you will be free to be with Elaine.

But the dread I had felt in the car was increasing to screaming pitch. I had such a bad feeling, and every step heightened my fear. I wanted to believe Kester, to comply with his wishes, but I was rife with suspicion. All the bad things that had happened to me could be laid at his door.

The fear on Elaine's face had been real, and I knew where she was. What's more, *they* didn't know I knew.

As the man held out the case I hopped onto the Nissan's bonnet, leaping for the wall. But the wall never came, only blackness.

CHAPTER SIXTY

I opened my eyes. My body lay dormant, like a scrunched up ball of paper that had been flung into a waste bin. I was over the wall, down between tracks of a railway line. Scraps of metal surrounded me. Floating flames passed above, the smell of ash in their wake. A high-pitched ringing filled my ears. I feared for the others; for no-neck, and the driver of the Nissan. The recoil from the blast had lifted me over the concrete wall that had shielded me from the impact. A path of my blood was spread down the incline where I had slid.

Broken ribs delivered a stabbing pain as I tried to get onto my knees. I had been right to mistrust Kester. Now I had to get out of here; get to Elaine before he and the others got word that I had survived. It was clear to me now that my demise had been intended. It suddenly made sense. *I wasn't just a decoy, I was a sacrifice.* And I had another problem; the blooded, shredded cloth that hung from me served as a reminder that I was disguised as Sadiq al-Barabi. Soon the authorities would be swamping the area and would find me. I couldn't let that happen, but as I looked for an exit all hell broke loose. Another explosion cracked open my eardrums. I held my arms over my head as debris rained down on me.

The second car?

For a moment I heard nothing, then the crackling sound of fire. Rolling onto my stomach, I crawled along on my elbows and what was left of my knees. Flaming debris was all around, burning fumes catching up with my lungs. The ringing in my ears rose further until it became inaudible. Suddenly sirens and screams joined the foray.

Then gunfire.

Two bullets smacked into the concrete beside me, chips of stone spraying out to hit me in the face. My instinct for survival warred with my pain and won. I scrambled for cover. A bridge provided it. From there I drew breath, glanced back to the bombsite, from where the shots must have come.

A black cloud of smoke smothered the area and was pursuing me. Shuffling along a ledge I was startled by a mass of red hair surmounted by a baseball cap that rose from inside a large cardboard box. A homeless man, shaking, frail, confused. At that moment I was hidden, protected, but I had to move. The shooter would be closing in. But where could I go, caked in blood, practically naked?

I moved toward the hobo. 'Please Sir, I need your jacket.'

'So do I,' he sniped, swung an arm. 'Fuck off!'

'Listen to me. You hear those gunshots? If I don't get out of here we will both be dead, I need your jacket.'

He stepped over the box, coughing and pawing at me. 'Get your own.'

'I'm sorry.' I grabbed his shoulder pads and lifted the threadbare coat off his back. He curled into a ball and moaned as I swiped his baseball cap. 'Keep quiet and stay still,' I ordered him. 'Help will come.' I then placed the box over him before pulling on the coat and heading up the bank of concrete. Crawling up the slope, fear consumed me. Every part of my body cried out in pain and jittered with adrenalin.

People were on the bridge, screaming, pointing. *Where is that shooter?* Having reached the top of the incline I was out in the open, half expecting a bullet. Keeping low I scrambled for a hole in a wire fence. A man landed near me. He had jumped from the bridge. With one leg through the hole I witnessed him pick up his gun and get to his feet. It was Al, the bald man from the house, and he had me in his sights.

'Taylor!' he called out, levelling his gun and following me through the gap in the fence.

More screams. Unable to run, I threw myself into a row of bushes rolling through a gap onto a gravelled footpath. A police officer saw me, his presence forcing Al to take cover.

I gestured toward the bushes, cried, 'He's got a gun!'

As the burly officer took cover I slipped into a narrow alleyway. It was long, tunnel-like and took me between brick buildings. I emerged at the edge of a bustling street. The only sign I recognised read 'Chinatown'. The place was rush hour busy, but there was no blending into the background. Up the road, police had started to move people on. They were running, crying.

Footsteps joined me in the alley. I had to get out, fast, but without being recognised. *Your face is on the news.* I pulled hard at my beard but it came out in clumps, glue retaining fluff. With no time to remove it I tucked my chin into the coat and walked out into the street. My legs were bare, my knees bloody, skinless. I was soon drawing stares and screams. LAPD would be coming.

In front of me, a Chinese family were about to get into a taxi. They stepped to the side in shock as I limped forward. The father ushered them away, leaving the cab free. Sirens blazed as the emergency services continued to arrive.

I ducked into the taxi, kept my face down, hiding it under the peak of the cap.

'Hey,' the driver wailed. 'You bleeding? I can't drive you. Grab an ambulance.'

'I'm fine.' I glanced sideways, spotted Al emerging from the alley, his eyes darting.

'Get the hell out my car,' yelled the cabbie. His fervent gesticulating demanded Al's attention.

Then Al saw me.

CHAPTER SIXTY-ONE

'Drive!' I screamed at the cabbie. 'I've got a gun.'

He sprang into action. 'Okay, be cool,' he pleaded. 'Don't hurt me Mister, please, I've got kids.'

As we pulled into the road, Al was left standing on the pavement, calling after me. He knew I had survived, and therefore, so would Kester. I had to get to Elaine, but the driver was eyeballing his mirror. He had other ideas. 'My God, you're that man,' he shouted.

I panicked. Ramming two fingers into the back of his seat, I warned, 'Just get me out of here or I *will* shoot you.'

He rounded his shoulders, cowering as he drove. Seconds later: 'There's a problem. They've blocked Spring Street. Looks like a police check-point.'

Up ahead I saw a road block, police stopping all cars and pedestrians. I couldn't fall into custody, not looking like this. There wasn't time to explain things to the police. My only advantage was that I knew where Elaine was. Soon she could be gone. Or worse. *Daughter or not, after Elaine's betrayal I could kill her in an instant.*

'Pull over,' I ordered. I had no choice but to exit the taxi.

The relieved driver obliged, screeching away before my door was shut, probably to alert the cops.

Now, sixty yards from the bombsite – forty from the check-point – the street was being evacuated, emptying of cars and people. I needed to think, but first I had to get out of sight. I ducked under a red and white awning, scanned for inspiration. Chinatown was awash with colour; lanterns and neon waiting to come to life. All shops at street level, housing above. One lot up, I noticed a restaurant and slipped inside.

'Blue Dragon closed, Sir,' informed a sturdy Chinese man with a side parting, blue jeans and a white smock. He stood back, gawped quizzically and stated the obvious, 'You hurt.'

Thankfully he didn't recognise me. 'Do you have a restroom I can use, clean myself up?'

'You need Doctor.'

I spread open my hands. 'I've no insurance. Please, I just need a minute.'

'Doctor, still help you.'

'If they treat me, they will deport me. Please.'

'No Visa?' His eyes widened, he looked again at my tattered clothing. Nodded; 'Upstairs, left side.'

'Thank you.' I staggered past the open kitchen. A large woman was chopping peppers, oblivious to me and the mayhem outside. Ascending the stairs, I looked back, praying they weren't calling the cops. I had to stop the bleeding and find some clothes. If I was to get out of Chinatown, it wouldn't be looking like this.

Once in the restroom, I eased the jacket off what skin remained on my left side. Every breath I took bit into my ribs, but I was lucky to be alive. I unwound the cloth towel from the wall, used it to pat my wounds. It was no use. I placed a foot against the wall and pulled hard, ripping the cloth from the wall. I then proceeded to wrap the towel around my ribs, tied it as tightly as I could. Ignoring the pain, I slid the jacket back on. Then I heard voices. Somebody had entered the restaurant.

The cops? Al?

Not taking chances, I crept out onto the balcony and peeked down through staircase spindles – recognised Al's smooth scalp and shaped beard. His narrow, suited frame rose and fell with exhaustion. He must have seen me ditching the taxi. Al held up a picture, got no reaction, until he reached for a back pocket and pulled out a form of ID. Suddenly the mood changed and a finger pointed up to the restroom.

Shifting myself along the balcony, I headed upward, to the third floor. My lungs rattled with ash. Several doors greeted me. I had to hide. I chose an office. After pushing a desk against the door I moved across to the window. Below, the people of Chinatown were being dwindled away, escorted into a bottleneck of fear and confusion amid the police barrier. The area to my right – near the bombsite – was now vacant but for bright uniforms and an assembling posse of hand held cameras. I yanked at the window hatch. It unlocked, but even without broken ribs, there was no getting down from this height. Not without being seen or risking death.

I saw a figure emerge, ghostlike from across the road, wiped disbelief from my eyes. It was Victor, going from building to building, pursuing me; his white hair flapping as he stooped to peer into every window. But I had a more pressing problem. Al was right on my tail. Soon he'd find the office and wonder why it was jammed. Fumbling for an object to use as a weapon, a telephone grabbed my attention. With my situation desperate, I thought about calling the FBI, but Elaine's safety dissuaded me. I couldn't risk being taken into custody. Given Kester's influence, trusting the FBI to save Elaine would have to be a last resort.

Think Ed. *Think*.

I noticed a menu on the desk. A voice popped into my head: *A smile will gain you ten more years of life.* Trembling, I pressed the keys, called the operator, asked for the LA office of the *Chinese Daily News*. I held as they connected me, then dialled 251, and asked for John.

CHAPTER SIXTY-TWO

I was trapped in the office, barricaded in by my own stupidity. I should have kept moving, but I'd opted to hide. And now floorboards creaked, alerting me to a presence outside the door. The handle turned, but wouldn't open. The door bowed; the desk held firm with my weight behind it. I lifted a lamp off the table, raised it above my head, and waited.

'This door.' It sounded like Al. 'Why's it locked?'

'It is office,' fired up an angry reply from the floor below. 'Listen Mister, the police are here. They asking for everyone to leave.'

The steps quickened; the police presence seemingly enough to remove Al. There was hot-footing everywhere, people passing on the stairs.

Then: A soft tap on the door. 'He's gone,' a voice spoke. Chinese accented. 'Quick, we must go, *now*, before police up here.'

Taking a leap of faith, I dropped the lamp, dragged back the desk, and opened the door. The sturdy restaurateur stood there with another man, slightly taller; his thick dyed orange hair came up to my chin. Struggling for breath, he introduced himself as Chang. Carrying a black hold-all and an expression of panic, he spoke to the restaurateur, 'Lee, keep the bald man away.'

Lee protested, 'But his ID? It say he CIA!'

They argued in native tongue, repeating the word *jingcha*. Then Chang turned to me. 'Follow me, Mr Edson.'

Mr Edson! From that moment I knew my call had succeeded. At first John Yeung had sounded stunned, but my talk of Kester Hardwick being behind the bomb – and being Elaine's father – had appealed to the journalist in him. By the time I'd finished talking, he'd sounded eager to help. He had sent Chang to my aid.

I followed Chang out onto a fire exit that dropped between buildings. Grimacing with each step, I struggled to keep pace. Left foot, right foot. Gravity, fear. There was no sign of Al. No sign of anyone. We reached the ground and entered a side door. I followed Chang through a wine cellar, tugging down my bloodied trousers and pulling the baseball cap low to my eyebrows. Still no one around. We moved into a kitchen, then into a small laundry room. Condensation hung in the air. Chang unzipped his bag, pulled out white chef's trousers and a navy waiter's jacket. 'Put these on,' he said, 'or anything else you can find. Yeung is on his way, he wants to meet you on Ord Street, outside the Jade Pavilion. In the meantime, wait here.'

I nodded, discarded the threadbare coat. 'How will he recognise me?'

Chang looked hard at me. 'You serious?'

I almost smiled, shook my head. It hurt.

'Yeung requested that I clothe you,' said Chang. 'Help you get out of here.'

'Thank you. You're a life saver.'

'Don't mention it.' Chang shrugged, 'Yeung reviews my food,' he said it as if it explained everything. He then left the damp room, locking me in.

With nothing better to wear, I pulled up the chef's trousers, biting into my lip to mask the pain. They barely covered my knees, and the jacket wasn't much better. I heard ripping as I buttoned it over my strapped up ribs. I looked like I'd been dipped in a charity shop. With my beard finally removed and ill-fitting clothes on, I wondered how much I still resembled Sadiq al-Barabi.

The door flew open. Chang was back, his face fearful, panting. He looked me up and down, apologised, 'Sorry 'bout the gear, they were all I could grab.'

I shrugged – painful error.

Lee joined us, closed the door. 'Baldy not hang around for police, but he be back. You better leave.'

Chang inhaled. 'Follow me. You have to meet Yeung, and it won't be easy. The Jade Pavilion is on the other side of the police line.'

A sound coming from the front of the building stopped us short. We stood in silence as a door closed. A deep voice echoed off the walls, 'LAPD, who's in there?'

CHAPTER SIXTY-THREE

Chang put a finger to his lips. 'Just me back here,' he said, nervously stepping out from the laundry room and into the kitchen. 'I'm Head Chef. I know I must leave, but food will go off if I don't prep these—'

'You must leave, immediately. We're doing a thorough sweep of all buildings.'

'OK, OK, I leave now,' said Chang.

Beep. A police-radio spluttered into life. Lee and I listened; exchanged glances as it crackled out an ominous message: *We have an IC6 sighted in Chinatown, possibly Sadiq al-Barabi. Proceed with caution.*

Lee's eyes were frantic, looking at me for answers.

'You might want to start upstairs,' advised Chang, attempting to stall the cop. 'The couple who rent the top floor are still up there.'

'No. I'll start down here.' Footsteps indicated that he was heading for the laundry room.

I tip-toed to the back door; through frosted glass I could make out a path running behind the buildings and a cluster of garbage bins by the door. I motioned Lee over, carefully opened the back door and invited Lee through. I followed, pushing him out. The door closed silently behind us. Keeping my back to the wall, I shuffled up against a drain pipe. Lee was already on his knees next to a large garbage bin. Twenty yards to our left was a cop with his back to us. He was walking towards another man with BOMB SQUAD stamped on his jacket. If either of them looked back we were screwed. I dropped down, joining Lee beside the bin. It shielded us from the large crowd gathered behind a police perimeter at the wide end of the alley. Any forward movement and we'd be seen. At the yellow and red police tape, a lone officer stood between us and the many frightened faces crammed in, eager for answers.

'We have no choice,' Lee whispered. 'You must go to police.'

'I can't.'

Lee tugged on my arm. 'But we hiding from law. This bad.'

'Listen, *please*, a woman's life is in serious danger. I need to get to her before I'm taken into custody, otherwise... Look, I don't have time to explain, but

I can't trust the police. The bald man who told you he was CIA is the one who shot at me.'

'But Mister, people recognise you, you on news. How you get to Pavilion building?'

'You have to trust me. I'm not who you think. Please, just tell me where the Jade Pavilion is? I have to meet John Yeung.'

He sighed an answer; nodded at the police tape, 'Behind people. Over there, across road.'

Lee was agitated; on the verge of turning me in. Needing him back on-side, I pleaded with him, my gaze never leaving the patrolling cop to our left. 'That bomb was meant to kill me,' I said, easing myself carefully out of the navy jacket and rolling it up as I spoke. 'I will call the authorities, I swear, but the minute I step out I will be arrested, or shot. They will see me as someone else.' The cop reached the end of the path and stopped. 'I have a plan. But I *need* your help.' I begged, 'Please.'

Chapter Sixty-Four

Apparently giving way to my plea, Lee reluctantly stepped out into the alley, moseyed towards the police tape and was soon in conversation with the cop manning the perimeter.

Come on Lee. Don't fail me now.

Just as I'd suggested, Lee stood crowd-side, keeping the cop's eyes away from me. I removed the baseball cap, screwed it up in the jacket, waited for my cue.

Do it, Lee. Make it loud. *Make it believable.*

Suddenly I wondered if it would work; if enough of the crowd spoke English?

Lee glanced into the alley, cried out, 'SUICIDE BOMBER!' Gasps became screams as I made a mad dash toward the police tape, running on adrenalin, carrying the bundled jacket in front of me as though it shielded a weapon.

By the time the officer turned around and pulled his gun on me I had stepped over the tape and was immersed in the crowd. Into chaos. Half the population of Chinatown scattered as panic ripped through the streets. Cowering down, I put on the cap, bent the peak forward, and draped the jacket over my shoulders. Head down, arms folded for protection, I drove through the pandemonium, stumbling, bouncing off bodies. Staying low and using the public as cover I zigzagged my way across the road. The corner of the block was soon in range. My hands shielding my face, I glanced up at the most prominent building in the area; saw the slanting roof rising ahead. A modern signpost read, THE JADE PAVILION.

People were pointing, hollering into phones.

I looked around. *Where is he?*

I didn't have long to wait before a car beeped. Bodies fled, revealing John Yeung sitting behind the wheel. He'd done it; delivered my wheels out of here. He leaned across. The car door swung open.

I fell in, tucked my legs under the glove box. John Yeung pumped the brakes and accelerator, learner driver style. More beeping. He yelled wildly, removing pedestrians from our path. Masses of them; crying, screaming, panicking. As we eased our way through the melee, I looked over at John Yeung. His jocular smile was missing. I was under no illusion about why he was helping me – his big break could have arrived. But first, he had to get me out of Chinatown.

'Thank you, John, you took a risk for me,' I croaked, still out of breath.

He nodded, clipped a kerb. 'You right. This risky. But one not refuse food because chance of choking.'

As the people faded, the roads busied and we left the blaring sirens behind.

By the time we joined the Interstate, I felt at last as though things were going my way. The traffic was backed up, but we were moving. I asked John if he knew where Lincoln Park was, and if he'd take me there. He answered: 'Yes,' and 'No.' He asked if I was able to drive, pointed out a sign for North Main Street, saying it would take me under the I5 and on to Lincoln Park. Except that we were heading in the opposite direction. John was anxious for me to find my own wheels. Clearly, he wanted me gone. It wasn't personal, he told me, but he was sure that I'd been seen, and the rarity of his imported Chinese car was concerning him. John was scared, out of his depth, desperate to ditch me before we were stopped. I couldn't blame him.

I began to worry that he was thinking about turning me in. I had already given him enough for his news story.

'Where are we going?' I asked, grimacing with pain that I could no longer hide.

'Next exit, I get you car.' He flashed a concerned look. 'Then you should go hospital, Mr Edson.'

'Not until I have Elaine with me.'

'You really believe Kester Hardwick would kill own daughter?'

'Absolutely. I've witnessed him kill, and I know he murdered his wife – Elaine's mother.'

John looked sideways at me. Something was bugging him.

'You don't believe me?'

'Another Chinese saying,' he said. 'Vicious as tigress is, she not eat own cubs.'

'I only hope you're right, John.'

With no sign of being followed we left Interstate 10; John firing questions about my relationships with Sadiq al-Barabi and Kester Hardwick. He looked bewildered, almost disbelieving, but curiosity kept him on-side.

He parked outside a Marriott hotel, in a two-space waiting-bay. 'Wait here, Mr Edson, Hotel has Hertz. Now I get you car.'

He left me alone with my thoughts. Deciding I had no choice but to trust him, I kept my head down; waited impatiently.

It was a long two minutes before he returned, handing me a set of keys and pointing out a yellow Chevrolet at the end of an adjacent parking bay. 'It is automatic; you can steer with right hand.' He then passed me his cell-phone. 'You know my office number. Good luck with Elaine.'

'Thank you, John. I owe you.'

* * *

332 / JOHN BAIRD

I got back onto Interstate 10 and scanned for North Main Street. The traffic crawled along. I was fearful of being recognised as Sadiq al-Barabi, but my fellow drivers seemed too tired or frustrated to notice. Whoever called it 'rush-hour' must have done so ironically. My broken ribs weren't complaining about the enforced rest.

Driving the Chevrolet Aveo to Kester's Lincoln Park townhouse, events since that fateful night in the park flashed through my mind. My thoughts soon turned to Sam. Had he survived? What shreds of life I had left amounted to nothing without him and Elaine. Defeat and desperation rode with me. I had no plan, no real hope, and no choice. I had to get to Elaine.

I turned on the radio. News of the explosion dominated the airways: *three fatalities*. My neck-less chauffeur? The Middle-Eastern men? Their deaths were my fault. If I hadn't agreed to the plan they would still be alive. I knew I had a duty to warn someone about my brother, and Kester. Help to stop them all. But how? Giving up Kester's location would be putting Elaine in danger. I just wasn't prepared to do it. I couldn't.

CHAPTER SIXTY-FIVE

As information of the explosion trickled in, Donnie Guzan mulled things over. He reached across and retrieved the witness reports; the sightings of Sadiq al-Barabi, shook his head at Tyler Derego. 'Sadiq al-Barabi isn't a suicide bomber.'

Derego nodded in agreement, 'But you still don't think that it was Sadiq al-Barabi?'

'No, I don't. The taxi-driver said he had a British accent. Come on Tyler, you saw Edson Taylor as clearly as I did. There's every chance the man identified in Chinatown was him. The suicide bomber rumour was just a ruse, to get out of the extended perimeter.'

Agent Beasley peered round the door of the small office, 'I've an update on the car,' he said. 'The Chery belongs to John Yeung, a reporter for the *Chinese Daily News*. Sure looks like he was the guy driving away from Ord Street. He's Chinese-American, has no record. As for your theory, Don, the Unit say early analysis concurs that the man identified near ground zero could be Edson Taylor. Whoever it was, they also believe he paraded as a suicide bomber to vacate the scene. Looks like John Yeung helped him.'

Guzan tried not to look too smug. 'OK, we need to know what connects John Yeung to Edson Taylor, *or* Sadiq al-Barabi.'

'We're working on it,' said Beasley.

'Good.' Guzan clenched his fist, bounced it on the desk. 'Pull up all traffic surveillance in a twenty-mile radius, and find that Chery Crossover.'

'Will do. One other thing,' noted Beasley. 'Preliminary analysis confirms that two of the victims are Syrus Meybodi and Ali Afshari. Sure strengthens the link with Sadiq al-Barabi.'

With the investigation suddenly moving at pace, Guzan took a moment to reflect on the death of the Iranians; if they hadn't evaded his surveillance they could be alive right now.

The phone buzzed, a voice informing Guzan that Ethan Knight was on line two. He took the call. Knight wasted no time. '$400,000 was just wired to a bank in the Cayman Islands, to an account that we traced to Kester Hardwick.'

Before Guzan could respond, line three lit up. 'Hang on, Ethan, got another call.' It was Agent Reinbeck at the Unit. 'We have a call from a man claiming to be Edson Taylor. He's asking to speak to you.'

'Fine,' encouraged Guzan. *Promising, Taylor's name had not yet been released.* 'Are we online for triangulation?'

'Affirmative,' said Reinbeck, confirming that the call's origin could be traced.

Guzan waited for it to click through, said, 'This is Special Agent Guzan.'

The voice on the other end sounded shaken 'I'm calling because I might not survive this and there are things you should know.'

'I'm listening,' said Guzan, nodding his satisfaction that the voice belonged to Edson Taylor. He thought he could hear a car shifting through the gears. Was Taylor driving – or being driven?

'When you questioned me, you wanted to know about Kester Hardwick.'

'Yes, where are you?'

'That doesn't matter,' dismissed Taylor.

A car beeped in the background. Guzan checked to make sure he wasn't the only one hearing it. 'Then what can I do for you?'

'A man named Sadiq al-Barabi – my twin brother – paid Kester Hardwick to arrange today's bomb, the purpose of which was to kill me. I was meant as a decoy to make you think my brother was dead. Two other men are involved, one called Victor, and a man who said I could call him Al. Both men were near the bombsite. One of them shot at me, probably Al. He had identification on him; CIA.'

Immediately, Guzan suspected Victor Lapenza; a plastic surgeon known for high prices and low ethics, but the other man? 'Describe this Al for me?'

'Bald, kind of a goatee beard, just under six foot, fiftyish, medium build.'

Guzan's shut his eyes. 'Anything else about him?'

'He wore a charcoal suit, was nervous looking. Oh, and he had twitchy eyes.'

It could only be Felix Proudlock. Shaking his head, Guzan said, 'Do you know where any of these men are now?'

'Maybe,' replied Taylor. 'They were at a place Kester called his *refugio seguro*; does that mean anything to you?'

Guzan knew what it meant, but wanting to keep Taylor on the phone, he hedged, 'Not sure. Can you tell me where it is?'

'I can't say. Not yet. Not until I know Elaine is safe.'

Exasperated, Guzan snapped, 'I'm sorry, I assumed you'd called me because you wanted to help?'

'I do. I called you because we've met and you know my voice. And because I wanted you to know who was behind the bomb. For all I know they could be planning another.'

'What makes you say that?'

'Isn't Sadiq a terrorist?'

'He is. So it's vital that you tell us what you know, failure to do so will—'

Taylor cut across him, 'Sorry, I don't know much more and I have to go.'

'Did you hear anything about a formula?' tried Guzan.

'No,' Taylor replied firmly. 'Good luck, Agent Guzan.'

'If you're trying to protect Elaine, tell me where––' The line went dead.

Guzan hit the interphone. 'Have we got him?'

'He's on the move,' said Reinbeck, 'just waiting on his location.'

Guzan opened line two. 'Knight, did you get all that?'

'I did. And I know what you're thinking; that this Al is Felix Proudlock, but––'

'Dammit, Ethan, one of yours all along,' said Guzan, angry with himself for doubting his colleagues; for excluding them. *Certain information has been leaking.*

'I still don't believe it,' Knight argued. 'We don't even know Edson Taylor was telling the truth. What's this *refugio seguro?*'

'It's Spanish; means safe house.'

'Figures,' retorted Knight, then, 'Taylor could be working with Hardwick; trying to confuse us. And we have no way of knowing he's not in cahoots with his brother.'

Guzan knew that Knight was right, but his instincts told him that Taylor was not a terrorist. 'He rang us remember; and his finger is pointing at a CIA official.'

'Or somebody impersonating one,' said Knight. 'But rest assured; we'll find Proudlock.'

Line three cut in. 'Edson Taylor's last signal came from Valley Boulevard, Lincoln Heights.'

CHAPTER SIXTY-SIX

Sat at lights, waiting to turn into Lincoln Park, I closed my eyes on the glare of the evening sun, saw it imprinted on my eyelids.

I began to wonder if I was right to call Agent Guzan. Maybe not, but my conscience had given me no option. Not after seeing the lengths Kester and his mob were prepared to go to. Guzan had seemed an OK guy; it was up to him what he did with the information. It was one less thing for me to worry about. Now I could focus on Elaine.

I opened my eyes just in time to turn into the park. Once inside the entrance, I located a small parking area. A handful of jalopies were lined up, not a hubcap in sight. This part of the park was quiet, the area behind the cars shadowed by bordering pine trees. Hopefully any vultures hiding in them would be more interested in the hired Chevrolet than in me.

Climbing out of the air-conditioned car, I felt the evening humidity drain my exhausted body. Restricted by broken ribs and the moistureless air, my lungs were dry to the point of collapse. I felt under my jacket, loosened the towel that strapped my chest. Like a soldier preparing for battle, I carefully adjusted my clothing, straightened out my short white trousers, fixed my baseball cap, and checked the glove protecting my bandaged hand. The pain in my hand was comforting; serving as a reminder that I had been up against it before, and survived. And not just with Kester's help, I reminded myself, for I had avoided his bomb. But my body was beyond tired. I was forced to rely on adrenalin; for one last effort. For Elaine.

I set off. *Now, Go seek!* Ahead, a brick building – housing a swimming pool – displayed a large map of the park, informing me that I was 100 yards from the Mayan pyramid. There was no point in planning my route; I would have to go unseen. And dressed in bloodstained clothing, it wouldn't be enough just to hide my face.

Slipping past the swimming pool, I noticed the baseball diamond was deserted. Keeping low, I made my way though the area, using the shelter of an occasional tree to catch my breath. Eventually, I reached a manmade lake with what looked like a boathouse on the far side. From my new position, I could see the top of the pyramid. A group of people were about to mount a giant pedalo, but I had to continue in the hope that I would be ignored. Not checking if I had been seen, I followed the path around the side of the lake until I reached the outskirts of the play area. Now I had sight of Kester's house and the window of the room where Elaine had been held. I wanted desperately to climb the pyramid, to peer into that window, but a couple of teenagers were mounting the slide.

The townhouse was part of a row of six, each consisting of three stories, every window lifeless. *Maybe I'm too late.* Despair gripped me by the throat. Then I saw movement at the third floor window. It was Victor; he had his back to me, but even from this distance I could make out his narrow frame and wispy hair. Never did I think I'd be pleased to see the man from my nightmares, but I was. Seeing Victor meant that I might not be too late. Elaine could still be in there.

Staying close to the play area's wooden fence, I edged nearer to the road. The front of the house was too open. Could I break in from the back? Tall trees lined the border of the park. Keeping under their shadow, I followed the road past Kester's house and waited for a quiet moment to cross.

Once at the rear of the house, I hung back and positioned myself behind a neighbour's fence. I could see Skid lounging against the back door. I pulled back, suddenly aware I had no idea what I was going to do next. I'd had a wild notion of getting in unseen and somehow carrying Elaine out. *Stupid!* Squinting through the fence, I saw past

Skid, to the external concrete stairs and metal fire escape. Possible routes in? Maybe I was deluded, but if I could just pull myself onto the escape I might be able to force open a window. *Worth a try.* But I needed to avoid Skid – *or silence him.*

My search for something to use as a weapon took me up a residential side street signposted Park View. I went as far as I could before the quiet street became visible to Skid. Still no potential weapon. Using a garage as cover, I entered the back of a garden, saw a birdhouse sat on a wooden post. With my arm wrapped around the post, I bent my knees and pulled it from the ground. My ribs protested. Silencing the escaping moan, I checked that I hadn't been seen, removed the birdhouse and carried the post back with me.

The realisation that these could be my final breaths gave me pause. I took a moment to myself. I had run out of fear. Sadness was my shadow, desperation my friend. I had nothing more to lose.

Hyped-up, I puffed out my cheeks and prepared to make my move towards the rear entrance: towards Skid. My mouth was so dry I couldn't begin to swallow.

The post was easily heavy enough to knock him out. So what if it was too heavy to run with; so what if my left hand was refusing to cooperate? I convinced myself that I had enough of a grip to wield the thing over Skid's bony skull and smash his daylights out.

I took a step towards him, felt a sharp nudge in the centre of my back. Froze.

Before I could swing round, a voice hissed: 'Don't make a sound. This is a .22 calibre revolver. Now, slowly place the wooden stake down on the ground.'

I did as instructed.

'Good. You have escaped death once today, you will not be lucky again, *brother.*'

Chapter Sixty-Seven

Every few steps the revolver prodded my spine, coaxing me back along the side street, away from Elaine. Thirty yards up, Sadiq ordered me to stop. We were alongside the back of an old, rust-affected van that poked out of an equally beaten-up garage. A hand searched me from behind, before shoving me into the back of the van. The door clanged shut behind me.

It was empty, but for the smell of gasoline warmed up by the heat that hung around relentlessly. I turned, tried to open the doors, but the van was locked. I peered out of a back window. We were high up. I could see Kester's townhouse; the place he called *refugio seguro*. Skid was patrolling the rear like a rabid guard dog. Then I saw my twin for the first time in the flesh. He was on his knees in the garage, bending over an inspection pit. The cover, a sheet of rusty metal was shoved to one side. He leaned over the pit, delved inside and pulled out a bag. Another bomb? He unzipped it. Before I could see what was inside, he quickly closed it up again and lowered it back into the pit. Then he stood, replaced the cover and kicked dirt over it before turning towards the van.

The door opened. Sadiq, my brother, trained his gun on me and ducked into the van. 'Sit down,' he said, slamming the doors behind him.

I dropped to the floor. He bent forward, staring at me. I read disgust in his eyes. He shook his head; sat down opposite me, cross-legged. He was wearing loose-fitting, black denim jeans and a brown vest. Pink scars covered his arms; lacerations like barcodes.

He pushed his gun away, sliding it noisily along the van's floor. It came to rest against the side, an equal distance from us both. I looked at him. Our features were the same but seemed to work differently; he had masked his disgust, the emotion on his face was unreadable. His brown gaze travelled slowly down to my bloodied left side.

'Show me,' he said, his voice a gravely, slightly accented version of my own.

I lifted my jacket, revealing the gash over my hip. Planting his hands down, he edged toward me transfixed, his head tilting, animal-like. Then he pounced. I raised my arms for protection, but he spun me round in an instant, crashing our bodies against the van. I was face down, my shoulders about to snap. Physically we should have been matched, but even without my injuries, I knew I was grossly inferior. Not able to loosen his grip I was confronted with extreme pain as he dug his fingers deep into my wound. When he released the pressure, the pain barely eased. Doubled over, I managed to sit up and face him. He was back against the doors, once more cross-legged, carefully inspecting the blood on his fingers as he spoke, 'You were meant to die for me. If I hear you speak or make so much as a whimper, I will hurt you. *Badly.*'

Taunted and tempted by the revolver, I glanced at it in frustration. With my energy dedicated to my breathing, there was no way I could beat him to the gun. He knew it; it was a refinement of his torture.

His glare was already back, enjoying my suffering. 'The nature/nurture debate has always interested me,' he said. 'Take identical twins, one born to Africa, to poverty and abuse, the other given a typical Western upbringing. No surprise then that one achieves great wealth, power and importance. And the other is weak, destined to lead a worthless existence. I had always wondered what if my shoes had been on your feet, would you have taken my path? Our mother could choose only one of us. Now I see why she chose me. You were the runt.'

What was he talking about? Through a red mist of pain I watched his unsettlingly familiar features. My only defence was to remain silent. As he continued to spew out his resentment, I kept quiet. Thinking.

'I'm told the only thing of meaning in your life is a woman.' He looked pityingly at me. 'Sudan gave me strength, success living off weak men like you. Fearful men. But fear is life. Pain is living. Before I had Gary Jasper killed, I gifted him the experience of fear and pain. It was his punishment, Sudan style, for the way he treated our mother.'

I thought of our father's cross-amputation, held onto my questions.

'I only wish I could have been there,' he rued. 'Maybe your turning up brings a second opportunity.'

I stayed quiet. Driven by anger, I twisted, glancing again at the gun. Intense shooting pains emanated from my nervous system.

'You want my revolver,' noted Sadiq. '*Now* you want to fight. To *kill?*' he laughed. 'There is hope for you yet, my brother.' Vigour entered his voice. 'I've a thought. On offer is the chance to redeem yourself; to prove your worth.'

He studied me for a reaction. Did he expect me to plead? I gazed into his eyes, schooling my face to stillness. Sadiq shrugged, broke eye contact. It was a tiny victory.

'I have possession of a bag containing half-a-million US dollars. In return for this money, Kester has a chemical formula that has been acquired for me. Unfortunately, after today's mishap my trust in him has diminished to the extent that I am no longer prepared to wire him the money. Aware of this, Kester has sent me a text message asking me to meet him at his *refugio seguro*; to bring the money in unmarked bills. Only now I find that you also know of this place. And in my mind that renders the venue unsafe – despite its pretentious name.'

As Sadiq continued his voice lightened, 'It is better that I get hold of the formula *before* he gets his money. That is where you can now be of help. You can enter that building – as you were already intending to do – and ask for my formula. Tell him we are now in collusion. *Brothers together*. You are the middleman. When you have the formula, he will get his payment. It will be amusing to fool him into thinking I have cut you in on the deal; that against all the odds we have discovered a bond,' he smiled, added, 'that blood is indeed thicker than water.'

When I remained silent, he said, 'You can nod your interest?'

Getting out of the van alive was enough to interest me, but a dilemma gnawed at my gut. *Can I bring myself to help this man?* The risks of abetting terrorism echoed inside my head. *What is this formula?* Warnings came in stereo, pulling me in opposite directions. But right now, getting inside Kester's house was the priority.

I nodded.

'Good,' he said. 'It was always my intention for your destiny to assist mine. This gives us a second chance.' He nodded, as if he believed it was all fated. 'Just to be clear, the money stays here until you bring me my formula. Then I'll hand you the bag. It's up to you what you do with it. Tell me now. Will you help? Or do I get to hurt you?'

CHAPTER SIXTY-EIGHT

6.40pm
Lincoln Park, Los Angeles.

Victor Lapenza inched up his shades, looked out over the park. He was worried, half expecting the Feds at any moment. Edson Taylor knew of their location, and that put them at risk.

He turned to his boss, who was standing beside him puffing on a cigar. 'We should make a move Kester, Taylor could have talked.'

'You sound as paranoid as Skid.'

'Oh?'

'He asked to man the rear. He's also worried about company, but we're safe here,' argued Kester. 'Taylor has other priorities; he won't talk.'

'And what of the formula?' said Victor. 'Is that safe?'

'I detect concern in your voice. Do you not trust me?'

'Not concern. Confusion,' he admitted, removing his sunglasses, waving them at Kester. 'Are you really intending to give this formula to Sadiq al-Barabi? I only ask because I'm not sure mass murder is what either of us wants.'

'Relax. Terrorism is not my style,' reassured Kester. 'The formula is deadly, no question, but Sadiq will be dead before he gets to use it, sell it, or whatever else he has planned for it. It's purely business, Victor, just like when we got three-hundred-thousand bucks for freeing him and four-hundred-thousand for delivering his brother. Only this time Sadiq gives us half a million and we kill him.'

'But then what are we going to do with the formula? I mean, if we never intended for Sadiq to have it, why have it developed in the first place?'

'Knowledge is power my friend. We don't have to use the formula; its mere possession is enough. We could expose a major government con.' He turned to Victor, smiled, 'Think of it as my insurance against them ever coming after me again.'

The intercom clicked in, the sneer in Skid's voice audible: 'Edson Taylor's here looking like a bomb's hit him. Apparently, he has a *deal* for you.'

Perturbed, Victor eyed the security monitor; waited as the images rotated. The entranceway appeared, Skid blocking the dishevelled frame of Edson Taylor.

Kester withdrew his cigar. 'Search him.'

As Skid reached up to frisk me, the smell of stale tobacco seeped from his pea-sized pores. His yellow teeth were grinding back and forth, sniffling and spitting out air with all the charm of a skin tag.

Once satisfied I was unarmed, he led me up the concrete stairway and inside the safe house.

I was pushed through to a front room. Victor was there. Without his tinted glasses I saw his small, green eyes for the first time, his gaze darting between a window and a monitor that was set into the wall. Kester was with him, his grey suit and hair unruffled. He waved a cigar at me, beckoned me inside as if he was welcoming a valued guest. 'The next words out of your mouth will be your last, so choose them carefully.'

I glanced upward, tried to swallow. Was Elaine still in the room above? From somewhere I dredged up a confident smile. 'If I don't walk out of here alive, you can say goodbye to my brother's money.'

For the first time I saw a hint of uncertainty in Kester's stony, blue eyes. Slowly swinging his body down into a leather seat, he sucked in air. 'You have my attention.'

'I am acting for Sadiq al-Barabi.'

Acting being the word, I thought ruefully. Being the middleman on my twin's behalf was gut-churning. My voice was shaky, and so were my hands.

I bit my lip and continued, 'Sadiq's waiting outside. He wants you to give me the formula. Once he has it, you will get your money.'

'What do you know about a formula?' said Victor.

'Like I just said, my broth—'

'Yes, your brother's outside,' interjected Kester coolly. 'Only Sadiq doesn't know of this address. Do you really expect me to believe that you two hooked up and you somehow led him here?'

'He was already here,' I protested, recalling what Sadiq had said, *Kester sent me a text message, asking me to meet him here.* 'And now he wants his formula. He said that if you kill me, you can forget about your half a million.' What little moisture I had left trickled down the small of my back as I watched Kester frown.

He wagged his cigar at me, half-smiled. 'I admire your persistence, Edson. This is a stunt to save Elaine. Sadiq al-Barabi is not outside, is he?'

'Then how do I know about the formula?'

Victor stooped down with short breaths. 'If he didn't get this information off Sadiq, we have to assume he got it elsewhere; the Feds must be on to us. Are you sure this place is safe?'

'Relax,' said Kester, brushing him away. 'OK, Edson. Let's say you are telling the unlikely truth that the brother, who wanted you blown to pieces, is now employing you as a middleman,' he spoke as though he were humouring a recalcitrant child. 'Those conditions are impossible. We don't deal without money up front. Sadiq knows that.'

'He no longer trusts you. And those conditions are not the only ones.' I paused, stared hard at him. 'I have my own condition. *Elaine.* She leaves with me.'

Kester smiled. 'It is as I thought; you clearly possess a suicidal infatuation with my daughter.'

His smile stayed. 'And you assume she's alive.' He crossed his legs.

I controlled the urge to plead with him.

'Say I agree to your demands,' he said. 'Do you really think your brother will simply hand over the money? The moment he gets that formula he will be gone. And you will be dead.'

Victor's eerie voice waded in, 'Sadiq won't spare your life; no more than he spared your father's.'

Victor was expecting a reaction. I disappointed him. 'Sadiq told me about Gary Jasper.' I squared up to Victor, towered over him like he'd done to me in my nightmares. 'You didn't come to England just to size me up, did you? It was you who performed his cross-amputation, let my father bleed to death?'

Victor stayed quiet, his eyes busily checking the monitor that flicked between images of the townhouse. I saw the front and back entrances, a couple of rooms. No sign of Elaine.

Kester exhaled smoke. 'Enough,' he snapped, his cool slipping.

I was undeterred. 'All *I* care about is Elaine. So if you have another suggestion as to how we might get out of this, I'm listening.'

Kester stood; his face purple, his eyes full of rage.

A buzz sounded. We turned to the monitor.

As the entranceway hit the screen, we saw Sadiq al-Barabi standing tall over Skid's fallen body. The little creep was face down. Bloodstained. Still as death.

CHAPTER SIXTY-NINE

The image shifted. We could no longer see Sadiq al-Barabi's brown, intense eyes filling the monitor, but we could still hear his voice coming through the intercom. 'My patience has run out,' he said. 'I'm coming up. We do this face to face.'

Looking pale and drawn, Kester put out his cigar. He stood, unlocked a cabinet and removed a gun.

Victor was jittery. 'Did you see if he had the money with him?'

Kester ignored the question.

We stood in silence, watching on the monitor as Sadiq made his way up the stairway. Suddenly the screen went blank. Victor pointed, shrieked, 'The security cameras are out! I don't like this, Kester.'

Guns readied, they squared up to the door. It crawled open. Sadiq appeared, his bare arms held out, empty. He walked into the room, his Glock sticking out of a back pocket. 'Never work with family,' he said, nodding in my direction. 'You end up doing the work yourself.'

'It seems our trust has waned somewhat,' said Kester. 'But the deal can survive,' he added encouragingly.

The three men faced each other and, for the moment, I was forgotten; I edged closer to the door.

'But not here,' said Victor. 'Skid's down. There's nothing on the monitor. We're exposed. I urge you both to put off the deal until we're out of here.'

Taking in the request, Kester narrowed his eyes. 'Tell me, Sadiq, how did you know where we were?'

'Your message,' he responded, a look of confusion reaching his face.

'I sent no message.'

'Then this is a set up,' cried Victor, putting his head in his hands. He turned to Kester, insisted, 'We must leave immediately!'

Kester nodded ruefully.

Then mayhem broke out. Sharp glass sprayed everywhere as windows smashed. We dropped to the floor as thick gas filled the room. There was shouting, accusations flying as we scrambled for the door. I heard footsteps disappearing upwards. Towards Elaine?

I was the farthest from the door. My eyes were burning, unable to open. Closing in on the stairs, I pulled my jacket over my mouth and gagged. Then I heard a voice at the top of the stairway. Then gunfire. A body hit the floor and fell a couple of steps. Elaine? I heard Kester. His voice muffled, struggling. I made out the words *old* and *liability*. The hall was full of the thick, suffocating gas. I grabbed my throat, headed after the footsteps, through the gas. Peeling open my eyes, I saw Victor on a stair near the top, right in front of me. *Dead.* His specs lay beside him, smashed; his head was a mess of brains, bone and blood. I climbed to my feet, stepping over his body. A loft hatch was down, a ladder dropping to the floor, but my attention was on the door to my left. Elaine? The door was locked. I kicked hard, then again, higher. It flung open, revealing Elaine. She was gagged, tied to a chair, wriggling like a dying fish. I ripped off her gag and opened a window.

As I untied her, I saw her eyes bulge. Felt her lungs fill with air. The air was hazy, relatively gas-free but now her image was starting to blur. I felt weak, grabbed hold of her, mouthed *I've found you.*

'Where are they?' she gasped.

Unable to speak, I motioned to the sky.

* * *

Back at headquarters, Donnie Guzan was listening in, glued to the unit feed as SWAT stormed into the townhouse. Conversing through gas masks, SWAT worked their way up into the tear gas.

It wasn't long before the first casualty was found. They identified Victor Lapenza, fatally shot. *Good*, thought Guzan, if Victor was there then he could assume that so too was Kester Hardwick. Good news flowed in; Edson Taylor had been recovered, alive.

Where the hell was Kester?

Another voice from the unit: Satellite had reported infra-red. Two bodies, moving away – one building after the other.

Was Sadiq al-Barabi with him, on the roof? There had been no reports from the chopper.

Guzan looked at his computer screen, brought up the image. There were two bodies seemingly running through walls. Unless? They were running *through* the roof.

SWAT was instructed to head into the garret. To block off each end immediately. Seconds later SWAT reported back; both ends were covered. They were moving in.

Checking his screen, Guzan identified infrared heat coming from directly between the SWAT members. Two bodies. *Thank God, they're still in the roof. SWAT has them trapped.*

Another call came in; they'd found a woman claiming to be Elaine McAdler.

Claire's alive, smiled Guzan, satisfied that by now the inside of the roof was secure. *Now for Kester.*

He imagined the scene. Dark. Dangerous. SWAT has night vision, he told himself. They were trained for this. Anytime now this would all be over.

The feed went quiet. Guzan held his breath, expecting a fight back. It never came.

CHAPTER SEVENTY

7.20pm
Westwood, Los Angeles.

CIA official, Felix Proudlock, paced the FBI holding room. 'This is outrageous!' he cried out to anyone interested, slamming his hand on the door. 'Bringing me here... *Big* mistake.'

After five minutes of confined isolation in the deliberately overheated room, he was joined not by a federal interrogator, but by Ethan Knight.

'Ethan. Get me out of here for heaven's sake,' he demanded, glad to see his fellow official. Knight looked tired, bloated; he always looked like he'd just eaten and usually had.

Knight shook his head in a look of disgust. 'It's over Felix, or should I call you Al?'

Proudlock's eyes sharpened. 'You trying to humiliate me, Ethan, is that it? As I told the thugs who apprehended me, I have been working undercover.'

'CTC has no knowledge of any covert position regarding Kester Hardwick,' said Knight, his eyes fiery. 'And as for bringing you here, that was my idea. After you made me suspect the FBI of leaking information I thought it fitting.'

'My relationship with Kester Hardwick goes back nearly twenty years,' argued Proudlock. 'It was instigated by the then director of CI himself. Without me you wouldn't even know about a formula.'

After tucking in his shirt, Knight pulled up a chair. 'Let's cut the shit. Where's Hardwick?'

Proudlock folded his lean frame into a seat, tugged at his flimsy beard. 'You don't have him?'

'SWAT lost him,' explained Knight. 'He disappeared through a ventilation system that had been doctored for a quick get-away. You have anything to do with that?'

'Don't be ridiculous.'

'You're in a bad position here, Felix. CTC deny that you provided any Intel on the formula. Your only hope is to start talking.'

'This goes above CTC,' claimed Proudlock, his sleeve chasing sweat across his barren scalp like a cheap paper towel. 'My position was too important to risk talking. For all I knew there was someone else on the inside. Ethan, please, this has all been cleared, you can check. CI has knowledge of my role.'

'What about the bomb near Chinatown? We found surveillance of you at the scene. Does CI know you're involved in that?'

Proudlock ran two fingers along the inside of his damp collar. 'I went there to question Victor Lapenza, about the formula. I didn't know about the IED until it detonated. By the time I reached the site I saw Lapenza going after Edson Taylor. I called out, but Taylor ignored me, disappeared inside a building. I kept Lapenza off his trail. Saved his life.'

Sensing a softening in Knight, Proudlock asked for a glass of water. He didn't speak again until he'd downed it. 'This all started way back. The director contacted me with a scenario that resulted in me winning favour with Kester. My hands were dirty – I was in deep, breaking procedure at will, but the director was happy. Then Kester got the murder rap. He occasionally approached me for information, but I pretty much kept my distance until his release. After I got wind of his link with the formula I decided to resume our relationship.'

Knight shook his head. 'What about sending SWAT into that abandoned clothes factory. That informant went through you, Felix. You trying to get back into Hardwick's good books by helping him kill Bruno Meyer?'

'Ethan, I…I'm on the right side here!'

'Course you are,' scoffed Knight. 'Meyer and that Surgeon deserved to die, right?'

Proudlock stayed quiet.

'What do you know about the formula?'

Proudlock's eyes narrowed. 'It involves fluoride in the water supplies. Fluoride can be poisonous and in certain doses, fatal. What the formula does is produce the dangerous effects, but with lower levels. Essentially it alters the strength of the existing fluoride, making the water deadly – undetectably so.'

'And you kept this from us?'

'If by *us* you mean the CIA, then yes. But the water companies were informed in the guise of an annual review. Their systems have been updated. I am assured there is no longer a risk. I decided not to inform CIA; if Kester had got wind of the fact that the formula was rendered harmless, he'd have dropped out of the deal with Sadiq al-Barabi.' Proudlock was refused a second glass of water. 'Look, Ethan, all I needed to do was stay under a little longer. Enough to uncover Kester's contact; the person he used to set this up. That's why I followed Lapenza to Chinatown. To find out what he knew.'

'Let me guess, this mystery contact has the formula?'

Proudlock raised his hands as if to say *finally*. 'So, as you said, let's cut the shit. Let me salvage what's left of my cover.'

'You are going to prison,' said Knight.

'I can give you names. Dates. You get to send Kester away for good. And I can find him,' insisted Proudlock. 'And get you the formula.'

Knight mused, got stuck on a thought. 'When your mission became a terrorist investigation you should have broken cover. This delay could have endangered thousands of lives.'

'Please, Ethan, I can deliver. Just give me an hour.'

CHAPTER SEVENTY-ONE

9.56pm
Lincoln Park, Los Angeles.

Lincoln Park was Kester's choice for the meet. He was familiar with the layout and thought it the last place they'd expect him to show. From the secluded West side he shifted up to the edge of the tennis courts. From there he took the night-vision monocular from his back pocket and waited.

Like much of the park, the courts were covered in darkness, but the monocular picked up a luminous green image from the South: *Sadiq al-Barabi*. Kester was impressed. Not so much by his cell-mate's escape from the house – it would have been easy for Sadiq to follow him down the purpose-built ventilation shaft – but his subsequent evasion of detection was admirable.

Kester was pleased to see that this time Sadiq had a bag with him. Though this was no place to take $500,000 for a walk, he reflected. After eight, the park was exclusively for drug users, and they were an unpredictable breed. Sadiq didn't know the area; Kester did, like the back of his hand. He knew he would need to be swift, but careful. Trust was a luxury he never afforded. Kester would not be surprised to find the bag devoid of money. No, he wouldn't trust Sadiq any more than he had to. The man was black after all.

Flipping his cell open, he placed a text to Sadiq's phone.

Head west. Under tall trees.

Watching as Sadiq picked up the message, Kester looked around, set off. If anyone was about, the trees would act as cover. With Sadiq also hidden under natural canopy, Kester discarded the monocular and placed another text.

Drop bag and gun. Wait for me.

After a nervous glance, Sadiq set down the bag and raised his hands. Either he had no gun, or he wasn't prepared to relinquish it. Kester banked on the former. Sadiq was standing, motionless but for his head, which ducked and twisted, frantically searching. He won't see me, thought Kester, satisfied that he was hidden from view.

He inched closer to Sadiq. When he could see the heat of his breath he decided it was time to make his move. With a hand on his gun, Kester stepped out from the trees.

'I have the formula,' he stated firmly. 'But first, you throw me the bag.'

Sadiq swung round, eyed Kester's gun, picked up the bag and flung it.

It landed at Kester's feet.

Keeping one eye on Sadiq, he bent down to check the money. He zipped open the bag.

What he saw were bundles of newspaper. What he failed to see was the agent behind him. He heard a footfall. Too late,

'FBI! Drop your weapon and show me your hands!'

In a flash, Kester raised his arms, but only to spring up behind Sadiq. He gripped tightly, holding a gun to his cell-mate's head. Looking around he saw they were encircled by FBI windbreakers. In the distance he heard the throb and thrum of an approaching chopper. Treetops swayed, a flock of roosting crows rose in protest.

'Back off or I'll shoot,' shrieked Kester, unable to hide the horror on his face. He kept his gun lifted, pressed high into Sadiq's cheek. 'You need him alive! Plans are set in motion.' He was forced to shout over the helicopter that had now arrived and was lighting up the area. 'Back off or I put a bullet in his brain. You've one chance to stop this.'

'You're bluffing, Kester,' the agent called back, removing his head-gear.

Recognising him as Donnie Guzan, panic struck Kester's face. Suddenly the rules had changed. *This* agent wouldn't require an invitation to shoot.

Guzan paced closer. 'Drop your gun and I might, might, just let you live. Inform on your friend here and you might be able to strike a deal.'

'I don't believe you,' screamed Kester, staring into Guzan's unstable, hatred-fuelled eyes.

Guzan cocked back his trigger. 'I shoot on three. To be honest, I don't care either way. One…' He took up position. 'Two…'

The gun slipped from Kester's hand. He released Sadiq; dropped to his knees a second before two agents landed on him. They knocked Kester to the ground, forcing his face into the dirt before cuffing him.

Spitting muck, Kester knew he'd been set up, but how? *By whom?*

He was dragged to his feet. Read his rights. Realisation and disbelief registered in his eyes. Standing alone was Sadiq al-Barabi. Uncuffed. Unguarded.

But it wasn't him at all.

It was Edson Taylor.

CHAPTER SEVENTY-TWO

Right on cue, Kester watched as Edson Taylor stepped back, pawing away his fake beard.

Lit up like a birthday cake, Kester cowered, tried to shield his eyes with his forehead. Given the FBI had Sadiq's cell phone, and password, he assumed the bastard had talked. Kester squinted at Guzan. 'What did you offer him? Diplomatic immunity?'

The agent glared back. 'If you mean Sadiq al-Barabi, he's dead. Died at your *refugio seguro*,' added Guzan.

Kester's mind melted as he reflected on the news. Who had set him up if not Sadiq? *Al?* He must have been implicated, covered his back CIA style. 'Fucking Proudlock!' he called out. 'The bald bastard's done a deal.'

* * *

Guzan nodded, grinning as he watched Kester Hardwick crumple. The *deal* was that Felix Proudlock would deliver Kester and the formula in exchange for leniency. It had all hinged on Kester believing Sadiq had followed him out of his safe house, and agreeing to make the exchange personally. They had been lucky on both counts.

'Proudlock's had plenty to say,' enthused Guzan.

Kester winced. 'Felix Proudlock,' he spat out the name. 'Don't believe everything *he* tells you.'

Watching an agent remove Kester's belt, Guzan gloated, 'You feel let down?'

'I am not the only one betrayed by someone close,' said Kester, looking at Edson Taylor, 'I may be a fool, but I don't ride alone.'

Guzan's eyes narrowed. He knew there was someone else working with Kester; Felix had said as much. But what point was he making? He shot a look at Edson Taylor. Had he been double-crossed by Elaine? She was Kester's daughter; it made sense.

The agent next to Kester stood up, caught Guzan's attention; having finished patting Kester down he was shaking his head.

He didn't bring the formula. Probably never intended to, mused Guzan. He came for the money, and presumably to kill Sadiq al-Barabi.

'This may be pointless,' conceded Guzan, waving a moth from his face, 'but I have to ask. Where is the formula?'

Kester smiled slowly. 'You mean, you don't have it?'

'You're in no position to play games,' reminded the agent. 'Cooperate, and you might avoid the death penalty. Get to retire in prison.'

'Death penalty? I don't think so. I have been away, how am I supposed to have organized anything? I know nothing of a formula and you can't prove—'

'We know you killed "Tino" Ricard and Victor Lapenza.'

Kester's face creased. 'Hearsay.'

'DNA, *yours*, found at both scenes. You're all over Tino's body.' *The ultimate evidence.* 'We recovered it in the hills, with help from Edson here.'

In fact they hadn't, not yet, but Kester didn't know that and with Taylor's directions, they soon would.

It was obvious to Guzan that Kester was taking this news badly; his shoulders sagged and a resigned sigh released facial muscles. All of a sudden he looked older. Beaten.

'Get him out of here,' ordered Guzan.

Arms outstretched and flanked by agents, Kester was led away. Twisting back, he called, 'Agent Guzan! I have to know something.'

The Agent raised a hand. The men stopped. Waited.

'On the count of three, would you have shot me?'

Guzan didn't answer. He just stood there, a smile passing his lips. He thought of his old partner, Cliff Donachie. Condemning Kester to a life in jail wouldn't amount to justice, but he sure hoped Cliff was watching.

CHAPTER SEVENTY-THREE

As a van loaded with Feds took Kester Hardwick
away, I could still feel his gun pressed to the side of
my jaw. My arms shaking, I sandwiched my head in
my hands. Agent Guzan walked over with an offer
of medical assistance, which I declined. Since being
helped out of Kester's townhouse I had seen more
than enough medics. But I indicated my desire for a
change of clothes. I had on my dead brother's jeans
and a long-sleeved jacket that hid both my freshly
bandaged hand and the bullet-proof vest that was
stretched over my now tightly strapped ribs.

'I'll see what I can do,' Guzan promised, 'and
thanks again for your help. We couldn't have done
it without you,' he nodded. 'You all right? Things
got a little twitchy back there.'

Some understatement! I said, 'I just want to collect Elaine and join Sam. The sooner we're all back in England the better.'

Guzan failed to meet my eyes. Then: 'I'm sorry, but you'll need to remain in custody a while longer. I appreciate your cooperation, but questions remain. Elaine is at headquarters now. She's instructed lawyers to act for the both of you.'

Lawyers? I was spiked with anger. The FBI had used me. Now I had served my purpose, *I* was in trouble? They were just like Kester: untrustworthy.

'I'm allowed a phone call, right?' I said belligerently. I still had something to offer, but I wasn't going to offer it yet.

Guzan screwed up his face, spoke through gritted teeth, 'You want to make a phone call, *now?*'

'Yes I do.'

He sighed, handed over his mobile and backed away to join his partner.

Turning my back on them, I moved into the open, between the trees and tennis courts. The chopper had gone, but there was still enough wind and conversation to mask my call. Guzan was watching me but he was far enough away for me to speak without being overheard.

The phone lit up as I made contact with John Yeung's office, gave my name and was put straight through. John answered on the second ring.

'Listen, John. What I'm about to tell you is very important.'

'Mr Edson. You okay?'

'Please John, listen carefully.'

'I understand. You give me story.'

'Later, yes, but right now I'm surrounded by federal agents. I need you to come to Lincoln Park.'

'Sorry? No understand.'

Speaking softly but as clearly as I could, I said, 'There's something I need you to pick up and look after for me. About twenty yards up a side street called "Park View" you'll find a scruffy green garage. There's a bag in there, hidden in the inspection pit under a metal sheet. There's money in it. A lot of money; be careful.'

'Maybe best if you tell police?'

'I don't know if I can trust them.' *Trust nobody.* 'It's nearly over John, the bad guys have lost, but the FBI aren't letting me go. I'm not sure why. *Please*, you must come now. Take the bag before they do. I will tell them about it, but only when I have to. That money could be the only thing keeping me alive.'

CHAPTER SEVENTY-FOUR

10.49pm
Westwood, Los Angeles.

Elaine was occupying interview room one. I was next door. Since finding her at Kester's townhouse, I hadn't spent a moment with her. After the medical team had finished with me I had been isolated – in FBI custody – until becoming embroiled in their plot to arrest Kester Hardwick. Seeing Elaine had warmed my heart, but it still ached without her, and paranoia clouded my thinking.

Sitting with me was my lawyer, Neville. He had the scrubbed presence of a choirboy, his hair too neatly parted, his jacket too loose. Agent Guzan and his over-tanned partner joined us, conducting my questioning from the other side of the sturdy table. Since Kester's arrest, the FBI's attitude appeared to have mellowed. They opened with talk of clearing up a few discrepancies, explaining that as far as the FBI was concerned, I was not a suspect in any of the day's criminalities, only a witness. My lawyer seemed happy enough; he had whispered previously that he was more concerned with my involvement in the stolen Hyundai from Lisa Connelly's apartment block; *If that Tiburon was stolen they'll be talking jail time.* I had forgotten all about it, but according to Neville, the police were waiting to talk to me about that and the condition of Sam Chapman.

As Derego made notes, I talked through my chance meeting with Sadiq al-Barabi, and what had subsequently taken place at the townhouse. I decided to come clean about my paranoia, citing what happened the last time I walked out of the FBI building. I voiced my fears that Kester knew people on the inside, people who could have me killed. Guzan tried to assure me that Kester had no presence within the bureau. He reiterated his gratitude for my assistance and expressed regret that I wasn't given protection. He added that he'd help quash my charge for stealing the car on account of my extreme duress. Young Neville grinned, looking as if he was about to recite a psalm.

With my concerns eased somewhat, I spoke about Sadiq's bag of money. The agents immediately perked up, leaning in.

'It was hidden in the garage I mentioned. There's an inspection pit beneath a metal cover,' I said. 'It's in there.'

Guzan angled towards Derego. 'Proudlock is still in the holding area. Find out what he knows about this?'

Derego was recorded leaving the interview room.

Eyebrows pinched, Guzan asked me, 'Why didn't you bring this up before?'

'In the park, when you said Sadiq al-Barabi was dead, I thought about it, but I didn't know if I should trust you. I've already been shot at by the CIA once today. You don't know what I've been through these past few days. And then, when I finally get Elaine back, you tell me I can't see her. Why? It made no sense to me. It's like there's something you're not telling me.'

Guzan looked perplexed. 'So what's changed?'

I shrugged, 'I suppose I'm not quite as angry at you as I was, but I still don't understand why I can't see Elaine.'

The door opened, Derego returned, swivelling his chair before sitting astride it. He turned to Guzan. 'Felix Proudlock denies knowledge of the money. His hunch is that it was to pay for the formula. It concurs with what we already suspect. That this was a third and final payment.' Derego looked down at his notes, then at me. 'Mr Taylor, you told us Victor Lapenza thought it was a set up?'

'That's right,' I said.

He turned to Guzan. 'It is possible Proudlock's lying; he may have sent that text message to Sadiq al-Barabi to get him to bring the money to Kester's townhouse. We know Proudlock had Sadiq's cell number, maybe he also knew about the garage?'

'Get someone out there,' ordered Guzan.

'Already done. We still have agents in the park. They're heading over there now.'

Regret clawed at my conscience as I thought of John Yeung. I had put him in an awkward position. I had to call him off.

Guzan locked his fingers. 'We need you to level with us, Mr Taylor. So I'm going to tell you why you've been kept apart from Elaine.' The agent sat back. 'The situation is that we had to question her *before* we allowed you both to talk.'

His face tightening, Guzan sighed, silent for a moment as if choosing his words. 'We know Victor Lapenza's gun was used to kill Sadiq al-Barabi. SWAT was instructed to capture everyone alive, but they arrived in the roof just before he was shot dead – a single bullet travelled through his windpipe. Elaine McAdler pulled the trigger. You told us that you blacked out from the gas shortly after you untied her. Well, while you were unconscious, she must have picked up the gun and headed up that ladder.'

I stared forward in denial. 'Impossible! You're telling me Elaine killed Sadiq al-Barabi?'

Derego nodded. 'She's confessed to it,'

CHAPTER SEVENTY-FIVE

The room fell silent as I took in this news. Elaine had admitted killing Sadiq al-Barabi. But how? Why?

Back at the townhouse, my focus had been on staying conscious long enough to find her. The next thing I remember I had been breathing through a gas mask, a medic talking to me. I recalled the moment she sat up. *Where are they?* I had pointed upward.

What had she done? She couldn't go to prison for murder. Not now. Not after everything we'd been through. But would she, for killing a known terrorist? I felt all screwed up inside.

'Is she in trouble?' I asked.

'That depends on why she shot him,' said Derego.

'He's a killer,' I cried.

'Relax, Mr Taylor. I'm happy with her explanation,' said Guzan, adding, 'She says it was an accident. And, like you said, he's a killer.'

Derego looked up at me. 'You said that your brother killed Skid. How do you know that?'

I told them again: 'Skid was alive when I entered the building, but when Sadiq appeared on the monitor, he was treading over Skid's body.' The image of Skid brought back my last memory of Sam; his body sprawled across the road. 'Please, agents, I know we have to go over this but you've gotta tell me about Sam.' I pleaded with them, 'Just tell me he's alive?'

Guzan said, 'The LAPD have the latest on his condition. They are waiting to talk. You'll be updated soon enough.'

'Then can we hurry this up?' I said.

'Fine.' Derego frowned, looked down at his notes. 'And he was at the foot of the rear entrance?'

'Who?' I took a moment to realise that he was referring to Skid. 'That's right.' I nodded a yes.

The agents exchanged whispers before standing. Reaching to turn off the recorder, Derego said, 'Interview ended 11.29pm.'

Out in the corridor our lawyers convened. They looked like father and son. Elaine joined us, head down, stepping out of interview room one. She looked worn. Then she saw me. As she bounded over a smile energised her face. She snatched my hand and I pulled her close; feeling the familiar contours of her warm body. My fingers brushed what felt like a mobile phone in her back pocket. Hugging me tight, she fitted us together perfectly. My ribs were murderous but I didn't care. Our embrace, her nearness, brought clarity back to my thoughts. Everything was going to be all right. We'd locate Sam. Fight any criminal charges together.

Derego waved us into the interview room, allowing us a minute together before the cops appeared.

'I need your phone,' I said to Elaine, a little hastily. It wasn't how I wanted to spend our minute, but I had to call John Yeung.

Expecting a different reunion, she hesitated before handing it over.

I smiled my thanks. 'Would you wait by the door, let me know if anyone arrives?'

Elaine sighed, wiped her eyes. 'If it's about Sam—'

'I'll explain later,' I said.

She agreed to wait in the doorway as I dialled up John Yeung. I had to stop him going to the garage. But would I be in time?

He responded sharply. 'No bag in garage, Mr Edson.'

'You've already been? I was calling to stop you. The FBI are on their way.'

'Already checked out garage,' he said. 'Looked under metal, found hole in floor, but nothing, Mr Edson. No bag.'

Somebody had beaten him to it. The FBI? 'When were you there?' I asked.

'Twenty minutes ago.'

Twenty minutes ago I hadn't even told the FBI about the garage.

I recalled Victor's screechy voice: *This is a set up*.

With relief that John Yeung was okay, I apologised to him, promised he'd soon have his story, and said goodbye. Without his help I doubt I'd have survived the day.

And what of Elaine? I looked across to where she stood keeping watch by the door. She looked back at me, hesitantly. How had she survived the bloodbath at her father's townhouse; more specifically, how had she survived her father? It brought to mind John's saying: *Vicious as tigress is, she not eat own cubs.*

I shot her a reassuring smile. She whispered forcefully, 'Police are coming.'

Two solemn-faced, uniformed cops, brushed past her and strode into the room.

One, a woman with a silvertan bob and matching shirt, spoke first, 'Mr Taylor. We have come to talk about Sam Chapman. I am afraid it's bad news.'

CHAPTER SEVENTY-SIX

I stood motionless as bile shot up to my tonsils. Forcing one foot in front of the other, I slumped out of the interview room. After seeing Sam in the road – so much blood the wrong side of his body – I should have expected this moment, but it had been too horrible to imagine.

Elaine invaded my space. Her red-rimmed eyes shone with tears. I thought of Janice and my grief extended to Sam's wife and kids.

Stepping into view was Guzan, sympathy plastered to his tired face. He must have already known about Sam's death – kept it from me – but he seemed genuinely moved, sniffing his condolences and dashing a hand to his moist cheeks. He turned to Elaine and thanked her, holding her stare and arm in the process. It was as though Guzan's tears weren't for Sam at all. Of course they weren't. Why would they be? I wasn't thinking straight. As he walked away, his steps quickened and I was left wondering what had just happened.

I looked at Elaine through blurry eyes. She led me back into the interview room, saying we could talk in private. Releasing my arm she took a double-take at my wounded hand; dark blood stained the bandage.

'One of us needs to call Janice,' I said.

'Already have,' she replied solemnly, 'after they told me about Sam I asked my lawyer for a phone.' Elaine's face reddened. 'Oh, Ed. She didn't know. Janice was unaware that Sam… that her husband was dead.'

'Oh God,' I covered my mouth with my hand.

'At first Janice was quiet, unresponsive. Then suddenly she erupted, sobbing hysterically. It was awful, Ed. I didn't know what to say to her.'

My tired brain and racked emotions tried to function. We needed to get home, to be there for Janice and the kids. But Elaine had killed a man. Would they let her go? 'What will happen now?' I asked her. 'To you I mean? The shooting…'

'It was an accident,' she said as if this would make everything all right. 'I didn't mean to shoot him. When you untied me I went after my father. I thought it was the only way to protect you. To protect us. When the gas disappeared, I saw a gun on the step above Victor. It was like a sign. So I picked it up and climbed the ladder. It was dark up there. Then SWAT appeared behind me. I didn't see them, only their light that flashed in front of me. I caught it reflecting off a gun. I heard steps in front of me, and jumped. The gun went off in my hand. It all happened in a flash. Then SWAT grabbed me and lit up the whole loft. When I saw his face I just collapsed. I thought I had shot you. Then they told me he was your twin.' She looked apologetic.

'He was evil,' I said. 'It was him who was behind the murder of Gary Jasper. I think he had Victor and Tino do it.'

She pulled me back into her. The feeling of love was undeniable; my heart and stomach swapping places. When we finally parted I stared unblinking, deep into her teary eyes as she lowered herself into a chair. I closed the interview room door. Another chair wailed in protest as I dragged it across the room. We sat close.

'I never thought it would come to this,' she sobbed. 'The plan to involve you had nothing to do with me. I came here to rid myself of my past, for good. I should have been back in England by now, explaining everything. My coming to LA was to end all the lies so that we could get on with living; not hiding. What matters right now is Sam's family, and us, Ed. Please tell me you understand why I came to LA? That you know why I had to keep things secret?'

'I understand.' I dipped a heavy nod, put a hand out to her. 'Will they accept Sadiq's death as accidental?'

'Agent Guzan owes me,' said Elaine. 'He says the FBI will do all they can. He expects any charges to be dropped.'

I pictured him thanking her, looked at her bewildered. 'I don't get it, why does Guzan owe you?' *For killing Sadiq?* 'The FBI told me they wanted my brother alive.'

'According to him, the FBI wants the credit for killing Sadiq al-Barabi. The press were set to be critical of his escape. The Feds can't claim the credit if the police arrest me for the crime.'

'So that's why Guzan owes you? Good publicity?' But even as I asked the question, I remembered Guzan's look of distress and knew there was more to it.

Elaine explained, 'When you were with the police, I spoke to Agent Guzan. I knew him from before; he helped compile the case against my father.' She stopped, studied my reaction. 'I don't know how much you know, but I saw Kester, my father, kill my mother.'

'I know that much,' I said.

'Mom was cheating on him with a man named Franco Biani. It was why Kester shot her. As an important witness for the prosecution, Franco was taken into protective custody, but he knew my father would be out for revenge. And to silence him. Sure enough, a man was sent to kill Franco – someone on the inside – but he escaped. It became too dangerous for him, so *I* agreed to testify if *he* agreed to disappear. We were close, me and Franco; he was like a father to me. Much more than Kester ever was,' Elaine looked down at her hands. 'We kept in touch, Franco and I. Had a pact that one day we'd visit Mom's grave together.' She sniffed hard, her eyes angry. 'Franco's spent the last fifteen years in exile, his own family unaware of his existence. And now his father, Guseppi, has gone missing, and Franco says Kester's behind it.'

I nodded blankly. 'Is that what you were talking to Guzan about?'

She twisted her head. 'Not exactly. I remembered Franco telling me that the man in charge of his witness protection was a good friend of Agent Guzan's. Some guy called Cliff Donachie. Franco told me about the night Donachie died; about how it was made to look like suicide. I've just told Agent Guzan what really happened to him.'

CHAPTER SEVENTY-SEVEN

Felix Proudlock sprang out of his chair as an exhausted Donnie Guzan crashed into the holding room.

'About fucking time!' said Proudlock.

Closing the door behind him, Guzan puffed out his barrel chest. 'Sit down, Felix.'

Proudlock stood his ground. 'There was no need for you to come down and release me personally.'

'You're not being released.'

'What? You back on the booze, Don? We have a deal,' argued Proudlock. 'You have Kester Hardwick in custody. I have immunity.'

Fisting hold of Proudlock's shirt, Guzan forced him back, slamming him against the wall. Proudlock swallowed air, his composure deserting him.

'Franco Biani survived,' said Guzan, releasing his collar. 'But I guess you knew that.'

Proudlock's face turned pale. 'You s...spoke to Franco Biani?'

'Anything you want to tell me, Felix?'

The CIA officer took a seat, held silent.

Guzan proceeded, 'Fine, I'll tell you what I think happened fifteen years ago. Feel free to join in if you know the words.' Guzan walked around the table. 'Kester asked you to find out where Franco Biani was being held. No big deal you thought. But then he wanted *you* to kill him?' speculated the agent. 'You went there. Alone. It was the early hours and Cliff Donachie was on the premises. He knew you, considered you friendly enough to let you in, but then he realised why you were there.' Guzan paused, watched Proudlock wriggling like a worm on a hook. The officer stroked his goatee whilst his flickering eyes searched for a get-out.

Guzan was tired; tired of the whole business; tired of double-crossing bastards like this one. He jabbed at Proudlock's chest. 'You were a threat to Franco Biani so Cliff did his job. He protected the witness, helped him escape.'

A twitch betrayed Proudlock's desperation but he remained silent.

'But why make it look like suicide?' asked Guzan. With his foot he pulled a chair out from under the table and slumped onto it, waited for the inevitable attempts at justification that were about to come his way. Knowing how close they'd been, he and

Cliff, the only option left for Proudlock would be damage limitation.

'You've no idea what it was like being under the thumb of both the director *and* Kester Hardwick,' said Proudlock.

Guzan angled a spot lamp onto the officer's bald head as the twitching picked up pace. 'Enlighten me.'

'I didn't go there to kill Donachie,' Proudlock said, bowing his head. 'You're right. I was there to kill Franco Biani. But I didn't even know if I could do that. I just needed to silence him. But Cliff knew why I was there. He sent Biani away, into the woods. It was dark. I had no chance of finding him. Couldn't exactly ask for a search party. When I realised Cliff had sprung me it came down to a decision. Him or me.'

Internally fuming, Guzan's hands clenched into fists as he struggled to keep his cool.

'I was under so much stress at the time,' defended Proudlock. His eyes glistened with unshed tears, his hands pleading for sympathy. 'The barbiturate pentobarbital I used to kill Cliff—' he stuttered into silence, swallowed. 'It could just as easily have ended up in my blood stream. That's why I had it on me. When I said it was him or me. Well it could have gone either way. You know how it was for Cliff back then; he was in such a bad way, it seemed like I was doing him a fav—'

'No!' Guzan shouted jumping to his feet. 'Don't you dare; don't even think it.' He wanted to pummel Felix Proudlock into the table; not stop hitting until he'd smashed his flinching face into eternity. He'd always found it hard to believe that Cliff would kill himself. But as much as Guzan hated Proudlock for making him believe Cliff's death was suicide, he hated himself more for believing it. Only he'd known how much Cliff loved his family and how badly their deaths had affected him. It was this that had swayed Guzan's belief.

'I didn't intend to dishonor him,' said Proudlock. 'I had to make it look like suicide. After his family died in the fire, he was a prime candidate.'

Guzan kicked away the empty chair. In an effort to control his wrath, he turned his back on Proudlock, tried to recapture the essence of Cliff's calming presence; but the more he thought of his ex-partner, the more angry he became. Tensing up, he slowly exhaled and let the anger seep out of him, causing his head to pound relentlessly. 'So who has the formula?'

Proudlock squeaked, 'What?'

'Come on Felix, you're going to prison either way. May as well spill.'

'As I said earlier, I don't know. But it won't matter,' insisted Proudlock. 'I told you. The water companies are now protected. The formula is no longer an issue.'

'Then you have nothing left to offer,' said Guzan. 'Enjoy prison. Say hello to Kester, if he doesn't kill you first.'

As Guzan turned his back on the crushed CIA officer he felt a weight lift from his shoulders. Maybe now his old partner could rest in peace. LA would finally know the truth about Cliff Donachie: that he died protecting a witness. It was fitting.

'Did you find the money?' asked Proudlock.

'No,' replied Guzan, leaving the holding room. 'Nice try,' he said, closing the door on Proudlock's future.

The FBI hadn't found the money. However, Guzan had a good idea who'd taken it.

ONE WEEK LATER

CHAPTER SEVENTY-EIGHT

Northampton, England.

The church chosen for Sam Chapman's funeral was packed full with members of the police authority, and about as much sadness and respect as was possible. The sky was fittingly subdued, the air moist.

The congregation even kept a lid on the hostility some of them felt towards Elaine and me for putting Sam's life in danger. Word had spread: they blamed Elaine for going to LA and me for taking Sam with me. Aware of the ill-feeling, Sam's wife, Janice, had allowed us to host his wake; an amazing gesture under such all-consuming grief.

After analysis of the bullet that killed Sam, Tino was deemed the likely shooter. The shell fitted my description of the rifle I had seen him wield from the BMW. *I'll shoot you like I shot your buddy.*

Only now was Sam's death hitting me. Despite Janice's show of support I was feeling deeply guilty. Not for taking away a loving husband and father of two young children, but for taking so long to feel its impact. Grief is a selfish emotion and mine had mainly been with Elaine. Being without her had scared me so much there was little room in my thoughts for anything else. Now she was back in my life, my world was coming together just as the Chapmans' was falling apart.

With Elaine by my side, I looked out to the garden where Sam's two boys were playing swingball. Both sons were aware of their father's death, but were yet to show it; yet to be swallowed up by it. I thought of my biological father, not his cross-amputation or murder, but of the unresolved. The unsaid. Then I thought of Elaine's father. The murder of Sam Chapman was duly added to the list of charges against Kester Hardwick – a rap sheet that also included the murders of Faustino Ricard and Victor Lapenza – among others. Fortunately, Kester's net of destruction hadn't fallen on Elaine's friend, Lisa Connelly. Having rented her Koreatown apartment, she was able to walk away with nothing but our deepest gratitude. Her own nightmare was finally resolved with the death of Bruno Meyer.

As for John Yeung, his exclusive hit the front page of the *Chinese Daily News* and was picked up by the Nationals.

My eyes and thoughts settled on Sam's two boys. Their tragedy had not been in losing a father. It had been in losing a father who loved them.

Janice ambled towards us, politely accepting condolences as she passed through. She joined us in watching her sons. Looking for the cracks. She asked if she could have a word with me and I led her into the dining room. A young couple ceased piling plates from the buffet as Janice walked over to the window. Once again her eyes found her boys.

The room emptied. She stood still. Her breathing heavy. Whatever she had to say wasn't ready to come. I filled the silence. 'Sam once told me that he believed in life after death – said he could prove it. Then he opened his wallet and showed me a photo of you and the kids.'

Janice squeezed her eyelids, gave a shallow nod. 'He used to say *we all die, we don't all live*.' A smile crept slowly over her face. Then her eyes hardened. 'Ed, there's something I need to tell you.'

'It's OK, Janice. I know.' *Not the only one betrayed by someone close.*

Since returning home, I had reflected on everything that had happened and come to suspect that Sam had betrayed me; that he was the one Kester was talking about when he said he had somebody keeping tabs on me. When I'd had time to think about it, I knew that that somebody had to be Sam. It was Sam who had helped to place Elaine in my inner circle; introduced me to her, even set her up with a job. I failed to see it at first, but there were other pointers to his betrayal. I should have heeded Lisa's warning – *trust nobody* – and not emailed Sam when I did. If I hadn't, Tino and Skid wouldn't have turned up in Koreatown. *Your friend led them to you.* Had he done so deliberately? The more I thought about it, the more I realised his behaviour had been strange. Like how he didn't want to go straight to the *Flesh* club when we left the airport; like how he went off somewhere when we checked into the hotel – he'd said he was going for a menu, but maybe he was calling Kester, letting him know I had arrived. Then there was the call Kester had made to him from Hardwick House. After Kester had spoken to Sam, he'd passed the phone to me. I remembered thinking it odd that Sam had uttered no objections to my vague explanations; nor asked why I had suddenly checked out of the hotel or why I wanted him to do the same. I had been too stressed to think much about it at the time, but it made no sense unless Sam knew not to make waves.

Janice looked sharply at me, then slowly to the floor. I sensed she was about to confirm my suspicions.

'Sam hated himself for it,' she said. 'You know he had been seeing a shrink for weeks?'

I shook my head. I hadn't known, but it explained why he recommended the Newman Clinic to me, and why Bobby, the psychotherapist I had seen, knew him. Some friend I'd turned out to be. I'd had no idea what stress Sam was under.

'You must understand, Ed, he didn't have a choice. He was approached by the CIA no less. It was all hush-hush, the officer wouldn't even give his name, insisted on using a code name: Al, I think it was. They asked Sam to keep an eye on you. He said they'd forced him to sign a secrecy agreement under the Terrorism Act. He thought it was ridiculous; that they'd confused you with a terrorist or something. But he decided that if anyone was going to spy on you, it was best if he did it. That way he could watch your back. But then they said they wanted him to watch someone else as well: *Elaine*. That was when they moved her into the area. He was told to help her settle, report back if her situation changed. He thought it was witness protection, that they just wanted weekly reports – what you were both up to and that. Nothing specific. He grew weary of their motives and started asking questions. That was when they offered him a backhander. He refused; said that might be the way they did things in the CIA, but not here; it was against his ethics to accept payment. Shortly afterwards he was given his first promotion. Sam always wondered if he'd been tested; if Al had influenced things in his favour. I told him he was being stupid.'

'Why are you telling me this?' I asked.

'I want you to know the truth,' she said, raising a hand to sweep her fringe out of her puffy eyes. 'I don't know if any of this had anything to do with what happened, but, the day you flew out to Los Angeles, that Al called again. Told Sam he was to

396 / John Baird

make sure you caught your flight and that he was to go with you.'

I recalled Sam's sudden change of heart; he had previously been adamant that my going to LA was a bad idea.

'Sam refused,' said Janice, 'but then they threatened the boys.' She looked up at me, her eyes filling with tears. 'Said they'd get hurt if Sam didn't go with you.'

I could see the pain leaking out of her. 'Really, Janice, you don't have to do this. I know that whatever Sam did, it was because he had no choice. He was a good copper – and a good friend.'

She shook her head sharply. 'The reason I'm telling you this is because Sam may not have been all you thought he was. I'm not sure he was honest with me. He told me he had refused to take any money, but a couple of days ago I found a building society account. It had forty grand in it. It's not proof of anything but… what if this Al was working for Elaine's father? What if Sam was—' she cut herself off, as if suddenly unable to speak ill of her dead husband.

I didn't know how much influence Kester had managed to gain over Sam – maybe I never wanted to know – but once Sam had served his purpose, Tino had been instructed to kill him. *His presence here was always going to be ephemeral.* I held my tongue, looked for words of comfort. 'Whatever Sam did, he was forced into it,' I said emphatically. 'I've seen how they operate, Janice. Believe me; he would have been given no choice. Whatever he did, first and foremost it would have been to protect you and the boys. Hold onto that.'

Janice nodded, squeezed my arm, spoke in a shallow voice, 'Thanks, Ed. That means a lot.' She left me alone at the window. I continued to stare out as she passed through the garden to join her sons. Her family gathered around the game of swingball. Grandparents kept score in a moving show of support that made everyone feel like an intruder.

Family members; their lives impact so much on our own, it's no wonder we try so hard to protect them.

Elaine came up behind me, put her arms around my waist; locked her hands in front of me. 'My father's got a lot to answer for,' she said.

'I think Janice knows. I think she knows Sam was working for Kester.'

Elaine released a hand, pointed out of the window. 'Look, Ed. That's the devastation my father caused; not Sam. Maybe Sam meant to tell you; maybe he was trying to protect you. Whatever the reason, it's because of my father that this family has been shattered. God knows what threats he levelled at Sam. Perhaps the same one he used against me. He threatened to have you burnt alive. He would have done so if I hadn't helped concoct the plan to fake my death. Right up to the last second in that furnace I didn't know if he was actually going to let me escape. It was terrifying, Ed. I couldn't let anything like that happen to you.'

She sighed, withdrew her arms from my waist, came to stand at my side. 'The point I'm making is that I had no choice. Maybe it was the same for Sam. We will go to any lengths, even while we hate ourselves for doing so, to protect the people we love – and I love you Ed; so very much.'

I reached for her, pulled her into my arms. She spoke, her voice muffled against my chest. 'After you were attacked in the park, I knew I had to do what my father said. I did it for our freedom, and now we have it. All we can do is repair as much of the damage as is possible.'

She tilted her head back and looked up at me. Dizzy with the warm scent of her, I lost myself in her gaze, consumed with the urge to never let her go. Elaine had gone to LA to put a line under her past. Finally, I was ready to put one under mine.

She was everything I had ever wanted and I had my everything back.

CHAPTER SEVENTY-NINE

Rancho Palos Verdes, Los Angeles.

Pulling up outside Guzan's house, Derego slipped his Saleen Mustang into park.

'So, do I get to meet Maria Garcia?' he asked.

'Nope,' replied Guzan, springing excitedly from the car.

'Uh-huh,' nodded Derego.

'What's that mean?'

Derego stuck his head out the window. 'You can't trust your lovely nurse with me.'

Smiling, Guzan shook his head. 'It's just that it's progressing nicely. I don't want you spoiling anything.'

'You can't trust her with me.'

'Not every woman digs the muscular, handsome look,' said Guzan, slapping the hood before heading down his path.

Derego called out, 'Does she smell of old people?'

Guzan waved two fingers. 'Goodnight, Tyler.'

Opening his front door, rose petals greeted Guzan, lining the carpet and leading through his home. Following the red trail upstairs, he pictured the lovely Maria lying there, like a pot of gold at the end of a rainbow. Yesterday's surprise was good enough, he thought, but this was something else. Yesterday, Maria had brought Mrs Donachie home with her, allowing him to tell Cliff's mother the good news about Kester Hardwick: news that the *big-faced bastard* was back behind bars; and with a death penalty in the offing that was the best he could hope for. But tonight – as petals led Guzan to the bathroom – he was hoping it wasn't Mrs Donachie waiting for him.

He wasn't disappointed.

'Wow,' he mouthed at the sight of Maria Garcia, naked but for the bubbles of his Jacuzzi bath. *Things don't get much better than this*. Grinning like a lottery winner, he quickly undressed.

Pouring from bottle to glass, she smiled, 'Champagne huh, we celebrating?'

'What do you mean?' he asked.

'All this,' she motioned to the petals, the Champagne, the bubbles. 'I didn't clock you as the romantic type.'

Colour washed from Guzan's face. *She didn't do this.*

'Get out!' he cried. *'Quickly!'*

Pulling Maria from the bath, he wailed, 'How long have you been in the water?'

'I don't know,' she fretted, 'fifteen minutes. It was warm when I got here.'

Guzan reached south. Yanked his cell from his pants. Dialled 911.

The setting sun poured into the windshield of Skid's new Mercedes as it cruised away from Agent Guzan's residence. Fumbling for his shades, stuff spilled out of pockets and onto leather upholstery. Realising the shades were on his head, he slid them onto his bulbous snout, rooted through the crap. Flicking a rogue petal off the crumpled formula, Skid wondered if it had actually worked. Obtaining the ingredients had not been easy, but he had needed only very small amounts and the packer at the 24-hour pharmacy had owed him big time. Skid smirked, thinking of the surprise that awaited Guzan. The bathwater had looked nothing but inviting as he had slipped away moments before the agent's girlfriend was due home.

Feeling beneath his seat, Skid found a capsule of blood. Blood that had helped him appear dead when Sadiq had arrived at the safe house in response to the text message; the fool had thought the message had come from Kester. Earlier, Skid had watched Edson Taylor arrive – nearly mess things up – and be frogmarched to the garage. But fortunately, Sadiq had been impatient; had come to the house himself just as Skid had planned. The bastard hadn't troubled to check he was dead; merely stepped over him. Skid had been banking on it. Relieved, he'd snapped into action, cut the feed to the monitors and darted off to swipe the bag of cash. When he reached the garage he'd looked back at the townhouse, seen FBI swamping the place. Watching from the inspection pit until the coast was clear he had then walked away with a cool half million. He grinned to himself. Skid the little rat. Beneath everyone's contempt. Always does as he's told. Hah!

After years of neglect – of refusing Skid a visit – suddenly Kester had wanted to know him again; needed him to become a contact; to secure a formula and to kill the scientists who had developed it. Skid had agreed, but had he been paid for it? Had he fuck! It was as though Kester assumed he was doing him a favour. *Skid owes me his life*, his boss would say. Well boss, when your life's worth shit, that's precisely what you're owed.

They had all underestimated Skid: from the twitchy CIA mole to old man Lapenza; all left wondering who the all important contact was. And all the time he was right under their noses.

Nobody's ignoring me now, he mused, tossing the capsule of pig's blood out of the window. He laughed; knew that his missing corpse had raised an almighty stink and a mass search for his whereabouts. He'd read about Guzan's arrest of his boss and the story of Edson Taylor's survival.